Also by John Balaban

Coming Down Again

. . .

JOHN BALABAN

. . .

A Fireside Book
Published by Simon & Schuster Inc.
New York   London   Toronto   Sydney   Tokyo

FIRESIDE
Simon & Schuster Building
Rockefeller Center
1230 Avenue of the Americas
New York, New York 10020

First Fireside Edition, 1989

Published by arrangement with the Author

FIRESIDE and colophon are registered trademarks
of Simon & Schuster Inc.

Designed by G.B.D. Smith
Manufactured in the United States of America

10   9   8   7   6   5   4   3   2   1   Pbk.

Library of Congress Cataloging in Publication Data

Balaban, John, 1943-
    Coming down again / John Balaban.—1st Fireside ed.
        p.   cm.
    Reprint. Originally published: San Diego : Harcourt Brace
Jovanovich, © 1985.
    "A Fireside book."
    I. Title.
PS3552.A44C6   1989
813'.54—dc20   89-34434
                         CIP

ISBN 0-671-67537-0   Pbk.

The astrologer's chart at the beginning of Chapter 17 is from *Ku Daeng: The Red Tomb* by
Konrad Kingshill, The Prince Royal's College, Chiang Mai, Thailand, 1960.

In Memory of
Stephen Carl Prescott, 1939–1974
and
Carlos Romero Mondragon, 1946–1979

"In big rivers, the fish run free."
—LAWA PROVERB

preface

On July 2, 1974, an event occurred that changed my life forever. Mr. W. T. S. Good, known as "the 'doyen' of the foreign colony in Thailand," died of a heart attack. Later events occasioned by Mr. Good's death involved my friends, my wife, and myself. I wanted to write about those events to understand not only what happened to us in northern Thailand but also to understand how we got there. Since I could not possibly know completely what had occurred with my friends, I decided to write a novel.

So this is fiction. No one in these pages is meant to resemble any person living or dead, including myself. I, too, am a fiction, albeit a happier one than I was before Mr. Good's death.

John Lacey
VIENTIANE, LAOS, 1980

Coming Down Again

prologue

Lacey's 747 banked down to Heathrow on a late afternoon so dark and drizzly that the dim yellow road lamps on the dual carriageway leading out from London appeared in his window as dull globes of phosphorescence, lone jelly fish in a sea of fog, rain, and city spew. As the plane circled lower, its path took Lacey over the gray looping Thames, once a pestiferous open sewer but cleaned up enough now to give old men in hooded slickers an excuse to set lines for perch. The plane passed the airport and circled over the Post Office Tower and the bed-and-breakfast hotels near the British Museum, where old ladies with Irish brogues were bustling past kitchen windows sliding with rain as they prepared trays to be laid the next morning before mute, uncomprehending Greeks and Syrians, before American and German backpackers and nervous Japanese fitted in tweeds. The plane flew over Hyde Park and Kensington Gardens, over the Round Pond where bundled-up kids, watched by au pairs in macs and scarves, launched little boats on the shallow pond stippled with rain-drops, and where the bird people, oblivious to the weather as they gathered by Peter Pan's statue, held out handfuls of seed for the shrill sparrows and the waddling pigeons that would eventually perch on their arms and heads offered up in bird-brained joy. Flew over the soaked Trotskyite giving a soapbox speech to a crippled pensioner at Hyde Park Corner. Flew over the glistening, dripping yews where proper men with bowlers and brollies went down on their knees for love. Flew over the hippie, tattered collar turned up, scratching the sidewalk with pastels—runny now with rivulets of rain—of the foods he'd like to eat. Flew over the M and L Club, a BBC haunt, where Lacey's friend, Jack Belfast, was waiting for Di to get off work as he tipped his pint of Watney's, dropped ten pence in the slot machine, and pulled the lever. Flew over Shepherd's Bush where Roberts and Prescott and Fay Cockburn were still sleeping. Flew over East Sheen. Flew over Dr. John Blake, another of Lacey's Vietnam friends, as he bicycled to the hospital past the Kentucky Fried Chicken just down from Sheen Lane, past the Hare and Hounds where Young's "real beer" was brought in each day on wagons drawn by brewery horses. . . . And flew—as it left Dr. Blake, with his wool cap pulled tight and his pipe bowl turned down, peddling through curb water on slippery brakes past the East Sheen bakery (aroma of pork pie and sausage rolls), the greengrocer (rearranging his Bibb lettuce), and the fish shop (where hundreds of forlorn walleyes stared at the ceiling from ice-packed trays)—to circle southwest back to Heathrow, over Richmond Park where herds of the Queen's own deer, coats steaming in the chill drizzle, huddled on hillsides thick with wet fern, under huge, squat, rain-black English oaks gnarled like the city through hundreds of years of plague, fire, war, Empire, and bombardment. "Courage," exhorted the gold-lettered signs on fields of red, yet this wasn't an imperial charge but merely a brand of beer.

1.

*W*hen Prescott and Lacey climbed out of the tube stop near Middlesex Hospital, Prescott cringed at the downtown crowds. He hesitated, hunched over. Once, in Saigon, stoned on acid, he had given Lacey a lift on his motorcycle, roaring up to checkpoints with barbed wire strung across the curfewed streets, where jittery Vietnamese cops jumped to their feet and took aim. But Prescott now knew that if he fell—tripped by some squirmy kid or pushed over by some mother intent on Christmas shopping—he could break a bone, his spine perhaps. His bones were now that brittle and weak. It would mean the end: lying in a hospital bed like a turtle with a cracked shell out on the road.

"I'll run interference for you," said Lacey, eyeing the crowd from the lee of the subway entrance. And he did, grimacing and pressing his fists together at the knuckles and thrusting his forearms and elbows forward like a Philadelphia Eagle posing for a kid's bubblegum card, as Prescott put one hand on Lacey's shoulder and shuffled behind, at arm's length. They headed down Regent's Street

3

with people veering out of their way, stepping aside and looking at them until other pedestrians barked their heels and hurried them along.

"Why didn't you write me?" Lacey asked, apparently of an Indian woman aiming dead at him who then blinked and looked away and sidestepped into the crowd with the ease of a Bombay stroller.

"I did. Didn't you get my card from Venice?"

"No."

"Well, I wrote you how Josiane and I were in love and how I love you and Louise and all my old pals."

"I didn't get it."

"Oh, come on, Lacey."

"Christ, how far is this hospital?" Lacey had just shoved an old man, who in turning around to glare at him had had his foot stepped on by a tall girl in stovepipe blue jeans and high heels.

"Near Tottenham."

"Let's get a cab."

"We're almost there."

"Yeah, but I don't like this plowing. Why are you going there? Why don't you see Blake? He's a doctor *and* your friend."

"Saw Blake. He gave me some palfium, but that's all he can do. He said to come here, register at the clinic, show 'em my diplomas, and then they'd send me upstairs to get zapped."

"What'd he say about your going to India and Vietnam?"

"Fine, as long as my stomach doesn't rot out, because when I can't digest my painkillers, I'm fucked. Also he says that if they radiate these fucking knobs—"

They stopped as Prescott pulled open his collar. His face was gaunt, his eyes exhausted. His chest was shrunken. At the back of his neck and on his left clavicle were several fist-size swellings.

"Christ, man, what *are* they?"

Prescott blew a puff of air as they regrouped into the crowd. "Cancer's plan. Hell, I don't know. Your chest's *bone*, isn't it? How can it shrivel?" If there was a whine in his voice, he dismissed it. "Sai Baba will save me."

"And who's this Sai Baba?"

"Sai Baba: southern Indian guru who materializes buckets of holy ash and Swiss watches and apparently saves a lot of cancer cases that the doctors have given up on."

"Uh-huh. Have Roberts and Fay met Blake?" Lacey did not want to hear any more about Sai Baba.

"No, no. I'm enough trouble for Blake. Roberts would badger him for dope, and Blake would tell him to buzz off. It'd be a short conversation."

"Good." Lacey turned the corner onto Oxford Street, where they slipped out of the pedestrian trample and leaned against a wall. "I feel," he said, "like a salmon running up rapids."

Prescott waited in a curtained stall among the many in the large room in the hospital basement. Lacey sat outside in the corridor on a tattered leather bench. Despite the number of people in the hall and clinic, the place was quiet. So quiet, in fact, that Lacey could plainly hear Prescott banging off loud farts that percolated from his cancerous colon. The farts were frequent, loud, long, and full of vibrato. The long walk must have shaken them loose.

Suddenly a voice called out angrily, "Will whoever is doing that, please stop. It is very rude."

Prescott's reply, of course, was another helpless burst, followed by a nattering bray. Lacey gritted his teeth and got up when he saw a doctor stamping down the aisle to Prescott's stall, where he threw open the curtain and demanded, "What's your name?"

Prescott looked at the young man in the white coat and could not suppress his smile. "Steve," he said.

"No, your *last* name."

Prescott was now grinning broadly. "What are you going to do," he asked, "arrest me?"

The doctor snatched Prescott's records from the clipboard on the metal tray. His frown fled as he read Prescott's Mt. Zion reports and Blake's letter. "Sorry," he said. He turned to look Prescott in the eye.

Prescott smiled at him with the good-natured curiosity he seemed to be adopting more and more as he got closer to death and discovered interesting things about the desperations that rankled ordinary mortals. "Not at all," he said. "I know it's awful."

"We'll get you upstairs to the specialists." The doctor scribbled a note, gave it to Prescott, patted his shoulder, which may have been the cause of yet another fart, and called out, beleagueredly, to the desk nurse, "Sister?"

In the elevator, Prescott drew stares as he inhaled and exhaled huge lungfuls of air. A lady in a tweed suit and matching hat knitted her eyebrows and frowned at Prescott. "Breaths of fire," he said in a confidential tone. He winked at her.

Prescott was on a German carrot juice diet, had tried a sautéed lemon rind cure, had drunk an extract of peach pits, had visited a Reichian masseuse, and had recently begun yoga asanas. He was doing all he could to keep from dying, including riding up on the elevator to have his cells ionized. He still was not certain that he was going to die, and he bridled at the suggestion, including any lapse in grammar that introduced the past tense of the verb in respect to his life: "What did you—" someone would start. "What *do* I . . . ," Prescott would correct.

At radiology, he was given a form: Stephen Carl Prescott agreed that he would not sue the hospital if his hair fell out, etc. Lacey signed below Prescott as next of kin.

2.

*W*hen Lacey moved in with Prescott, he could see why Prescott preferred the relative comforts of Roberts's place to this dump off Portobello Road, a one-room walk-up that belonged to a guy named "H," once the sound man for the Jimi Hendrix Experience and more recently for a large discotheque in Hammersmith. Two weeks before Steve moved in, H had rented a rowboat in Capri and managed to drown himself. Fay had a key to his place, which was now Prescott's until the landlord got wise. But it was hard to get to, except by cab, and it was just one large room with a sink, and you had to climb three flights of narrow stairs, past landings strewn with garbage bags and dirty diapers, past the single stinking bathroom where if you wanted hot water to shave or wash you had to keep feeding a gas meter with ten-pence coins, and, perhaps worst of all, past the other tenants: a filthy young woman who was always screeching at her whiny little boy on whose upper lip lay a dollop of green snot, two gays whom Steve suspected of having broken in and stolen some of H's records, and an old man in a uniform indicating some sort of public service who stopped Lacey on the stairs once to ask him in a smug, knowing, quiet tone, "What's wrong with your friend?"

Lacey stared at the man.

"He looks pretty sick," the old man ventured with an ugly smile.

Lacey thought of kicking the old fart down the stairs. Instead he turned to walk back up and said, "He's got a bad cold."

"Looks worse than that," the old man called after him.

The room had a chair, a stand-up closet, two bare mattresses thrown on the floor, and a single, bare light bulb that Steve left burning to ward off roaches and neighbors. Prescott's stuff was thrown about the room: books on cancer cures, his manuscripts, unwashed clothes, a hi-tech German juicer. There was also a huge stereo system and stacks of records, all of which had been given to H by record companies. And an electric heater that Fay's friend, Thomas, had given Prescott and that kept them warm on one side or the other as they slept, wrapped in ragged cotton blankets, beneath the bare bulb Prescott would not turn off.

Awful nights. Each time Lacey awoke, he looked over at Prescott, lying on his back, naked to the waist, chest caved in, ribs protruding, eyes staring at the ceiling. Lacey awoke that way so often he finally thought he was dreaming the scene. "You alright?" he asked once, just to see if he was dreaming or if Prescott was really awake. "Alright," came back the reply, almost immediately, but from a place very far off, somewhere Lacey had never been. Finally, awaking again to see Prescott up and standing before the high sink, stretching up to try to piss into it, Lacey asked him to turn off the light. "In a minute," came the faraway voice. But it took some minutes, for Prescott could stand there and stand there while nothing happened. At last, when Lacey woke again, the light was out. But was Prescott asleep? "Steve?"

"Yeah?"

"Christ, man, go to sleep."

———

They didn't spend many conscious hours in the hole, at least not Lacey. When they were there, they brightened the atmosphere a bit by listening to H's records: to Jimi Hendrix, to the Stones' new *Goat's Head Soup*, to Elton John's "rocket man burning up in the air alone." Prescott seldom felt like eating and, knowing how uncomfortable it was for Prescott to sit for long in a restaurant, Lacey obliged by grabbing his food on the run: meat pies at bakeries, sliced ham at the pubs, Wimpy Burgers. One night, leaving Prescott to practice his asanas, Lacey went out just before closing time to get something at a pub near Nottinghill Gate. It was a drizzly, fogshifting evening like the night of his arrival. Portobello Road was deserted except for the odd car that came along sloshing rainwater in a sheen of filthy ripples. He felt rotten and alone. It was rotten leaving Louise alone at Christmas. He should have brought her. Since returning from Vietnam, he left her alone too much in their falling-down farmhouse. He didn't like to think of her alone, amid fields surrounded by rednecks in house trailers, poachers whom Lacey was always running off the land. Christ, he thought, she'd be safer walking down this foggy poorly lit street at night, and then heard, as if on cue, a groan and a scuffle from the dim road ahead. He walked forward quietly, making sure the backs of his heels touched first and his soles rolled forward noiselessly. Through the separating mist he saw two men standing over a third lying on the wet cobblestones. The guy was on his back, his hands up to protect himself—without success—as the two men on either side of him alternated kicks to his ribs. Jesus Christ. Lacey could get by them, but how could he stop them?

"Can I help?" he asked cheerily as he walked up out of the fog.

The two thugs stopped kicking, looked at Lacey, and then looked at each other. They were both about twenty. One of them had a severe David Bowie haircut; the other, a Rod Stewart shag. "'E's aw mate. 'E won't come with us," Bowie explained.

"Bloody lie!" squealed the guy on the ground. His shirt buttons had popped off and his paunchy little belly showed beneath his

9

leather jacket. "They's about to kill me." A bloody front tooth lay on his neck.

One of his shoes—a flimsy yellow pump with a blocked-up heel—was flung off in the gutter. Lacey considered the situation and walked over to pick it up. As he did, through the fog he noticed a car parked by the curb just a bit up the road. Two dots of cigarette light glowed in the rear seat. This was hopeless, he thought, as he walked back to where the guy was still lying in the street. They were all drunk; perhaps they'd had a falling out. Anyway, he had got them to stop kicking and that looked like the best he could do, even if they started knifing the guy in the car.

"Come on, Arnie," one of the assailants was saying, "we'll get you home."

"Yeah, come on, Arnie," Lacey said. "You're pissed. Your friends want to get you home." Lacey smiled at the two. One winked. "Here, come on, now, put on your shoe."

"They ain't me friends; they wanna kill me."

"Naw, Arnie. You wooz startin'. It's over now."

Lacey helped Arnie up, said good night, and walked on. Three blocks up, at the pub, he took a stool at the bar and asked the middle-aged barmaid for a hot sausage roll and a half pint of the best bitters. No point calling the cops, he thought. Either way now, it was settled. He downed his pint and ordered another. He had come to say good-bye to Prescott. He had also come to gather with his Vietnam pals. Probably a mistake. He was playing hooky from his awful job. He sipped his mug.

3.

*L*olling about. Drunk. Stoned. On New Year's Eve. They were slumped in the stuffed chairs and sprawled across the two double beds in Prescott's hotel room. In Prescott's room: billed to an American Express card he would never pay; on Prescott's methadone: just as they had smoked his heroin in Saigon, except for Fay, who was prancing about Soho then. In Saigon they tapped 95-percent-pure crystals into half-emptied Marlboros, the skag was so cheap. Now the skag was free, provided by the National Health Service to their dying friend, who, after radiation, was looking better, feeling better, and eating again, and who seemed, as he sat in his throne of pillows, in good spirits. *Radiant,* he said. No pain, no problem.

Just the same old Saigon scene, thought Lacey. Roberts was telling a story from one of the double beds. Prescott was there offering the deft joke. And Whiting had his camera. But the girl now was Fay. Fay, with her auburn, hennaed hair still damp from the shower, sat naked next to Roberts. Her large brown eyes were weary, her features sharp. Big hips, small flat breasts. Her arms terribly bruised.

"Well, don't *stare* at us," Roberts said, interrupting his own story.

A radiator hissed in a corner. Fay patted the bed beside her, and Lacey shuffled over to sit by them. When Fay helped him off with his jacket, he saw again her jagged, broken nails and, in the lamplight, the left side of Roberts's face, swollen and red and turning black.

Whiting was filming. He sat forward in the dark leather chair just in front of a spotlight trained on the two beds. At the moment he was filming Roberts flipping a clasp knife at the thick heel of Lacey's boot. He missed almost every time and once nearly stuck Lacey in the calf.

"Cut it out, you guys," Prescott said.

Relieved, Lacey pulled back his foot. Stoned mumblety-peg. The advantage, or disadvantage, of drugs was that it turned your puny threats into mythic encounters. Something quite the reverse had once brought them together.

Whiting flicked off both his spot and camera. "Heavy duty," he said in his nasal Georgia drawl. He was short and muscular, sported a wiry blond beard. He was beginning to bald. In Vietnam, he had filmed the war for CBS. Now he shot car ads for some Dallas agency.

"As I was saying," Roberts continued as Whiting switched on the spot, "a party for Thomas's—the guy who owns our house—new discovery, a black blues singer named Preston Jones, a waiter from Detroit who Thomas got a one-night gig at Ronnie Scott's in Soho."

"The best place in town," Fay said.

"Mind if *I* tell the story?"

"Oh, stop," she said and, hand under the covers, grabbed for his dick with her broken claws. Roberts rolled away. "C'mon, tell the story," she said.

"Well, Preston's gay, about forty, and he'd never had a break like this, so he was in heaven, belting out Bill Withers's 'Lean on Me' and crooning Joe Williams's torch songs. He figured I was famous somehow so I got a lot of his personal attention."

"And didn't you like it?" Fay said sweetly.

"What? When he was sitting at our table? I mean on our table? Christ, he was singing so close to my face, he fogged my glasses." Lacey started to unbutton his shirt. Fay helped him.

"Anyway, after his last set—Sonny Stitt was the main bill— Thomas took us all to a pub nearby where he bought everybody— the whole pub—drinks. Preston was ecstatic and flirted around, even with some women and these Welsh working stiffs who just glared at us and drank Tom's booze." Roberts pointed to a cigarette pack next to Lacey, which Lacey flipped him. Roberts took the last cigarette and lit it, crumpling the pack and tossing it at Prescott's head, now slumped in sleep in the next bed.

"Toss it again, man," Whiting said, retrieving the pack from the bedcovers in front of Prescott. "I didn't catch it the first time."

Meanwhile, Fay pulled herself belly down across Lacey's lap to lean over the edge of the bed and fish for a bottle of Scotch that had rolled underneath. Her wonderful full fanny was just below Lacey's face. He grinned and looked up at the ceiling.

Roberts coughed smoke and grabbed for the bottle. "Gimme that and keep your ass out of my friend's face." He took the bottle from Fay. Along with the bruises, his face was puffed from booze. He was thirty-seven.

"Well, it's quite alright," Lacey said, trying to sound British.

"Why, thank you, love," said Fay, who now leaned against him.

Roberts took a slug and gave the Scotch to Fay, who took a swig and passed the bottle to Lacey, who took a swig and passed it back to Roberts. Whiting, looking through his camera, waved off the bottle. When Fay leaned back against Roberts, Lacey got up and walked over to the window sliding with rain. One story down in the parking lot, he saw the attendant, an Indian kid of fifteen or so, dressed in blue jeans and a tight-fitting, yellow silk jacket with an elastic waistband. In the lamplight under a dripping metal eave, the boy was tumbling out lighted cascades from an electric yo-yo. The dingy wall behind him had been spray-canned: Wogs Out. Lacey watched the skipping streaks of light and thought about Louise spending New Year's alone. In three days his classes started again. Behind him, Prescott was snoring and Whiting had cut the spot. Through the drizzled window, Lacey watched the tumbling yo-yo. This was Saigon *transmogrified* to London. It seemed all wrong. As before, they lolled about, wandering in and out of the vagaries of each other's dreams and into the misworkings of each other's drunk or drugged minds. But, in Vietnam, they also *did* things. Roberts had gotten the blueprints for the tiger cages to the *New York Times*. Flynn and Stone never returned from their last roadblock in Cambodia; Abrams got fragged near Quang Ngai. Horowitz was murdered in the Delta. He was the strangest, Lacey thought. Horowitz did not drink or smoke or whore or hang out with the crowd holed up in the apartment on Tu Do Street. An ex-Marine, paying some private penance, he lived in an isolated village near Ba The Mountain in the middle of the Delta. Villagers called him the "poor American" because he wandered the Delta on foot, in flipflops, in cutoff blue jeans, carrying all his possessions in a burlap sack because . . . who knew why? He was the first of them to die. "So what happened?" Lacey asked, turning from the window. Whiting relit the room. What did Horowitz say, what did they all say, Lacey wondered, when death came trundling up?

"Well, when the pub closed, Thomas invited everyone back to our house, including the four Welshmen, and that's when the trouble began. Preston, who thought they were all for him, went out in the garden with one guy and then came back in, socked and sobbing. Thomas, a big, blond guy with shoulder length—"

"Whom we call the Gentle Christian," said Fay. Lacey nodded and slumped into a chair off camera.

"—*hair*," Roberts continued with one of his authoritative male rumblings, "went over to the guy as he was coming back in and asked him why he had socked Preston. Not hostile, just curious. 'E patted me bum,' the guy said. 'Well,' said Thomas, who did a first in classics at Oxford, 'Hylas in limine latrat'—which he told me later is from Virgil and means: Hylas has crossed the threshold. Anyway," Roberts went on, seeing that Lacey was losing interest, "then Thomas says to the guy, 'I daresay if that's the worst that's ever happened to you, you've lived a charmed life.' Now, Thomas towered over this dark, little runt by about a foot, but the guy punched him in the gut anyway, and when Thomas doubled over, the guy busted a glass over his head. Then one of the runt's friends kicks Thomas in the ribs as he falls to the floor."

"Jesus," Lacey said. Fay shook her head in agreement.

With one eye grimaced behind his camera, Whiting said, "Heavy duty."

"Well, I had been watching these dudes, so I picked up a board that Thomas had left in a corner after nailing up cold frames for the garden and I whacked the second mother's head and laid him out cold."

Roberts was death with timber in his hands. Lacey remembered how Roberts had K-O-ed a young Vietnamese hoodlum whose gang had cornered Roberts in some whore's room in a part of Cholon the cops never went into, a part ruled by renegade, black GIs so zonked and heavily armed that if MPs ever went in, they went in with APC, and grenade launchers. Roberts had gone berserk. He broke off a table leg as the punks crowded toward the door. He whonked the first in reach. The kid dropped like a fawn and the gang ran away. Lacey looked at Prescott collapsed into his pillows.

"Then the first guy hits me in the right temple and I bang my left one on a table as I go down. But the best part was Fay, who sees this and goes crazy, jumps on the fucker's back and rides him around the room clawing his face and biting his neck. Biting his fucking neck."

Fay smiled at Lacey past Whiting's camera and showed her pretty white teeth.

"Then everybody got into it: the two other Welsh creeps and the rest of the party. We beat them up and threw them out in a heap on Sweet Williams Crescent. And today I was in the pub saying good-bye to everybody and the bartender says they always pull that. I told Thomas and he says, 'Dear me, they should be better at it then, shouldn't they?' "

Roberts was finished. Lacey smiled weakly and slumped farther down into his chair, groggy with the methadone or perhaps just from nerves. On New Year's Day, the next day, they were leaving for India. At least Prescott and Roberts and Fay. Not Lacey. Nope. In three days he would be teaching again.

"What?" said Roberts. He was up and rummaging in his luggage. His boxer shorts dropped over the crack of his ass.

"Lizards, leaping," Lacey said, again making jumping motions with his hands.

"Gotcha," agreed Roberts.

"Do you think," Lacey mused, "the record player's still playing?" When they had cleaned Prescott's stuff out of H's apartment that afternoon, they had left H's hi-fi blaring the Stones. Just left it on; no reason to turn it off. H was at the bottom of the sea, and his newest album, the Stones' *Goat's Head Soup,* was droning out on automatic replay, "Coming down again. Where are all my friends? Coming down again. Coming down again."

"Slipped my tongue," Fay sang as she toweled her hair, "in someone else's pie . . ."

"Fuck you," Roberts muttered. His doped, lethargic brain took her singing as a crack.

"C'mon, man," Lacey said, "don't spoil the farewell."

"Alpha-FALpha!" Whiting was stunned by the drama of it all. He stepped back to get both Roberts and Fay in his frame.

"Lacey, wake up." Fay was shaking him. Her tits wobbled as she shook him. Whiting switched on his spotlight.

"I'm awake." He pulled himself up in the chair and looked around the blurry room. The digital clock in the TV read midnight. The New Year. Prescott was propped up on his pillows. His mouth was wide open. His eyes, closed.

Fay pulled away the sheet that covered Prescott. His skin was yellowish; his flesh hung loosely on his big bones. They all looked at him for a minute, a little awed by the wreckage. Then Fay reached over and took Roberts's glasses and placed them on Prescott's peter, transforming it into a long nose, and his thatch into a woolly head of hair. Prescott, the man with axial heads, snored away out of one of them.

Whiting filmed: Roberts, laughing on the other bed; Fay, shaking her finger at Mr. Dick Face as if he had just said something rude. Lacey, weaving, collapsing back in his chair. Whiting had filmed a lot of bodies in Vietnam, and parts of bodies; all this was just as important, he said.

"Confirms my suspicions about feminists," Lacey said.

Fay just smiled. *"He's* not very nice around women."

"He never did very well with adults," Lacey admitted.

Lacey watched Fay as she slugged at the Scotch bottle and wondered if her whiskey voice really came from drinking whiskey. Her remark reminded him of Steve Prescott's priapic pursuit of Saigon bar girls, women who were like small, wicked girls, and of how, last summer, when he had gone to San Francisco to see Prescott after he first got sick, he had found him the day after surgery alone in his hospital room, lying on his back, eyes open and staring at the ceiling. A clear plastic hose was taped to his nose; the end prodded down his esophagus into his stomach, suctioning up a green, spinachlike slime and pumping it out his nose and along the looping tube before emptying into a gallon glass jug by his bed. Prescott's pierced right hand was taped to a tube that ran from an IV bottle. And, under the sheets, a catheter, having been poked through his penis to his bladder, emerged, draining brownish bubbles along the four or so feet of tubing into another jug. And yet, a week later, when he was dismissed with a raw football stitch running from his sternum to his navel, vowing never to return to a hospital, Prescott insisted that he and Lacey drive down to the nude beaches below Santa Cruz. He could barely walk, but he could *see*.

"Say some poetry," said Roberts. He knew the Vietnamese custom: whatever a poet said this New Year's night would come true.

But Lacey hesitated. Roberts, sitting on the edge of the bed, was now fiddling with the powder and spoon he had taken from a shaving kit. "Heroin?"

"Hope so," Roberts replied. "Me first," he said to Fay sitting beside him. He jabbed his arm with the hypodermic she had just filled. Roberts gave himself half. Fay held out her bruised arm. Roberts fluttered his eyelids to regain focus and concentrated on the syringe in his hand and the blotched, black-and-blue arm in front of him.

Now Lacey saw why Fay's arms were so bruised. He had thought it was the fight, but apparently Roberts, who always hit himself first, was already zonked by the time he stuck Fay and, fearful of hurting her, he was too gentle. He didn't depress the hypodermic hard and fast enough. Her subcutaneous blood was rinsing back and spreading under and into the puncture faster than the solution was being shot in.

"Some poetry," Roberts repeated, calling now from the edge of dreamland. He and Fay were slumped against each other and looking into Whiting's camera with slitted eyes.

"At my back," Lacey said, "I always hear Time's winged chariot drawing near—"

"*Hurrying* near, asshole," Roberts muttered.

"—And yonder all before us lie, deserts of vast eternity." Time's winged chariot, indeed. On the island in the Mekong where Lacey had lived for a while, the kids would tie little paper chariots to the fist-size cockroaches that combed the cement walkways above the river. The clumsy bugs would clatter about pulling their fluttering loads, which, when the unwieldy insects took to the air, became tumbly kites that the wind carried out into the muddy river. Tomorrow, his auld friends would fly off—fly back—to Asia.

4.

Roberts lay on his left side on a reed mat and studied the rain trickling down the inside of the decaying wall of his prison cell. Large spots in the stucco had bulged out and rotted off in the weeks of relentless rain. The cement where the stucco had flaked off was white and powdery and dusted away under his fingernail to reveal a substructure of crude brick. The mottled surface was already more brick than stucco, even though Roberts, like the other prisoners, had finished the wall himself in May, only two months before. They had worked from aluminum basins and bags of USAID cement. The bags displayed an American flag, hands clasped in friendship, and a motto, in English and in the funny, indecipherable curlicues of Thai: "Help people help themselves."

The rainwater slid down from the ceiling just below the palm thatch eave, on the jungle side, and trickled through the stucco cracks and collected in the urinal drain that slanted along the base of the entire wall. Actually, Roberts thought, as he coughed out a mixture of rough tobacco smoke and damp, tubercular air, he was lucky. The monsoon rain was a godsend—it flushed the urinal that entered his cell through a hole in the wall from the cell above and then ran into the next cell down. The drain connected five cells before dropping into a terra-cotta culvert that led to the shit pond at the east end of the prison.

The rain was tattering wildly on the flat, torn banana leaves that grew on the outside of the prison wall, producing tiny racemes of yellow fruit that ripened before they were the size of your fist. Roberts had reached out once to grab one through his tiny barred window and then couldn't get his hand back through the bars without letting the fruit go or, as he finally figured out, by working it through with the fingers of his other hand. A monkey trap. You hollow out a coconut and put some fruit inside. The monkey sticks his hand in the hole just big enough for his extended fingers but too small for the hand clutching the fruit in its fist. The monkey is too stupid to let go, and is caught. It was how they had caught him and Fay. With all the dope they were certain to get across the border, why, he wondered, had they been so stupid as to carry two ounces of hash across. Too stupid to let go. Greedy monkeys.

The rain was slapping the flat banana leaves, leaves as big as a man. It was boiling the surface of the stinking pond and flushing it clean. Roberts sat up on the wooden bed with its plaited reed mattress and reached for the bhang he had bought from a guard. The surface of the bamboo cylinder, actually just a sealed tree segment that served as a crude water pipe, was stained with sweat and dirt. Roberts stuffed the bowl with a wad of dark Laotian tobacco so strong it made him dizzy for the first few seconds after he drew the smoke down through the cooling water. "Fucking one smart move," Roberts said to himself as he relit the pipe, took a long drag, blinked, and leaned back against the wall. "My one smart move." Two months ago, when he saw that his English Rothmanns would run out fast if he weren't released soon, Roberts had given his last five packs to a guard in exchange for the bhang and what he figured was a month's supply of the Laotian tobacco. When that ran out, his Swiss army knife had got him about six months' supply of tobacco plus a blackish brick of compressed hashish nearly ten times the size of the plug that had landed them in jail.

Out in the prison yard where sheets of rain rippled across the flooded earth, geese were honking forlornly as they waddled to shelter. They piped like saxophones with broken reeds. Roberts turned his head to look at them as they gathered under the protective timbering of the watchtower at the far corner of the triangular yard. They bobbed their snaky necks and ceased their wailing to preen their dirty feathers and settle down. The geese came and went through an opening in the wall directly below the jakes that stood pyloned above the east end of the shit pond. They sometimes startled Roberts, paddling beneath his feet as he squatted on the planks. Somehow they managed to maneuver through stretches of concertina barbed wire under the shit houses. Roberts would linger, watching them navigate the razory coils of it, deceptively overgrown in trellises of blue morning glory. Sometimes the geese would leave a feather or two floating behind, which the little shit-eating fish—carp of some kind—would bat about. Once a goose tripped a claymore mine in the outside moat on the far side of the wall gardens. Blew out the bank and mulched the prison wall with a papering of banana leaf, duckweed, and spatters of goose feathers and goose flesh.

The prison was primarily a police station, a little district outpost near the border crossing at Chiang Saen where the steep jungle mountains of Burma and Laos join the more open slopes of northern Thailand to form the Golden Triangle, a series of steep, forested north-south ranges and remote valleys thinly populated with Shan insurgents, hill tribes, bandits, and private warlords. Their prison was Thai (situated somewhere called Feng or Fang, as nearly as Roberts could make out) and its layout was American: a triangular A-camp like those the Green Berets set up in the more contested regions of Vietnam. At each of the three corners, built up on a scaffolding of palmetto logs and rough-sawn timbers, was a forty-foot watchtower thatched with palm leaves. From his cell, Roberts could see only the tower facing him and in it the ponchoed guard sitting in a chair before a Browning automatic rifle mounted on a tripod. The small post was pretty well armed. Border Patrol Police. Roberts had seen M-16s and .45 "greaseguns" and grenade launchers and, sitting in the yard on a swivel mount, a large new mortar that was belt-fed and cranked like a Gatling gun. Every bit of their issue was American. Roberts was resentful. Ingrates.

He had counted forty-five prisoners. Thirty-four men and eleven women, including Fay. Only two sides of the prison triangle were cells, each with a small barred window facing either the jungle or the terraced paddy surrounding them beyond the moat. Opposite the forest side and facing the prison yard, each cell had a half-wall, the upper part and the door in iron bars and the lower of brick and stucco. The women were permitted cotton curtains to cover the barred sections of their yard walls. The small cells were shared. Only Roberts, Ko Pisan, and a Chinese dope smuggler had individual cells. Fay could have, but she chose to share.

As long as the prisoners didn't bother the guards, they weren't locked up and were free to visit or roam the yard or even help the guards spear the little bandicoot rats that skittered about the outside moat. Despite their possibly carrying rat-bite fever and plague, they were fried up as delicacies by the guards, who spent hours stalking the banks for them with long, bamboo poles tipped in sharp, iron tridents. Only Ko Pisan, a mad Karen tribesman who had murdered his mother, was locked up. He had hacked her up with a machete. Roberts had tried to talk with him once. The guy's eyes bulged and his lips trembled with rage as Roberts spoke to him in demon language.

"When's your trial, man?" Roberts had asked.

The Karen started trembling in his neck and shoulders, and his knuckles whitened as he grasped the edge of his wooden bed.

"You gonna get a lawyer?"

A guard came over and shooed Roberts away. The guard made hand motions near his head to indicate that the pop-eyed Karen was crazy.

"I know," Roberts said, "hyperthyroid."

The rest of the prison consisted of an office and interrogation room, barracks for the twenty or so Thai guards and their chickens and three pigs, a separate room for receiving the Nae Amphur, the district chief, and a small arsenal. Gardens, flooded now by the monsoon, produced beans and pumpkin, cabbage, and taro. Under one of the watchtowers, a bunker had been dug and roofed with sandbags. Within a radius of seventy-five miles roamed: Burmese police, the Thai Liberation Army, Shan rebels, Pathet Lao, North Vietnamese, Meo bandits, and Chinese warlords, heirs to the Kuomintang army that Chiang Kai-shek had abandoned in Indochina. And never too far away was the U.S. Air Force, swarming like bees after the hive had been poked to pieces in Vietnam.

Coils of concertina wire were strung across the tops of the prison walls and along the far side of the moat and where the pond met a mountain stream that plunged over boulders and shot around fallen trunks, then quieted down in the less steep forest and terraced paddy surrounding the prison. Across the moat lay a helicopter pad of steel mesh. A single dirt road, impassable now except for half-tracks, led from the prison, bridged the stream, and disappeared into the forest.

Roberts stood up, put down his water pipe, and pulled his sweater off the back of the chair. He tugged it on over his head and eyeglasses while slipping his bare feet into the flipflops that one of the other prisoners had made for him out of an old jeep tire. Maybe, Roberts figured as he shuffled out, keeping to the wall under the stormy eave, maybe he'd better talk to Fay.

The eave shot streams of icy water onto the muddy earth where the prison yard joined the cement walkway aproning the cells. Cold muddy water spattered Roberts's bare feet as he slipslapped along. The rain's roar was deafening: a fierce tympanic assault of gutter gurgle, leaf spatter, metallic plunks, and the sizzling sweeps of rain-sheets hissing through the upper branches of the forest and tearing across the thatched roofs and the muddy prison yard. Every now and then cold drops caught Roberts on the neck as he passed the cells where prisoners were playing cards on their wooden beds. The dope smuggler was playing Chinese chess with the young guard whom he had commissioned to bring him special meals. Neither looked up as Roberts walked by. In another cell two men had wrapped themselves up in cocoons of mosquito netting to doze and wait out the rain, and, in the next cell, the acrid smell of opium hung about the open door. Two middle-aged men—one in fatigue pants and a checked cotton shirt, and the other wrapped in an Army blanket—reclined on the wooden bed where they shared an opium pipe. Roberts shook his finger at them and said, in his atonal version of Vietnamese, "Ma Den. Ma Den." Black Phantom. Black Phantom. Roberts shared his small vocabulary of Vietnamese generously, especially with those who did not speak a word of Vietnamese. The two men were Shans. They smiled back slowly with heavy, sleepy eyes at the big-nosed devil who had penetrated, for an already forgotten moment, the depths of their opium dreams.

Farther down, Roberts passed Ko Pisan's cell and, glancing in, saw the man squatted to shit in his urinal instead of using the removable steel can sunk into the cement floor. Roberts was ready to wave hello, but the Karen was glaring at the floor and did not seem to note the shadow passing before the bars of his padlocked cell.

Roberts shuffled on. At the corner under the watchtower, he avoided the mysterious red oil drums and cautiously stepped over a monstrous sow banked with squirming, suckling piglets. One cell up, he pushed aside the curtain and walked into Fay's room.

Fay and her Lao cellmate were lying next to each other, naked except for their panties. The Lao girl was running her long finger-nails along Fay's back and shoulders and arms. She smiled at Roberts when he walked in. The women looked dreamy and half asleep.

"Keeping warm?" Roberts asked as he sat down and helped himself to Fay's huge, brown-wrapped Shaiyo cigarettes. A bottle of strong Singha beer was on the rickety metal table. He looked around for an opener.

"Piss off." Fay spoke in a languid tone. But she tried to be encouraging. "Listen to the rain," she said. "Isn't it lovely?"

"Not even nice. I've been listening to the rain for two months now."

He worked the bottle cap into the corner between the table top and one of its folding brackets, but the metal was so soft it bent. Roberts puffed out air forlornly. Finally Mai stopped swirling her long nails over Fay's back and sat up, revealing large flattish breasts with dark brown nipples. She took the bottle from Roberts, set it carefully between her front teeth and pulled it open. She took a swig and handed it back.

"Merci." Then Roberts laughed and coughed. "Shit, Fay, if we'd had her choppers at Thomas's party she could have decapitated those Welshmen."

Fay grinned and drew a blanket around herself and Mai. They settled against the wall, spotted like the others with stucco rot and blossoms of gray mildew. A Thai calendar hung on the wall to the left of Mai's head. It showed a woman with her head cocked to one side and wearing an ornate gold headdress. Her long gold fingernails were touching her face. The woman's face was powdered white and rouged. Fay's was almost as pale. Mai's skin was very brown; in the sunlight it was golden, marred only by a large vaccination welt on her shoulder and a scar at the bottom of her chin. She was a whore and a club dancer who had left Vientiane for Chiang Mai when the foreigners disappeared. She was in the slammer for rolling a drunken Thai officer from one of the border towns. Instead of trying her in

Chiang Mai, they had sent her to Feng at the convenience of her accuser. The funny thing was that Roberts knew her or, rather, thought he had seen her act three years before when she was a novelty dancer at the White Rose bar in Vientiane. Mai's act, if indeed she was the same girl, was a strip dance that ended with her sticking a whole pack of cigarettes into her labia majora, lighting them, and somehow making them puff smoke.

"Fay."

"What?"

"Wot do yer think," he tried to mimic her, "is 'appening?"

"Perhaps, darling, they don't know yet."

"Do you think they mailed the letters?"

"Mai says no."

"Pourquoi tu pense ce la?" Roberts's French wasn't bad.

"Jeno sais." Mai's was. Her English was no better. She shrugged underneath the blanket and smiled at Fay.

"Christ." They had written to Mary, Roberts's mother, who had only to call up Walter Cronkite to spring them; they had written to the American consul in Bangkok, to Fay's father, to the British consul, to Lacey. Months ago, three months ago. No reply. What the fuck was happening? Christ, things went sour the day they left. They should've left Prescott with Lacey and gone on alone. But it had been too late to back out. At Heathrow, at the frisking gate, Thomas and their friends sang a good-bye chorus from *Hepatitis,* the latest London musical, a spoof on hippies flocking to the mystical East. "The burning ghat is where it's at." Fucking Lacey. If Lacey didn't answer something was wrong. Lacey had a conscience as predictable . . . as fucking gravity or something . . . as the spectrum of argon. No, they hadn't heard. The Thais were fucking with them. The goddamn dinks didn't even seem to know who he was. Once again his dead papa had deserted him.

5.

*I*t still rained every day, but not all day. Usually, in the early morning, the sun fluttered around Roberts's cell like one of the prison chickens that would sometimes wander in, cluck about, sense some danger in its little pea brain, then panic and drum its wings until it found the open door again. So, each day, despite the rain, Roberts was awakened by a rooster of a sun. Long before Roberts actually got up, the sun would shake through the foliage into his cell until he thought he heard it squawking. What he heard were the raucous dawn songs of the forest birds: lorikeets screaming in the bamboo brakes across the moat and stream; barbets piping in the screw pines that thicketed the jungle floor in a curtain of rootstalks; flame-red parrots cawing from bobbing top branches in a poisonous upas tree; spotted babblers, bush warblers, antic magpies combing the cavernous hollows of a banyan; chattering mynahs, and, farther away—where the flatter rain forest gave way to steeper hills choked with magnolia, teak, oaks, chestnuts, firs, dwarf bamboo, and coffin trees: pheasants calling; whistling quail.

Roberts—like Fay and Mai, who slept together—slept inside a dingy canopy of old mosquito nets strung above his bed on bamboo rods. Mai had stitched them together with cotton patches and seams to keep the malarial bugs away. Each dawn, if he actually opened his eyes, Roberts could observe the mosquitoes chilled and clinging to the gauze where they had waited out the night like tiny vampires, waiting for Roberts to toss a leg or an arm against the netting. Sometimes, when he woke and batted the netting to shoo them away, they were too fattened with his blood to fly.

This morning in mid-August was like all the others since May when the monsoon season began: a long opium dream in which nothing moved, nothing happened, a dream in which the mind fixed on a spot for hours, frozen like the mosquitoes stuck to the net. Roberts lay on his woven mat on a wooden platform until the bird noise and the sunshine made it impossible to linger. He opened his eyes and thought of his father, of his sister, and wondered if his mother or Lacey were doing anything for him. He tried to imagine what his son looked like now, if he missed him still after all these years, what story his ex-wife made up to explain his absence—and the presence of the new daddy. From the forest edge outside his cell window, a monkey screamed. He thought about Fay, but not much. She was doing better than he. She was nuts about Mai. Fay got along. Shit, she had even taken to Prescott. Sat up with him, read to him, fed him, wrote his last letters. He didn't have to worry about Fay.

Around eleven, as usual, the sky was overcast; by noon, the sound of rain drowned out everything except the scratchy melody that floated through the rain sheets from a tower guard's transistor radio. Before the deluge gathered all its force, Roberts crawled out from under his netting, slapping at the mosquitoes before they sailed away, coughed, spat out the door of his cell, and stepped into his flipflops. He slept in his clothes, which Mai washed when they got too rank.

He shuffled over to the latrine trough already gurgling with rain-water and pissed. At first the piss wouldn't come, and then it shot forward with a jab of pain. Roberts wondered if the opium, which they were smoking quite regularly now, was causing the trouble. All three of them had stomach cramps, hot and cold chills, and indifferent appetites. Their muscles ached. Or maybe, he thought, thinking once more about his father, he had the old man's prostate problem. Maybe malaria. Who the fuck would know in a hole like this? He tugged up the heavy brass zipper of his cutoff jeans and shuffled out the door, kneading the muscles in his stomach and in the small of his back.

At Fay's they drank, as they did each morning, instant coffee mixed with thick, sweet, condensed milk. They sat about listlessly and smoked Shaiyo cheroots wrapped in brown paper until finally—resigned to the emptiness of another day—they roused themselves for breakfast. Always the same sort of breakfast. Mai had saved the sticky rice from the day before. They ate with their hands a cold ball in which she had mixed a little dried fish. Not really awake, they ate quietly from aluminum pans. They had to pay for any extras. The coffee was a luxury; the sweetened milk was nearly impossible to get.

The guards liked Fay and Roberts—and tolerated Mai—because the two big noses were always in need of extras and were willing to shell out hard cash for favors. Fay wondered if they were being kept without trial or representation simply because they were such good sources of revenue. They were, after all, probably the biggest thing ever to hit the little border post at Feng. Roberts, considering their isolation more darkly, wondered when their captors would figure out that it would be a lot easier just to kill them and take their money, cameras, baggage, watches, rings, clothes, shoes. Maybe they didn't dare kill them, he finally decided, because too many people might remember their getting pulled off the bus at the border last April or because too many prisoners could talk, or even a disloyal guard, or, by now, Border Police from nearby posts. So why didn't they just confiscate their stuff? Instead, the guards were doggedly solicitous. One brought Fay a leaf monkey with a wonderful silver mane and beard. It was a sad creature, very quiet. She kept it for a while, encouraging it to frisk about her cell, until one day when she saw it plucking and eating its lice. After that, they kept it tethered to a stake under the eaves. They fed it sweet-potato shoots, rotted bananas, and, every now and then, some greens. All of which, of course, Fay had to pay for. Sometimes it ran about and climbed its post, but most of the time it sat hunched and half asleep.

Coffee. Condensed milk. A little pork or wild boar. Catfish. Mangoes. Mosquito netting. Pillows filled with the downy floss from bombax trees. A little stoneware grill. Beer. Rice whiskey in an earthen jar. These were the favors that the guards were pleased to sell them. And opium. They were, after all, in the Golden Triangle, perhaps the world's largest source of illegal opium, where the mountain tribes—the Yao, Miao, Akha, Khun, Karen, Lahu, and Lisu—prospered only through the cultivation of hilltop fields of poppy and where several armies—the remnant Kuomintang; the Thai insurgents, the Thahan Pa or "soldiers from the jungle"; as well as the Thai and Burmese military—competed for control of the raw opium.

The Shans wanted the opium to finance their rebellion against Burma. The Burmese wanted to keep it from the Shans. For the Chinese troops, opium had become their only means of livelihood once Chiang Kai-shek had retreated to Taiwan. For the Thai Liberation Army—Communists loyal to China but on uneasy terms with the Vietnamese, the Khmer Rouge, and the Pathet Lao—opium not only meant money for payrolls, arms, and bribes but also a means of controlling the mountain tribes who grew the poppy. This meant *all* the mountain tribes, for the poppy was the only cash crop possible in the weak laterite soils of the steep hills where villages were always shifting as forests were cleared by slash-and-burn swiddening, planted in poppy, corn, and rice, exhausted in seven or so years, and then abandoned. The mountain peoples augmented their meager diets with game, squash, spinach, wild hairy camus, corn, and low-yielding, high-altitude rice. But opium was their means of existence.

For the Thai Border Police and the regular army, opium was a double bonus: the Americans paid their government to pay them to burn the unlicensed fields, to interdict the mule caravans threading through the mountain passes with Shan or Chinese armed escorts, and to confiscate the opium. But the orders were ambiguous or, at least, conflicting. They were also told to leave the mountain people alone lest they turn to the Communists. And, besides, opium was valuable. The area's only industry. How could they simply destroy it? Instead, they sold it. They scolded the mountain people for growing the poppy, but they let them harvest the opium and sell it to the Yunnanese Haw retailers who sold it to the big warlords. And then the Thais captured it, reported the confiscations to the American Drug Enforcement Agent in Bangkok, and sold it again to other middlemen, mostly Chinese, who reduced its bulk by a crude refining in Bangkok, from where—through the complicity of still higher officials—it was shipped to Hong Kong and Marseilles. There it was further refined into heroin, diluted, packaged, and made ready for the streets of Europe and the U.S.A. In moving from Feng to Bangkok, a kilogram of raw, compressed opium increased in value from fifty American dollars to two hundred.

Roberts, for all his canniness about drugs and his curiosity about Southeast Asia, knew very little about these complexities of survival, economics, politics, and corruption. But he knew that his prison at Feng was in the dope business: in the drizzly sky beyond Fay's window he watched as a police helicopter dropped to its pad across the scummy water. Right now, a pistoled army officer and a soldier with an M-16 were ducking under the whooshing blades and holding onto cap and helmet as the blade wash whipped up the puddles of water all around the mesh landing pad. At other times, Roberts had looked out and seen the Border Police off-loading what he knew to be packets of opium wrapped in burlap.

And the hills farther to the right of the window—far above the terraces planted in banana, taro, beans, and rice—swayed with bright, rapturous, washed cups of full poppy blossoms. Now, in August, as the rainy season was winding down, the white variety, *na ying*, was starting to flower. From their cell windows, Fay and Roberts could watch an entire Miao village of some forty families and their Karen hired hands spread through the fields like grasshoppers as they scoured the bright rows, weeding and thinning the early *na ying* and planting the later-blooming poppies—the red-and-white, the purple, the red, and finally another white with a high sap yield, the *ying pang gler*.

"Someday," Roberts said, sucking his sore right gums, rubbing the itch between a thumb and a finger, and still looking out the window at the gray, broken clouds into which the departing helicopter was rising, "someday that chopper will land and a tall roundeye in a white linen suit is going to get off holding a briefcase and . . ." He turned to see if Mai and Fay were listening. Mai was rinsing their breakfast tins in a pail of moat water. The oil from the dried fish swirled on the surface; the few abandoned rice grains rocked to the bottom of the pail. Fay looked over from the chair near the shaky folding table where she was rereading an issue of *Eve*, a feminist magazine. With her long nails she scratched her pubic hair beneath her panties and waited for Roberts to finish. "And in that briefcase . . . will be orders for our release. We will shake hands with the guards, give them back their sad, shit-assed monkey and also the leftover opium, gather up whatever they haven't stolen from us, and then climb into our bird and whirl away."

"Oh, no tell me so sad," said Mai, whose English was developing after nearly four months of close confinement with her European jailmates. "What I do, you no here?" The glare of pail water rippled on her scarred chin. She was smiling. She was happy. Fay and Roberts had been her biggest break since her sister had sold her to a Chinese restaurateur when Mai was only twelve. "New cherry make Chinese man strong," she had explained. She was sold for $200. Whatever the results for the restaurant owner, for a year Mai's family was rich. Yes, she was a lucky girl. Her parents were gone, but she had Fay. Whose skin was smooth and white as coconut milk and just as sweet. And Roberts, whom she found easy to please.

"And whirl away," Roberts repeated thoughtfully as the chopper disappeared to a gnat-size dot.

"Should that happen, ducky, the first thing I'd do is put myself in hospital." Fay pulled away the elastic band and looked down at her mons veneris to see what the hell was itching her. "Can you imagine soap and hot water and clean, starched sheets?" She knitted her brow. "Paul," she said, "what is this?"

Roberts turned away again from the window and looked over to see where Fay was pointing. "Well, I'd guess that's your cunt."

"No, come on. What are these spots? Measles?"

Roberts yawned, pressed his palms into the sides of his belly, coughed hard and sat up from the bed. Mai dried her hands on the ass of the pair of Fay's blue jeans she was wearing. She walked over and stood next to where Roberts sat on the edge of the bed. Fay stood before them holding down the elastic band of her panties with her two thumbs.

She was stippled there with about a dozen hard, red, crusty dots. The little lumps looked angry and some of them had erupted in pus.

Roberts looked at them, touched one very delicately with an index finger and hissed a long "Ssshit." "*I* don't know," he said looking up at her and shaking his head. "You got 'em anywhere else?"

Since Fay, as usual, was wearing only her panties, it was easy to find out. She stood still with her arms up and her hands clasped behind her head as Mai and Roberts combed over her body. A soft, white, English girl's body, nurtured by summery mists and spring fogs and unblemished by the sun. Opium had made Fay thinner than she had been since she was twelve. She had lost a lot of weight in her hips; her ribs showed. Her face and back and legs were clear.

Roberts sat back and watched Mai, whose hands, as in all corporeal matters, were quite practiced. Mai was silent and intent as her hands passed over Fay's white body. She stopped and turned to Roberts when she found one red spot starting at the aureole of Fay's right breast.

"Make turn," she said and Fay turned around, but as she did Mai grabbed her elbow and pointed for Roberts to look. Her elbows were inflamed with hard, dry lesions. "Bend down." Fay turned around again and grasped the edge of the bed with her two hands. Mai pulled down the back of her panties. Her large white fanny shone in the drizzly daylight. Roberts got up and came around to look. At the base of each pretty buttock, which Mai was now pressing up and apart, were hard, angry lesions like those on her elbows as well as the pustulating kind scattered about the pudenda.

"Well, love? Bedbugs? Measles?"

Mai was silent. Roberts watched. Fay stood up and Mai pulled her panties back. Now Mai sat on the bed and made Fay kneel on the floor with her head in Mai's lap. Nimbly, Mai's fingers separated and plucked the fine strands as she searched for lice. There were none.

"Jungle rot," Roberts said now that the inspection was finished and Fay stood up again.

"Ducky, what do you know?"

"I know we're in a fucking rotting jungle. Look at my fingers."

Mai frowned and took Roberts's hand and pulled him down beside her. Between the fingers and on the sides of the digits there were the same dry crusts and red lumps. Mai smiled ruefully; she also found a dirty gray track just under the skin of one finger. "Fay," she said, "get Mai needle."

Roberts looked at her with suspicion.

She pressed about the welts with her hard thumbs. "A baby animal," she explained. "I take him out."

"No you don't."

"No hurt, papa-san. You see. Permettez-moi . . ."

Fay was examining her infected nipple. She was beginning to remember a story her mother had told her. "Love," she said. A story about the London blitz and the shelters. "Perhaps we'd better see."

"No hurt," Mai repeated. But it did. Quick as Mai was at working into the lump of a welt and pleasurable as that sharp pang was for a second, still it hurt like hell in the next second when she poked deeper and then came away, smiling broadly, with a little white dot about a sixteenth of an inch in diameter.

"Oh, God, Paul."

"What? Goddamn it, what?" he repeated as Fay covered her face with her hand and began to cry.

"Scabies. We've got scabies."

"How do you know?" The anger had left his voice. His tone was cold and tentative.

"Mother told me that people got them in the shelters during the blitz. Like that. A little white mite that burrows under the skin."

"What do you do?" He pulled his hand back as Mai started to go after another welt.

"You put yourself in hospital," she wailed and went on sobbing.

"Wait a minute. Wait a *minute.*" But Fay was bawling. "Look, Mai obviously knows this stuff." Roberts put his hand under Mai's blouse and gave her near titty a squeeze. "Mai, you got 'em?"

"No yet. I get. Maybe now already."

"What do you get it from?"

"Dirty man. Dirty girl. Maybe dog." She paused to point outside the door. "Maybe monkey. Bar girl always get."

"Yeah, I know, occupational hazard. But what do you do?"

"I fuck some man, some girl."

"No, I mean what do you do to get rid of it?"

"Rid? Comment?"

"Make go away. Se debarrasser *de.* Guerez." Roberts made throwing away gestures with his hands.

"Oh." It was a big "oh" accompanied by her wide, scarred smile. Mai knew the answer: "Go hospital or baby animal go everyplace body."

"Fuck-an-A," Roberts groaned. Fay sobbed all the louder.

6.

*T*he last shots were fired into a pack mule. The big, bare-headed Negro in fatigues, his belled cheeks running sweat, squeezed off a burst into the mule's head as it lay on its side, front legs pawing the air, haunches shredded by the mortar blast that had blown open its twin saddle packs. The mule wrenched up its neck and legs and then collapsed into a heap of meat and bloodied opium.

At the last shots, the fifteen or so other mules stamped momentarily, flicked their long ears, and huddled unattended on the red-clay hillside above the forest stream. Once the mule was dead and the staccato reports had echoed out of the cramped valley, the black man heard a nasal Thai song yammering in the grass where a transistor radio had fallen next to a dead guard. He turned and fired his M-16 again, shattering the voice and jags of plastic through the tall weeds.

"Hey, Beta, maybe Kor wan' tha'."

Beta turned to the young Asian walking toward him and wiping his face with the checkered cotton scarf draped around his neck. The man used the AK-47 he was carrying to point toward the shards of the radio. He was thin, about five-foot-five, with high pronounced cheekbones, very dark eyes, and black, straight hair cut just about his shoulders. Along with his sandals and homespun pajamas, he wore an Atlanta Braves baseball cap.

"Whiney shit fuck yo' mind." As Beta spoke he studied the craggy ridge line high above them, where some of the caravan guards had fled into the bamboo thickets.

Once again, crickets and locusts pitched their seesaw trills about the hillside. Below, where others had fled, the jungle stream plunged loudly through the rocky shallows where screw pines rose up in a basketry of russet roots some three feet off the forest floor. Their palmlike fans sheafed upward and rustled with the leaves of wild banana. Green babblers shrieked in the treetops. A gibbon, walking the trunk, scolded them from a pandanus tree, its enormous bulk laid across the jungle floor.

"Chom," Beta called and his Asian friend turned and looked where Beta pointed: A flock of lorikeets had swarmed out of the treetops on the far side of the bank, about a hundred yards away.

"Both si' covah'," Chom said, and soon they heard more small-arms fire near the spooked birds. "We make blocking force, jus' li' Jimmy say."

"Yeah, like Jimmy said." Beta fished in his canvas ammunition bag for a fresh clip. Then he took another M-19 rifle grenade from his bandolier and fitted it into the launcher below the M-16 barrel.

Chom waved down to a man by the stream bank who was waiting under a banyan with a string of fresh mules.

"Seems like only two dead," Beta said.

They walked together up the trail. A bright green snake whip-lashed away before Beta's heavy boots. Chom called to a turbaned man leading a Yunnan pony down toward them. He was younger than Chom. Around his neck was a string of grenades—the Soviet kind with handles—and a small clay Buddha housed in a silver casing. Near the amulet hung a red thread holding a prayer that had been whispered and cinched into its knot. The boy smiled as he led the pony down and spoke to Chom.

"Him say we have siktee' good mule."

"Sixteen, huh? We did okay."

They found three caravan guards dead.

"All Loi Maw. All Chini'," Chom said as an older man in rubber sandals brought him the dead men's guns and papers and Taiwan watches.

Two others were wounded. One had shut his eyes as he lay on his back and slowly rocked his head left and right. He thrashed his legs and groaned; blood drained from both his ears. They looked at him and walked on. The other was a kid in Hong Kong sneakers. His fatigue shirt was far too big for him. He had been shot through the hand and was just too scared to run with the others. He sat near the trail holding his shattered hand.

"Him?" Beta said, as he and Chom sat down on a mossy boulder next to the boy. Beta picked a fern and twirled it in his giant hands. The boy stared at him wildly.

"Him Shan, not Chini'."

"Uh-huh. What we do with the li'l fucker?"

"Let him go. He go."

"But he'll talk."

"He our ca'ing car'."

"Uh-huh. Callin' card. And him?" Beta pointed to the boy sprawled on his back by the trail.

"He die." And with that Chom motioned to one of his men standing by the other boy. The man put his old M-1 to the boy's head and pulled the trigger. Once again, a report bellowed through the little valley, and the locusts ceased, and the birds along the stream rose up in a screech and flew off in silence.

After a moment Beta said, "Ain't the same without Jimmy."

7.

The rain-swept village was set high—three hundred feet up in the steep, forested mountains that now hissed and seethed under the monsoon. Chom, wearing a sweater, his scarf snugged about his neck, his baseball cap pulled down, sat cross-legged near the dripping eaves of his aunt's thatch-roof house. From a tin cup, remnant of a Japanese mess kit, he sipped *yog law* coffee into which his aunt had stirred a thick, yellowy dollop of sweetened condensed milk. He puffed Lao tobacco from a calabash pipe and watched the rain.

The small taro field near the mountain stream that rattled through the village was now filled with rain and runoff. Soon the bright green taro shoots would unfurl and choke the shallow basin, and when the dry season came again and the taro had been harvested and pounded into meal, the children would go hunting for frogs hiding in the mud cracks, as he had when a boy in his father's village farther west.

Chom watched the tree line just past the pepper field where the branches rose and fell with the squalls. And behind the bamboo hedge—the living fence separating his aunt's yard from the neighbor's—he saw a bougainvillea tremble with rain and drop crimson petals on the muddy track that ran between the houses. The yellow gourd blossoms were flat and dripping on the trellis above the gate; the ragged leaves of the banana shook in the rain. Chom reached over and picked up the skin of the papaya half his aunt had given him on a slice of banana leaf; he shoved it through a floorboard crack to the pig penned below him. The pig awoke and grunted.

The house, like the others, was raised on teak posts. Chickens and pigs roomed below; his relatives, above. The water buffalo was corralled at a neighbor's where it had more room. It was a good village, small. They had patches of mint, garlic, sweet potato, cassava, pumpkin, cucumber, and peppers, some groves of jackfruit, papaya, and banana, and a few terraces of upland rice. There were even two kapok trees; his aunt had made pillows from the thick silk in the seedpods. The money to buy the fruit trees, to purchase the land, the seed, the pigs, chickens, and water buffalo had come from opium. Here his Lawa relatives and their Skaw Karen associates could prosper out of the reach of the Thai authorities, Thais who had taken their old lands and who had taxed the Lawa out of their patrimony of centuries. Once his people had built the great wats in Chiang Mai; then they were driven into the hills by the Lanathai lords; and when the Prince of Chiang Mai himself was driven out by the southern Thais, all their lands were lost. Once they had been rich in elephants, silk, and gold. Now they lived like monkeys in a strange forest. But now he had guns and with guns he had opium and with opium he could regain their wealth. And it was, he thought again, a good village. The Karens who sold it to them had done so only because they could no longer deal with the village spirit living in the immense banyan that dropped massive weaves of aerial roots through the only level spot in the village. So the spirit was already looking out for the Lawa: no helicopter could land here. No roads led here, and the Border Patrol Police were so ignorant of the mountain peoples that they probably did not even know yet that the Karens had moved out and that the Lawa had moved in. No roads for miles. Just mule trails. Akha, Lisu, Hmong, and some Haw from Yunnan lived in villages in the hundred or so square miles from here to the Burmese border, but they grew or sold opium and so they kept to themselves. No opium, Chom thought, must ever be grown here: no Black Phantoms to destroy his people, no competition to annoy his neighbors, no excuse for the Thais to come and take a look. Chom puffed the gourd pipe and blew a cloud of smoke at the rainstorm. He decided he should talk to the tree spirit sometime.

He sipped his coffee—maybe they could grow coffee—and looked at the spirit house that he had made from upas wood and set on a post in the yard. The paper furnishings would be soaked. He'd have to replace them. It was good the rains had come so soon after the ambush. He felt safe. He could smell the little silvery river fish drying in the flat basket behind him, and the mold in the dip nets hanging in the rafters, and the tobacco hanging there, and the herbs from the garden and forest, and the roots his aunt ground up, and the stack of charcoal under the cooking tray, and the orchid his aunt had wrapped in a sheaf of bark and bundled to the porch pillar. He heard the rain splattering on the steel plowshare leaning against the pen at his feet. He sipped his steamy coffee, tasted the tin from the rim of the cup and felt good.

Despite the rain, he heard Beta walking toward him through the hedgerows. He knew him by the way his big feet slopped in the muck. Like the Lawa, Beta had no home. But the Lawa had each other. Beta was like a lone monkey in the forest. Very sad. Even Jimmy was gone.

Beta wore a hooded poncho. Coming up the ladder, he could barely squeeze his broad shoulders through the floor door. Chom heard something knock against the ladder as Beta shoved his shoulders through. The Ingram.

"Hey, Chom."

"Here. On por'."

Beta came out, his big boots squeaking water. He sat down beside Chom and struggled out of the poncho, then pulled the sling of the Ingram over his head and set it down. Chom pushed an earthenware jar toward Beta. Where the damp bottom had been, a family of earwigs wriggled away. Beta lifted the woven straw cap from the jar and looked in. He picked out a giant moth with a long snout and flicked it off into the downpour.

"Lord," he said. He took a reed straw from a packet on the wall and poked it into the rice whiskey. He took a pull. "Lord."

"You see Jimmy?"

"Uh-huh."

"Any bettah?"

"No. He ain't gonna be better. That Crane's no doctor, nor his ol' lady. You know what he told me?"

Chom leaned back to listen.

"He told me his wife go up to that Haw village 'cause some chil' dyin', you know, an' this girl she's 'bout ten, got fuckin' plague an' his Missus shoots her up with some kind of antbiotic an' tells the girl's family—now get this—*that the kid would make it* if they became Christians. How's that."

"Bad."

"Yeah, an' you think Jimmy's gettin' any better?"

"What happen to girl?"

"Well, these Chinese are Moslems you know, and they say no, an' few weeks later the kid dies. Reverend Crane seemed to think it was wrong for his wife to say that, mind you."

"Maybe we should take Jimmy to MPs."

"He wouldn't want that."

They listened together to the rain rinsing through the roof thatch, spilling into buckets, plopping in the path puddles, ripping the taro field, and washing the fog-wreathed forests all about them.

"He gonna rot in this rain. Chom, he just sitting there like a dead man."

Chom took a drag on the pipe and offered it to Beta.

8.

*F*ather. Father. Father. How many times had Roberts called in his heart when as now, in September, weeks after the start of the scabies, he needed rescue. No rescue had come, even when the powerful rescuer loomed close by. As close as the mirror, as close as his own practiced male voice which also resembled his father's. Who now was dead. Whose death was like another trick—the most devious and unfair—that made their mortal combat all the harder for Roberts to win. Banker and statesman. Fame fixed in death.

He drew deeply on the long heavy pipe that Mai held for him as he lay on his side, his right cheek flattened on the square white porcelain brick with its finely crackled glaze. An opium pillow. Roberts took the pipe to his lips and was careful to suck a long continuous drag so that the opium rosin—which Mai had liquefied over a small alcohol lamp—would not coagulate and clog the pipe's pinprick hole. His head swam as the smoke bloomed in his lungs. Letting it go, he sighed a great blue cloud and watched a memory come rolling back through time on its billows, slapping like dock water at the soiled feet of the others sprawled on the wooden bed: Koi, the old guard with the smallpoxed face who lay next to Roberts; Fay, sitting on the bed in the sunlight by the window, watching the fighting fish, each alone, circling like a thought in its large earthen jar. A familiar memory. A painful memory. Same-same, as the dinks said. Him and his sister together, sitting alone on the boat landing at their prep school in Rhode Island. Waiting. Waiting for their father, as always. Picking at the pier, tossing into the water some wood splinters and tar chips and the cracked mussles that gulls had abandoned. The bright glinting water. They had boasted to the others that their old man, who hadn't seen them for months, would come sailing up the bay at noon—he had telegrammed them. They skipped lunch and waited for their father's sailboat. At two, they stopped inventing excuses. At three, they walked back to the school in silence. Paul arched the stick he had whittled high up into the oaks at water's edge. Paul Roberts was thirteen; Jane, fifteen. It was hide-and-seek. They'd play it forever. Paul, aggressive, clever, tireless to compete; Jane, looking for any excuse to quit and find some private haunt where her neglectful father became only silence. But Paul set out in search of redress. If he couldn't have love, he wanted justice. When the old man didn't want him around, he would just show up. A thirteen-year-old who wasn't so cute, asking some actress or diplomat's wife to dance just as his father, flushed with booze and making the best of his son's surprise visit, was saying how he hoped the boy would become a stevedore or a truck driver so he could see America straight-up, the way he had. Children fight hard for love, especially when the odds are hopeless. Love like murder. The little VC against the U.S. Army: winning sometimes, but at terrible, disfiguring cost.

Mai sat cross-legged, working the opium, slicing a chunk from an oily, unwrapped brick, rolling a wad between her fingers to heat it slowly, powdering the wad with large doses of Chinese aspirin to ward off the headaches that came with withdrawal, and then heating the wad at the end of a long needle—at first right over the little blue flame of the alcohol lamp and then in the tin where it simmered and liquefied. Friendly blue flame like a Bunsen burner's. Then she transferred the shiny bubble to the tiny bowl of the pipe and applied the flame. When she did that, Roberts was already sucking in again. It was important; otherwise the pipe would clog and the opium would be wasted and everyone would have to wait while she reamed out the gummed pipe. But there were time and opium to waste. Lots. Lots of both.

He rolled over on his stomach and looked at Koi's pitted mug as the pipe was passed to the guard. Fay was now kneading the muscles in the small of Roberts's back. He had rolled over slowly, fighting nausea, and now he closed his eyes as he felt her rough, scabby hands pressing into his back and buttocks, which were also crusted with sores. The scabies sores were painful and got infected easily, and the skin was raw from the home remedies that Mai applied along with the needle she used to probe out the mites, trying to get them before they could lay eggs in the tunnels that they bored in the flesh. She rubbed them with coal tar and kerosene, with alcohol, with pungent Tiger Balm that soothed the itching and that she sometimes mixed with a solution of opium. There was no hospital. They were allowed no doctor. They were red and raw and ugly. They had had no trial, had not been formally charged. They weren't even on a prison roster. They could not go to Chiang Mai; nor could a doctor be summoned. Bua Miang, the fat district chief, was adamant.

"You are charge," he had told them, "very serious crime. You no leave until try."

Trial he pronounced "try." They had stood before him in his room on the barracks side of the prison. He was sitting on the edge of his army cot before a card table on which lay their passports, and stuffed into each passport was a sheaf of papers in Thai. A glass of warm beer, in which a dead fly floated, was next to their papers. Major Miang was wearing one of Prescott's shirts pilfered from their luggage. His belly bulged against the buttons. He held a handkerchief to his sweaty head.

"So let us have a trial," Fay had said. "We plead guilty."

"No possible. No judge."

"Mr. Miang," Roberts began in a serious professional tone. "We have been imprisoned for six months. We will be glad to pay any fine you think appropriate, but we must see a doctor."

"Very sad, pretty girl like Miss Fay." When he smiled, he flashed a row of gold buck teeth.

Fay smiled. Scabies doesn't affect the face. Her smile was pretty and the rest of her was properly covered for their interview.

"But no."

"My father was a rich man. He knew the President of the United States."

This was not the right thing to say. In fact, it was the problem. Major Miang made a motion as if shooing a fly and the guard—old Koi—shuffled up to his feet and pointed to the door with a jab of his M-16. Their interview was over.

And so here they were. Yet another day of smoking dope with their captors, who had imprisoned them for smoking dope. Mai was singing her own version of "How Much Is that Doggie in the Window?" ("How ma as the daggie in window?"). Koi was off in dreamland, with his M-16 propped against the bed and the peeling stucco wall, and Fay, wrapped in a cheap cotton sarong, was thoughtfully poking her finger in the fish jars trying to induce the needle-jawed creatures to fan their sail-like fins and attack.

"Be it ever so humble," Roberts said. No one replied, although the leaf monkey chained outside screamed as a mangy cat crept close to scout the monkey's food. Roberts dangled his arms off the edge of the bed and wiggled fingers aching with scabies and smelling of coal tar. Like Mai and Fay, he also wore a sarong now, because his jeans made his crotch itch more. In front of his extended hands, a large cockroach with an egg capsule protruding from its rear end shuffled along the wall to a clump of roaches feeding on another, dead, upturned roach. Their clothing and food stank of roach excretion. Strung out on opium, Roberts watched the huge bugs with dispassion. "Fay," he said, pointing to the insect cannibals when she turned.

"Lovely," she said, and rolled over to place her head on Mai's lap. Mai brushed Fay's hair from her forehead, extinguished the lamp, and put away the pipe and opium. She leaned down to kiss Fay on the mouth and then sat up again. Fay closed her eyes and Mai began stroking her face.

Fay and Roberts didn't fuck much anymore unless the three did it together, Fay on Mai or Mai on Fay and Roberts bringing up the rear, doggy-style. The doggy in the window, looking in at two cats, at the soles of their feet, their buttocks and backs crusted with scabies. Roberts didn't have the appetite to demand more. Just as the opium made him stop eating, it also curtailed his appetite for sex. Often he couldn't get an erection, even watching the two of them; and often, when he could, he couldn't come. It was as if someone had strapped a dildo on him. He'd pump like a whippet, break into a sweat, and, after several minutes, give up. This was fun for both Fay and Mai, who would straddle him and then ride his appropriated member, but boring for Roberts. Sometimes, when he came, he had a lot of pain as the nerve ends at the base of his urethra misfired in anesthetized sequences.

He liked Mai okay. She was a cheerful and professional fuck. Her skin was less ravaged than Fay's. She understood that for all of them to stay happy, she had to please him. She cooked, washed their clothes, massaged them, negotiated with the guards for their needs, prepared the opium—no small skill—fucked them, and doctored them, inventing dreadful cures that their desperation persuaded them to accept, like the white salve she made from boiling a bar of soap and then mixing the solution with cheap, red kerosene. But she had also stolen Fay. Or had he just lost Fay? Maybe Prescott had stolen Fay. Roberts yawned in resistance to this task of analysis of emotions. He really didn't care about other people's emotions. But something had happened in Bangalore. Fay wasn't the same after that.

Roberts studied the roaches busy devouring their brother and confident in the calm, opiated, dim midday light. Those fucking bugs were too much. At night, he burned a light trap in the room, setting a small kerosene lamp on a brick in a bucket of water. At dawn the surface was littered with floating and still-fluttering bugs: papery moths with snouts; huge, pale June bugs shaped like guitar picks; leaf borers with great, horned heads; gallflies with pink, segmented bellies; leaf binder flies with yellow waists and thick, red, faceted eyes. Rice bugs with pop-dot red eyes and katydid-green legs infested their food. Mosquito larvae wriggled in the steel drum outside where they stored the drinking water. The trick there was to keep a film of kerosene on the top so they'd hit it when they wiggled to the surface for air. Silverfish had gotten into Fay's knapsack and onto a photo of her father. They had eaten his face away. Mai picked their heads for lice and pinched and poked their flesh for mites. If the dinks just kept 'em long enough they'd all be gone without a trace and nobody would have raised a hand. The way you fed crickets on potatoes.

"I am not a potato!" Roberts screamed, slamming his hand on the bed and knocking over the alcohol lamp.

Koi blinked open his eyes but did not stir. Fay, however, sat up and looked at Roberts.

"Hey, man," Mai said soothingly, "sa va. No sweat. I rub you now."

Fay motioned Mai to keep still. Then Fay leaned over and touched Roberts's hand. "C'mon, love," she said. "We'll be out soon."

"You fucking sure you want to rouse yourself?"

"Paul . . ."

Roberts glared at her. He knew that his anger made so little sense that he couldn't even find an accusation to continue on. He knew she knew. It was just resentment. Her and Mai. The whole fucking, stinking, bug-ridden deal.

Just then a police whistle blew in the yard and there was a clamor of voices and the sounds of feet running across the dried mud. The monkey was screeching, and finally—before Paul and Fay could get to the door—there were three pops of a carbine.

When they looked out, prisoners and guards were milling at the door of Ko Pisan's cell, where the guard who had fired the three shots was waving another to come over. Fay and Roberts shuffled out, although the sun hit them like a mortar and their stomachs lurched into spins. Mai followed them, though she wasn't as hopeful about the entertainment. By the time they got there, the crowd was turning away. People would struggle forward to get a look inside the cell and then would walk away without speaking. No one seemed interested in a long look.

It was Ko Pisan. Naked and dead, lying before the door of his cell with his bulgy eyes staring up at the ceiling. The ceiling and walls were spattered with the smashed carcasses of geckos, the tiny, clucking lizards that ran upside down after flies and mosquitoes and that were some amusement to most prisoners, except sometimes when the geckos forgot themselves up there and went to sleep and plopped down to the ground or onto a sleeper. Ko Pisan had been dead for some hours. He was cold when the lieutenant felt his pulse.

"How'd he do it?" Roberts motioned for Mai to ask the guard.

"He say him eat opium. That way Karen people kill self here."

"How much opium?"

Fay looked at Roberts nervously.

"He say him brother bring him last week. Him no good man. Kill mother you know? Village say better he die."

"Yeah, he never was any fun. But how much did it take?"

Mai asked the guard again, who shrugged off the question. "I dunno. Maybe ball like you put inside you hand."

Fay turned away and started back to their cell, but Roberts stayed. He had his father's scientific curiosity. General Bullmoose. In fact, Roberts was the first to notice the flat, shiny, inch-wide, white ribbon that was slowly rocking out from under Ko Pisan's buttocks. When the Thai guard rolled the Karen over with a shove of his black army boot, they saw a tapeworm—already about three feet long if unraveled—leaving the dead man's body through his anus.

"That too bad," Mai said, meaning "too disgusting." "I go back."

"Well, it's one way to get rid of those pesky mites." Roberts grinned at the guard who had also turned away in disgust.

"*Comment?*" Mai asked, and then not bothering about his clarification, she said, "Paul, cher, you me go back. I give you back rub."

Roberts, shuffling beside Mai, stumbled back across the prison yard, muttering "one potato, two potato." Across from them the sizable piglets were squealing and trotting after their weary sow, her tits hanging down like a collapsed accordion as she edged off behind the red barrels—What were those for? Roberts asked himself again—underneath the main watchtower. The sun was so strong it made him sick in his stomach. Where was Jane, he wondered. Their daddy was in heaven with the saints, eating steak at "21" and telling Happy Rockefeller not to worry about the boy. Their mother? Watching the ocean off Maine. Drunk as a skunk; brain as salted as a clam's. His son? Riding a tricycle underneath the oaks of his new daddy's Pennsylvania house. Lacey? Professing. Prescott? Dispersed ashes rolling over slowly along the bottom of the Ganges. Paul Roberts? A little sweet potato roasting on a grill for extralarge roaches wearing Border Police uniforms.

9.

The Karen's suicide occasioned a holiday for the prisoners. Since it was important to keep on good terms with the local hill people who had employed Ko Pisan and his brother, the Nae Amphur had radioed his assistant, the Kamnan, Snit Puaree, to let the prisoners out while the mountain villagers came down to claim the body. The Thais had adopted a policy of accommodation with the minority groups in the North—a reversal of an earlier policy of exploitation and assimilation that had driven the minorities into the arms of the Thahan Pa, the Communist "soldiers from the jungle." The King annually spent large personal sums on the hill tribes, who lacked schools, health clinics, doctors, legal representation—in short, the rudimentary protections of civilized society. The Nae Amphur and his Kamnan were in accord with the new policy. Officially they still discouraged opium production, but unofficially they looked the other way. At their small outpost near Chiang Saen, they simply avoided looking up—to the terraced, red-clay hillsides spotted with white-blossomed fields, where the harvest of early fall varieties was already in full swing as the villagers lanced the fertilized pods and collected the sap twice a day. The new policy meant opium cash in everyone's pockets.

The Nae Amphur's decision to let out the prisoners just made good sense. In several ways. Nobody really trusted the Miao or wanted them circulating about a small prison whose population included several of their tribesmen, the Chinese trader with whom they had done business, and Shan revolutionaries from across the Burmese border. Furthermore, the prison needed an airing. A spirit airing. Ko Pisan had been possessed by a demon. The Miao, for whom he had worked, would capture the evil spirit and beat it before it left his body. His soul would be put at rest, and he wouldn't bother anybody anymore. It was common sense for everyone concerned.

At seven o'clock before the chilly mists had been burned off the dense thickets, the guards, one shouldering a Browning automatic rifle, opened the gates and headed toward the forest stream, which had been dammed into a pond bordered by mud flats, sandy spits, garden plots, and, on the far side, a rustling sea of jute swaying twelve feet high in the breeze. The BAR was set up on the dam at the spot where the stream was partly diverted into the prison moat.

Three guards remained in the prison. The others—along with the Kamnan, a jaunty young man with an oily pompadour, shiny boots, and a Browning .45 strapped to his side—called the prisoners out of their cells, grouped them in the yard, counted them, and herded them outside. Some of them marched shrouded in blankets and blinking like owls in the sunlight that was shafting through the treetops where lorikeets and blue-green rollers screamed. Mai and Fay carried their cotton blankets, three cheap Chinese towels, a pot of dried pork and sticky rice, and Prescott's blue leather flight bag, which contained their valuables and whatever remained of his: cameras, traveler's checks, some cash . . . and Prescott's last notebook. Old Koi, his M-16 slung across the back of his shoulders and his arms draped over it, ambled beside them while balancing a canteen full of boiled water from a webbed belt that dangled from the rifle's barrel. He had become their personal guard. Their interests were his. Like Mai, he worried about their cash holding out. Roberts, who had cramps in his legs, shuffled behind them in his flipflops, muttering "all sentient beings" as he led the leaf monkey by a rope. When the group finally halted to squat on the lower, cracked-mud shore, a young Thai—a truck driver arrested for smuggling Chinese laundry detergent—knelt down and vomited.

Holding his big automatic in his hand, the Kamnan told them in a strident pitch how far they could wander without being shot. To make his point, he directed one of the guards, a young thug with a shredded ear, to pop a few shots at a breadfruit tree some yards away at the edge of the forest. Even before the huge spiny fruit splashed apart and fell to the ground, the forest birds stopped screaming and a flock of egrets quietly lifted out of the shallows where the stream plunged away from the forest. Then Snit Puaree, still holding his pistol, pointed sternly at the BAR. The gunner fired a short burst into the thickets of bamboo and screw pines, lopping off whole trees at waist height. As the birds whirled out of the thickets, the Kamnan continued to shrill at them. "Snit's in a snit," Roberts whispered to Fay, but she only frowned and moved away. Fay was tired of Roberts's lame jokes. She wanted to be alone. Even Mai was milking her like a cow. She wanted to think, to let the sun wash her skin, to feel the cool mountain water, the clean air.

With the burst of the BAR, the egrets flapped a little faster on south across the paddy. Fay's gaze followed the birds as they flew over the Hmong, as the Miao villagers called themselves, who had been waiting under some large fig trees below the prison where the moat and the stream rejoined. Taking the shots as their signal, the Hmong—the whole village, it seemed—set out single file across the paddy dikes onto the dirt road leading into the prison. The lead man was carrying a gun.

"How thoughtful," Roberts said as he watched the line enter the gates. "They're changing places with us. That's really white of them." He tied the monkey to a sapling as the group broke up into its usual segregations. The Kamnan holstered his pistol and walked back to the prison, *briskly* one had to notice, while the guards took up their positions: two by the whispering jute field into which you could disappear in just a few steps; one at the head of the stream where you might scramble over rocks into the jungle; and several behind the gardens plotted out before the flooded rice fields.

Fay found a spot on a sandbar away from the crackled shore, a clean place where she could slip her scabby feet into the cold water. She lit up a brown Shaiyo and offered a drag to Roberts, who was digging his toes in the sand and trying to figure out what to do. Fay brushed back her red-gold hair, closed her eyes, and turned her face up to receive the morning sun. The cicadas chirred. The jungle birds were calling again. Roberts took another drag and studied the water.

"Hey, breakfa'," Mai called as she waddled over with a thermos of coffee mixed with sweetened condensed milk. They were rationing their supply, but this was a holiday. She held out three tin cups for Roberts to hold as she poured. "Koi, numa one!" she shouted back to Koi, who was sitting against a bamboo fence topped by sprays of yellow flowers and new, tiny gourds. He waved his fatigue cap and smiled. Chapeau. The coffee was his gift. He had made it at dawn . . . and at no extra charge. "You be ni' me, I be ni' you" was his motto and only English phrase.

"Coffee."

Fay didn't open her eyes. Roberts put her tin cup into the sand beside her.

"Thanks, love." She took back the cheroot and returned her face to the sun.

"Hey, Fay, look!"

She looked in the direction he pointed. Across the jungle side of the pond, near the stream head, little blunt shapes were poking up from the shallows. Some rippled to the shore and wiggled out of the water. Others hobbled on their fins into the exposed, knobby roots of a huge wild nutmeg tree that had scattered its great, spidery breather roots down to the water line.

"Gobies," Roberts said. "Beach-skippers." He was excited. He knew fish. As kids he and Jane had an elaborate aquarium in their father and mother's Boston apartment. Hobbies were encouraged. They kept the kids out of the old man's hair. For the gobies, the kids had two tanks: one held water and was filled with loaches and gobies, and the other was a terrarium filled with ferns and mosses. The two tanks were connected by a Plexiglas tunnel through which the gobies crept to feed on the crickets kept in a cage where they sang all day and night.

"You go look at them."

Roberts sucked his bleeding gums and looked at her. She hadn't opened her eyes.

"You okay?"

"Super. You and Mai go."

Mai tugged at his sleeve and jerked her head to go. With Koi ambling behind them like a man minding sheep, they circled the bank, past the other prisoners who were sprawled around the pond or playing cards in the shade.

". . . in Vietnam." Roberts's loud voice carried across the water to Fay. He was explaining something to Mai. Everything in his bloody head entered by way of a gate called Vietnam. Fay was sick of it. It was one of the first things she had detested about Prescott. When he hit London, all he and Paul could do was swap exploits. They reminded Fay of her father, who thirty years ago had led a regiment of Gurkhas when the British recaptured Rangoon and opened up the old Burma Road. Although he had been retired after the war, he still styled himself Colonel Cockburn, took pride in her allowance, cluttered the house with Gurkha swords and garish Buddhist bric-a-brac, and chatted with boozy cronies about wogs and the lost empire.

No, she hadn't liked Prescott at all, not at first, not until India. In London, the Vietnam banter bored her friends, whose conversations centered on Sassoon cuts, trendy clothes, and the last party . . . the party last night. There was a party every night. They wondered why she had taken up with Roberts. Taken him in, actually. And Paul was certainly at his worst around Steve Prescott, forever pushing about, trying to impress Steve by what he too had seen in Vietnam. Seen deeply, clearly. "Do you remember when . . . ?" Fay was excluded. They only sought her envy, the way children boast to another who didn't visit the zoo, who didn't spot the whale spouting offshore. And then there was this unpleasant passion *to prove* something. Fay doubted that Vietnam really had been so mysterious, so thrilling, so *essential*.

And they were chauvinist pigs. Roberts, who had been quite charming for an American, took to telling boorish tales to her feminist friends just to shock them: The "steam job" parlors in Saigon. The whores in Kowloon. The knotted string they stuffed up your hole and yanked out as you came. Bargaining with a refugee girl for a blow job behind the central market in Phnom Penh. Steve was even worse, because where Paul bragged with bluster, Steve was obsessed. He actually preferred small, childish women and rejected the friends she had first introduced him to. How sad . . . to be excited only by someone over whom one has utter advantage. How vain and insecure. Prescott, Fay had told Paul, was a cryptofag and added that she was going along on the Indian junket not to comfort a dying friend but because she was bored in London, had never been anywhere but Paris, and the dope and the plane ride were on Steve, or rather his American Express card and his Master Charge.

But before they reached Delhi, she felt like an undertaker. When the Sikh customs official—turbaned, bearded, with steel bangle on his wrist, sword at his side, and smelling something like rice pudding —boarded their plane, Steve was so weak and sick he had lost consciousness.

"What is the trouble?" the Sikh had asked them, his intonation hanging in the air. "Is he sick?"

"Yeah," Paul had said, "he's sick."

"A disease?"

"Cancer. We're taking him to his mother."

"Oh, my God," said the Sikh and cleared the plane that he had been about to quarantine.

The taxi ride from Bangalore, where they had hoped to meet Sai Baba, to Puttaparthi, where the healer actually was at the time, was dreadful. Puttaparthi was a hundred miles from Bangalore—and three thousand feet lower, in a baked mountain basin where temperatures hung between 110 and 120 degrees.

Fay paused to sip her coffee. Paul and Mai were chasing gobies, while Koi sat on the gigantic roots, pointing out a fish with his M-16. About twenty feet below her, two skinny, brown kids from the valley had brought three water buffalo to wallow. The guards had let them through and now the boys were staring at her from the crackled mud of the shore. The road to Puttaparthi was like that. Instead of frogs hiding in mud cracks, there were humans hunched under scrubby trees. As they drove through villages, the taxi nudged the crowds of gaunt women in dusty saris balancing bundles on their heads. Aimless cows, emaciated bullocks, bony horses. Their sweating driver leaned on his horn and screamed at the beggars swarming to their taxi like flies. Despite the heat, they had had to roll up the windows until they got outside the towns, when the bucking taxi—shocks long gone—would pick up speed and honk past dilapidated buses that lurched about and spewed black fumes. Their luggage scraped across the gritty floor of the boat. Steve was scarcely awake, his head on its ghastly neck bobbling against the sweaty seat as the taxi rocked left and right. On the open road, they splashed cow pies, banged across potholes, and obliterated two dogs that their manic driver did not bother to swerve for.

They hung around Puttaparthi for four days, sleeping in dormitories on patched air mattresses on the concrete floor. Ten to a room. The air leaked out of the mattresses by morning. The loo for the men was a fly-infested hole in the concrete floor; their shower, a faucet at the back of the dormitory. It was too much. Each day they carried Steve into the town to eat at the Paradise, the only restaurant with refrigeration. They drank Cokes and ate bananas that Fay examined for broken skins. The orange-drink machine at the restaurant whined with flies when it wasn't working; ants paraded through the popcorn maker. It was dreadful. If Sai Baba didn't save him, Steve said he wanted to try the psychic surgeons in the Philippines. But he was sure this would work. Well, he was and he wasn't. Fay concluded that he simply willed himself into belief, all the while knowing it was a game.

During the day, she sat with Steve in the courtyard before Sai Baba's porch. They sat under a banyan tree, a monstrous centipede that sent down branches that became roots, that became legs on which the tree walked slowly, growing over the decades. The pale buttresses flowed down like tallow. The magpies squawked in the tops, while below—holding slips of music sheets—she and Steve hummed *bhajans*, prayer songs, along with the thousand or so devotees waiting to see Sai Baba. All during these days of sitting on grass mats, Paul kept trying to get them an audience. The situation was bad, Steve simply couldn't survive the heat or lack of proper food. Even the water with which he drank his methadone could kill him if he got dysentery.

They picked up Sai Baba stories while they waited in the crowd. A German told them about an American named Cowan who had died of a heart attack in Bangalore. Pronounced dead at the hospital, his nose and ears stuffed with cotton, his death certificate signed, he was wheeled off to the morgue. Two hours later, Sai Baba visited the morgue and whispered into the ear of the corpse on its slab. "And now, go see him in Bangalore," the German had said. "Cowan is living there with his wife."

Steve liked that story. For him it was more to the point than the *vibhutti*, the sacred ashes that Sai Baba materialized with a wave of his hand. Or the gold rings, Swiss watches, *japamala* rosaries, and sacred medallions that the Master produced from thin air and gave to his devotees at *darshan*, "the blessings of the Lord," which occurred at eleven and five-thirty each day.

It was only then that they saw him, but across a sea of the faithful: a small, dark, stocky young man with a large head made yet larger by a black, kinky Afro. He had bushy eyebrows and large, fleshy lips that glowed pink against his dark skin. Earlier pictures, when he was first discovered to be a teenage Baba, showed him to have been quite handsome: angelic and sensual, earnestly looking into the camera from a strict yogic lotus position, with a mass of black curls ringing his face. Now he was a trifle gross, padding about in an orange muu-muu (with *big* sleeves, Steve had sadly noted), smiling and patting people on their heads and asking them what they wanted or leading the whole group in the singing of *bhajans*. He was not interested in seeing Steve, although cancer cures were his specialty. The best Paul brought back was a *japamala* bead that hadn't even been materialized but merely handed him by an aide, who told him it would be better for Steve to try to see Sai Baba at his mansion in Bangalore. They left—taking the taxi back, killing another dog, running more buses onto the shoulder, and finally returning to cool Bangalore, where they got a hotel room together and waited for Sai Baba.

At the end of the week they tried again for an audience. Paul got fierce—a sign of friendship, Fay wondered? Anyway, he forced their way through protesting lackeys past the vestibule and into the inner house where he and Fay *laid* Steve in front of the door from which Sai Baba would emerge to give *darshan*. Poor Steve, conscious but unable to walk, lay there looking up at them, twiddling his thumbs in mock boredom and humming a dum-de-dum Bugs Bunny imitation of a *bhajan*. It was his kind of *bhajan* and was sincerely addressed to all powers that monitor the realms of life and death. The cosmos, he had told her, had a lot of humor. He lay there between two large, pedestaled, gilded, wooden elephants reared up on their hind legs. Next to him were a chair and footstool covered in red velvet, some roses in a vase on a wicker stand, and on the wall a bright pastel lithograph of Sai Baba.

"Well, no one can doubt you're a believer," Paul had said, a little loudly, as he hovered by Steve in case anyone tried to get him out of the doorway.

"It's like an old Ramar movie," Steve said. "You know, beautiful maiden offered in sacrifice."

When, after two hours of waiting, Sai Baba appeared at the door, he looked down at Steve, smiled, *stepped over him,* and began blessing the crowd, which had risen to its feet on the veranda and the lawn outside. Steve blinked wide in disbelief.

"Baba," Paul had called, bowing. "My friend is dying. Please save him."

"Sweets, sweets," Baba replied, materializing with a flourish of his hand some candy, which he gave to Paul and to Fay and to several standing nearby with clasped hands.

"Oh, Baba, hey, *please,*" Steve said in a hoarse voice. "I've come from the United States to see you," adding on the Atlantic miles.

Sai Baba smiled. "I know." He turned to look down at Steve. "You have pain, yes? You take drugs, yes? You have cancer. I hear you calling me for weeks. You must take this . . ." And with that he leaned over and showed Steve his empty palms. Then, from his right palm, gray sacred ash poured forth onto Steve's mouth and chin. Steve tapped it with a finger and gave it a close look. Straightening up, Sai Baba turned to Paul and gave him a packet of holy ash that an assistant had handed him. "Let him take this with water, twice a day. I will visit. Where are you staying?"

"The Paramount Hotel."

"No. You go to my friend, Lady Baldwin. She will arrange everything. I will visit you there."

10.

M ai and Paul, preceded by Koi, were returning with presents for her. Talking with Mai, Paul ambled behind carrying the M-16 by its sight grip, its barrel carelessly pointed at Koi's booted feet. Oblivious, Koi beamed childishly at Fay and held out his cupped hands. She looked at him the way one might regard a burred-up setter fetching home a squirrel. Good ol' Koi, dark and doglike. The dimples of his smallpox scars were pitted with black dots that stippled his whole brown face. The whites of his eyes were yellowish from malaria most likely, or hepatitis, or from any one of the hundred or so diseases that left the locals jaundiced.

"Well, how much will this cost, Koi?" She smiled.

The old guard grinned and turned to Mai for a translation. He shook his head no-no-no and slowly opened his hands, carefully pressing in one index finger to hold down his catch: a cicada with two sets of brilliant wings and a strangely pointed head like a green-nosed Concorde. It was more exotic than a jungle butterfly. The front overwings were emerald green, mottled in bright yellow; the back underwings were brilliant yellow with brown tips. Koi gave the bug to Fay, who let it sit in her opened palms. Gathering itself slowly, it sprang off in a wild leap for freedom, fluttering out over the pond and landing on the surface with a smack—which was quickly followed by another smack as a fish lunged from the cold bottom for the kill.

Koi gestured for his rifle back from Paul. Paul returned it matter-of-factly. Fay watched him closely as he handed it over without even looking at Koi and turned to reach into the woven plastic bag that Mai carried.

"Now, look at this," he said. In his two hands he brought out a bug as big as a puppy. It was soft pale green and shaped like a leaf. It even had veins like a leaf, and its horned head revealed no eyes or mouth but looked like a sprout on a branch. Only its four-inch spiny legs—which slowly sawed the air in a arthropod attempt at escape—gave it away as a living creature.

"Ghastly. What is it?"

"A grasshopper. And lunch for Nixon." The leaf monkey's name changed with whimsy. "Koi says you can fry them and eat them."

They moved up the bank to where the monkey was seated— shaded and tethered to a tree—in sad contemplation of the forest. He screeched and stamped and took the grasshopper. Fay was quick to look away, but she heard the initial crunch.

Fay and Paul walked off as Nixon tore at the bug. And while Mai and Koi were working bamboo poles into the sand for a blanket awning, Paul and Fay sat down on the shore. Sand flies were zinging by their ears.

"The fish here are fucking far out. I used to pay five dollars for Siamese fish. The pond here is stuffed with them. And loaches too. This pond's worth about ten grand."

"If you got that gun again, could we get away?"

Roberts looked at her, shooed a sand fly from her bare shoulder, and tossed a pebble in the water. His tone dropped. "I don't think so. I thought of it back there. But we're in no shape for running. The scabies' nothing serious, but we aren't eating, we get no exercise, and we smoke opium. We can't run, and we don't know where to run to."

"Could you kill Koi?"

"Could Koi kill us?"

"I don't know, really. He's very good to us."

"Well, I know."

"What shall we do?"

"They like us. Maybe we can just cool it and talk our way out slowly. You know how gobies survive the dry season?"

"How?"

"They just cool it. When the monsoon's on and the fields are flooded, they are out there swimming around in the rice fields. The locals catch them by torchlight right in the paddy. Then the dry season. The fields dry out. They harvest the rice and the paddy is bare as a bowl. But no fish. Where did they go? And as soon as a rain washes the field again, there they are. Big fish."

"How?"

"When the drought comes they go underground and burrow in wet mud pockets, wriggling out when the rains return."

"And if the drought lasts?"

"They bake, I guess. Like a fucking casserole."

"Paul, look at us. We're baking."

From a common pot, the four of them pawed up dried pork and cold, sticky rice. Koi brought them two big bottles of beer that he had stuck into the cold stream last night. From the gardens behind them, he had filched two long papayas: fragrant and orangy-ripe. Mai sliced them by balancing the fruit against the sole of her turned foot.

Fay looked at Koi with amusement. (Would this man kill them if they tried right now to make a break?) "Mai," she said, "tell him my father would make him headwaiter at our hotel. He's got the touch."

"No," Roberts interrupted, "tell him her father will make him a headwaiter if he's good to us like this."

"How you say? Fay make him waiter if he ni' you?"

"That's it," Roberts said. He wondered if her Thai was better than her English.

But the compliment seemed to get through to Koi, who, leaning against the snaky root runner of a pandanus tree, burped on his beer and snapped them a salute. He threw the monkey the papaya skins and settled back against the tree, rifle across his knees.

Fay leaned back to doze in the shade of the awning. Mai had plaited a diadem of flowers in Fay's hair: white, five-petaled frangipani, star swirls with soft yellow centers. They smelled fresh and heavenly, nearly overpowering the odor of coal tar that rose from the arm she draped across her forehead. Paul and Mai wandered down to the water to bathe with the other prisoners. Fay dozed . . . and remembered . . .

He talked about his novels with some regret. All unfinished. About Sandy, his bar girl. With regret. Their affair unfinished. Fay never met a more utterly lonely person. Yet he wasn't maudlin; in fact, he was funny. His condition, he said, was everyone's, his just more visibly subject to time and death. The cancer nodes had reappeared in his joints, and he could hardly walk. The universe was at him, hammer and tongs, but he was still hopeful—and amused. One day, when she came to read to him in his room at Lady Baldwin's vast bungalow, he showed Fay a poem he had written:

> He was a sad man.
> Everything he said was so fucking funny.
> Because the funny are only telling
> the sad truth.

He told her lots of sad truths. How he had tried to get back a girlfriend, even though he was pretty sure he didn't want her back. "She said she'd love me *no matter how awful* I became. I treated her badly to feel my lovableness. What would I have done with her?" How he left Saigon to wander around Java, playing with whores, and then went back to the United States, where, plying his tricks with teenyboppers on the boardwalks below San Jose, he felt like a pervert for the first time. And accepted his identity with ease. How one night he had to sleep under the boardwalk because he was so doubled over with pain that he couldn't move. "The hunchback under the boardwalk," he'd said, "a solitary mister."

"So you think Sai Baba is a fake?" he had asked her. He lay on his back on a foam rubber pallet, covered to the waist with a sheet, staring at the ceiling fan slowly stirring the room. Sai Baba's *japamala* bead—a dried nut of some kind—hung from a string on his neck. He looked like a beached flatfish, his chest sunk onto his bones and his bones knobbed with cancer that swelled against his yellowish flesh.

"Well . . . ," she said, putting on her knees the volume of *Sathya Sai Speaks*.

"Why can't a fake cure cancer if you believe in him? The main thing is belief."

"Why not?"

Fay sat up under the blanket awning. Koi was nodding off against the tree. Paul and Mai were now drying on the sandy bank. Fay reached for the blue flight bag and pulled it over, undid the zipper, and rummaged for the notebook that she was supposed to have mailed to Lacey. Steve's jokes, his sad truths, had brightened up a moment but had disappeared on second thought. So she kept the book. She still hadn't decided whether to let the notebook go, this *Skag Journal Continued* which was just a schoolkid's copybook. A week of writing, scrawled over the blue-lined sheets in a hand loosened by methadone and cancer. The first page, March 15, began:

There was once a man
who wrote beginnings to novels.
wrote hundreds of them,
thousands.
When he died they found
all these brilliant
beginnings of novels,
94,078 of them.
Such a brilliant man.
So much confidence
in himself.
Brilliant beginnings.
No better beginnings
Anywhere.
As far as they go.
No critic has ever
perceived a flaw in
his plotting,
as far as it goes.
The first step:
setting the scene.
Never have greater
scenes been set,
as far as they go.
Usually the description
of one object.
Never have better
objects
been described,
as far as they go
etc, etc.

———

Did he mean it as a poem? And the following, did he mean it as a letter? Undated, it was addressed to Paul, but did he mean it for her?

Dear Paul:

You don't know me, but remember that time you were fucking that girl—no, not your wife, that other girl—and you were so sure no one was watching? Well, I wasn't, Paul, but my camera was. Of course you don't have to believe me, Paul. It's quite possible I've just made the whole thing up.

Fay lit a cheroot and read on. Some of this was hard to read. The handwriting got progressively larger and looser.

MARCH 17

If you live in a foreign land, you may have no very clear idea of what they're doing. But they have a very clear idea of what you're doing. (I may hazard a guess as to what they're doing.) They're sure because they've talked it over. They all agree about what you're doing. If in the United States you meet a Turk, say, you develop a sort of idea of what it might mean to be a Turk. But it's a very different idea from the one you'd get in Turkey. Them Turks aren't outnumbered over there. They're the majority.

MARCH 17

> *Socrates*
> *a man forever*
> *asking questions,*
> *so people would*
> *thinkhehadanswers*
> *Buthedidn't.*
> *I believe that Socratic*
> *irony*
> *isn't irony at all.*

The
poorfuckjustdoesn'tknow.

MARCH 17

Sexes.
Two of them.
There are just exactly two of them.
That's remarkable.
Why should it have
to be this way?
Hangonasecond.
I'm going to go
hookupforasecond.
I've got
one right here with me.
It just is not
the same
sitting around,
a couple of guys.

MARCH 18

What about the
hypochondriac doctor?
The poor guy must
be a nervous wreck
(and he knows what
that means:
nervous wreck.
He doesn't have
just a vague
metaphorical notion).
He knows what his

nerves look
like right now.
And what they
will look like dead.
And he thinks about it
(there is a small
body of us whose
job it is to
remind others of
their mortality).
(Thought it had me there.)
Every stroke I write
is a drumbeat of mortality.
Thrive, ye
drumbeats of mortality.
May your numbers
be legion.
You can leave the summing
up for somebody else to do
when they have instruments
for recovering all old thoughts
that everybody who
ever lived has thought.
There will be political
leaders of the states they
will have then who
will insist on having
that information.
So it doesn't really
matter if you don't
get it all written down
or on film or tape.
Don't worry. Somebody

else will recover it all.
So just
relax on the recording angle.
Okay, buddy boy?
The next question is:
what do you feel like doing?
Do it.
And don't start getting
uptight about all
those dirty thoughts.
Nobody cares. Everybody
else thinks the same.
And that is the
family of man.
That's what we're
all in together.
We might as well enjoy
one another.
We're only going through
this thing once,
my friends.
Howsoever many
children you beget,
you've only got this
one trip yourself.
So take care of
yourself a little.
Don't be so
hard on yourself.
You're by far your
most frequent
companion.
Might as well strike

up a friendship.
Now they're all
going to rush me:
"He's a dualist."
These guys who've
got it all figured out.
Hear that, Lacey?

This is what happens
when you're alone.
You hear yourself.
You are conscious that
that is yourself you
hear.
When you're with a
crowd,
You only have
yourself barely
there somewhere
nagging.
And it's in a
state of irritation
at all the interruptions.
Forget about that
death (yours).
It has nothing to
do with you.
It's somebody
else's problem.
I can guarantee
you it won't be a
problem to you.

A few days later, on March 23, in the evening after dinner, she came over, from the Paramount, where she and Paul were staying, to look in on Steve. How hot it had been, 90 degrees or so, but so very humid. Her blouse had stuck to the taxi seat when she got out at Lady Baldwin's. Paul didn't come. He didn't show up much. He had lost interest and was waiting for Steve—how could he just abandon his friend? was there no one he cared about but himself?—was waiting for Steve to get on with his next act, dying, so they could continue with their next act: the flight from Delhi to Mandalay, the train south to Thazi and then the narrow-gauge, double-diesel train across the Shan Plateau. How surprising to pass from steaming jungle to grassy plains ringed by peaks, some of them snow-capped and dotted by pines. The train traced parts of her father's treks, to Taunggyi, Kunhing, to Ta-Kaw where the deep-trenched Salween River edged through a gorge, its surface littered with jams of teak logs. From there through alpine valleys, at 5,000 feet or so, to Keng Tung in the Burmese Golden Triangle, then south again to the border crossing at Hawng Luk, just above Chiang Saen, where she was . . . She couldn't get over the Shan Plateau: vast banks of scree, whole mountainsides bare in loose rock. The kind of thing you saw in Norway. And as their train chugged through narrow gorges and little valleys, she saw pines and rhododendron, oaks, and, as the valleys winked open, she saw forest clearings, men cutting wood, mahouts driving their elephants, dragging logs out on chains. The lower stretches were bushy with dwarf bamboo; the upper hillsides dotted with blue gentians and columbine—alpine flowers growing a few degrees north of the equator. Imagine. It was lovely. Until Hawng Luk. That smart-ass was looking for trouble. Foreigners rarely passed from Burma into Thailand, especially through the Golden Triangle. He busted them for a pittance of hash. Oh, why hadn't she ditched it like Paul had said? Just forgot. He punched her for forgetting . . .

By the 23rd, Steve could walk only with help. Someone—the girl at the hotel desk whose father had just died of cancer—had warned them that Steve's bones might snap if he were handled roughly. The father's spine had snapped as the nurse was easing him back into bed. . . . *Why* did Paul have to punch her? Bruised her arm. She punched him right back. Straight in the side of the head. Broke the frame of his glasses. She wasn't going to let the bastard get away with that. Big scuffle and shouting match. That clinched it. The cops took them off the train.

Steve lay that night on his pallet as she read him Lacey's letter, the first to catch up with them after being posted to Puttaparthi. In the living room, Lady Baldwin's nasal, operatic, old lady's voice rose above the others as they sang *bhajans*. Thursday and Saturday nights were *bhajan* nights. They sang English versions. The melodies, which seemed to Fay less strident but more whiny than Christian hymns, still gave her the sense of listening outside a church. "Tell Steve," the letter ended, "that, if you guys don't get to Saigon, I've written Clyde to make sure Steve's bar girl gets the old Boileau camera. The guy at AP has it now. Clyde will make him hand it over. It ought to get her a few hundred bucks." Or something like that. Lacey was a bore. Kind, but boring . . . and that's why they were counting on him now. What was he like in bed, she wondered. You could tell a lot about a man by the way he fucked. She once slapped a man and shoved him off her when he came just after entering her. But you couldn't always be sure about a man who could hold it either. Paul could hold it, but fucking him was not exactly a thrilling personal experience. There was no one there. Just a dick. His mind was missing in action, somewhere else, in Vietnam, or settling some grudge with his father. Once they took Polaroids of each other naked. She lay on her back holding her legs apart in the air. Paul the same way. The photos turned out reddish, like medical photos. They looked like corpses, scary. Paul fucked the way that huge grasshopper sawed at the air with its legs. Mechanically. It could be good for a girl if she didn't think about him. But you couldn't go on like that forever. It was like fucking a bug, a hard chitinous body, built for defense, empty inside. No wonder he loved Vietnam; the war must have set him free from himself, from his father, from everything. Could his father fuck, she wondered? Right now, she had Mai at least, although she also considered the Kamnan—or perhaps even the lout with the torn ear who could shatter a breadfruit at thirty yards.

> *"Start the day with love.*
> *Fill the day with love.*
> *End the day with love.*
> *This is the way to God.*
> *Shining in the lotus heart,*
> *Beyond all changes, unreal and real."*

She really wondered what those sots singing hymns really knew about love. Did Steve know less? This poor American cowboy whose pony was his penis? She listened to them chanting in English and in Sanskrit. They were winding up.

> *". . . yato va imani bhutani jayante*
> *. . . That from which each has come*
> *and into which, after annihilation,*
> *all will merge."*

To her surprise, she heard Steve mumbling the chant. She remembered wondering: Had they been there that long? A week and a half and no visit from Sai Baba? Just this officious cow spooning porridge into Steve, which she washed down with *vibhutthi* and water, after chasing off his friends because they drank and Sai Baba did not permit it.

"Help me, Fay," he had said that last night.

"Steve, you'd better use the pan." She reached for the bedpan, but he was already propped on his elbows, leaning to the left and pulling in his legs to get up. He crouched, then slowly stood, an act of unimaginable pain that no amount of palfium or methadone could mask. As he rose up on his own, his sheet fell from his waist to the floor. He had been big. The big bones stood out at his hips and knees and shoulders. His skin draped across his bones like sailcloth. His dick hung like a rope; his scrotum, a dried leathery sack of stones. And he was smiling. The fucker was smiling as he lifted his cart-horse knees and shambled past her.

"Ta-ta, love," he had said. Ta-ta.

"Where are you going?"

"To take a piss. To look at the stars. Haven't seen the stars for some time, you know." He rocked forward on shaky feet. Fay moved aside as he crossed the hall, which opened to the living room where the last *bhajan* was being sung, and went out onto the veranda. He stopped at the garden rail and, grasping it with both knobby hands, tilted back his head to look up at the stars looming large near the equator: Berenice's Hair, the Lost Pleiades, Cassiopeia's Chair, and his favorite, Orion, the star-belted Hunter about to cast a spear of stars, the lonely mortal made divine from unrequited love. Divine and more lonely: stalking the heavens each night as the constellations wheeled about the Pole Star, his prey always in sight, his star spear always raised. But never hurled.

Still holding onto the railing and still looking up at the heavens, Prescott leaned forward and pissed. The urine splattered the flag-stone walk; some of the nearest crickets stopped their trills. Then he turned and walked back, flailing his arms slowly at his sides like a man walking through surf. Lady Baldwin's guests, now breaking up and leaving the singing room, saw him as he reentered the hall. They stopped dead and shut up. The only smile in the room was Steve's, who nodded at them all: A naked, ravaged corpse stood before them with a smile. They stood still as Steve gazed at the wall with its life-size portrait of Sai Baba. With an effort, Steve crossed his arms reflectively, mindful of his audience, and considered the painting the way a man might regard a painting in a gallery. He studied the portrait with a widening smile. As he turned to go, he crashed to the floor like a chimney sweep's bag of chains.

Even at death, Fay thought, he was the funny man telling a sad truth. If he was the loneliest man she had ever met, he was also the most alive. She regretted never fucking him.

The girl at the Paramount recommended the city's new crematorium, the Electric Crematorium, as it was officially called. They took him there in a cab late that night. Paul was drunk. Really drunk, *and silent.* Usually when he was drunk, he was blabbing at her. As they were getting Steve out, Paul decided he wanted the *japamala* bead around Steve's neck. He got his Buckknife out. His hands were shaking and he used too much force: the cord sprang apart and the knife sliced into Steve's neck, leaving a gash that did not fill up with blood. Stupidly, they both looked at Steve to see if it had hurt him. But no smile appeared; his lids did not blink open.

The Electric Crematorium—Cremo A-Go-Go, Paul dubbed it— did Steve the next day. At 2:00 P.M., the girl at the desk rang up to them. "Steve's here," she said brightly. Steve would have liked that. He was there alright. A taxi had brought his ashes: in a can of Hershey's Chocolate still hot and filled with white flakes and porous bits of bone.

They telephoned Lacey on a radio line that blanked out if both parties talked.

"Steve's—"

"Hello? What?"

"Steve's—"

"Where is he?" Finally Lacey paused.

"He's here."

"How is he?"

"He's okay. He's dead."

"Oh."

"I got his ashes here in a can of hot chocolate. A hot can of hot chocolate. Got that?"

"Yes."

"What should I do with them?"

"Give me some. Give me some for his mother."

"We're going to put some in the Ganges, where it starts in an ice cave at the Himalayas."

"Good. What then?"

"Then on to Saigon."

"You sure that's smart?"

A gun went off inside the prison. The monkey screeched as if it had been shot and jumped on its tether, pulling down on the branch. The head of the clan had fired an old flintlock to salute the soul of the dead. The funeral ceremonies were over. They had taken all morning and had been complex and unnerving. First of all, they were Blue Miao, or Hmong Njua as they called themselves. Ko Pisan and his brother, although raised in Hmong villages, were Karen. But their father had refused to become Christian with the rest of his village. Ostracized and having no place else to go, he had hired on as an opium harvester with the Hmong. The brothers, then, despite their Hmong wives and clan links, were somewhat dangerous, since they fell into no clear spiritual hierarchy. "Fish in the water; birds in the air; Hmong in the mountains" ran the proverb, and it meant that the Hmong had little to do with other peoples, whether from the valleys or in the mountains.

The village now had to attend to the Karen soul to keep it from turning on them. They accepted the task gravely, after much debate on procedure, for they had never buried an outsider before, were no innovators by tradition, and collectively found the whole affair repugnant. The burial required the utmost attention and tact.

They had filed into the prison in their finest attire, with the clan head in the lead, holding the red-tasseled flintlock, its stock studded in silver. The brother followed, his head wrapped in a white bandanna. He held joss sticks in hands pressed together in supplication. The women wore their dark blue, deep-pleated hemp skirts. Some wore blue bibs embroidered in silk and decorated with their wealth: Indian silver rupees stamped with the images of Edward VII or William IV.

The first task was to appease the house spirit, the Sier Klang of the prison cell. Even before removing the body, which lay naked on an army cot, the shaman entered the stinking cell, chanting and burning incense and calling to Sier Klang not to take offense. He explained that Ko Pisan was not a Hmong, that his death was not an affront to any Hmong spirit. Then the shaman—his teeth as spare as an old hound's and his eyes glazed and heavy with opium—cut the throat of a white rooster that the brother had fetched into the cell. Using a special curved knife, the shaman swept the rooster's throat while the brother held the head in one hand and the feet in the other. At first the bird just looked about wildly. Then it thrashed its wings against the brother's extended arms, and gradually, as its blood spattered to the floor, it blinked asleep. Then, in the center of a white sheet of paper about ten inches square, the shaman dabbed some blood and stuck it with feathers from the rooster's breast. He stuck the paper to the wall facing the door.

That done, he called in Ko Pisan's four children to wash the body and clothe it. When they were finished, they placed on their father's feet the special leather shoes that had been made by men from another clan.

Outside, some women ground the rice for a feast while the men squatted in groups around the prison yard. The place was very unhealthy. The air was thick and smelly. The Kamnan—who sat in a chair in front of his office drinking beer—commanded their respect, but as a jungle cat would: something that could hurt them and that they would just as soon kill. One group of men was cutting firewood; another group was hammering at the heavy slabs of the coffin. Among the women, the dead man's wife was being consoled. The funeral was at community expense. Both Ko Pisan and his brother had been absolved of all debts.

The tapeworm had been saved in a lidded earthen jar. It was the shaman's judgment—gained in a trance—that the evil, harassing spirit had tried to escape in the worm. The name of the spirit was Suter Sublong, "the fire and blood spirit." The jar was brought into the bright yard and the shaman danced around it, chanting, naming the spirit, striking at it with a light wand, and commanding it to depart. Then, in a moment of inspiration, he called for kerosene, lifted the lid, poured some in, and threw in a match. When the conflagration jetted up from the jar, the Hmong murmured approval. This spirit had been the real worry; it could cause madness, suicide, violence, and it could disrupt their harvest. Their shaman had been very clever in catching it. It would be so beaten and burned now that it would be a long time before it tried to return—and when it did return it would be more cautious.

Then the family, and as many others as could fit into the cell, entered with smoking joss sticks. Outside, the shaman sacrificed a dog and gave it to the women for the feast. Then he reentered and called on Ko Pisan's soul: to return to the body where it now would be safe and to be kind to the village that had shown it so much respect. They burned paper spirit money so Ko Pisan would not be poor in the other world.

Finally, they ate, first offering some dog to the Kamnan, who took it happily, red-faced from the beer and a whole morning in the sun. The feast continued past noon. At last, the head of Ko Pisan's wife's clan fired the flintlock. The village filed out, bearing the body in a coffin slung from a jute stretcher that sagged between two men's shoulders.

Fay stood beside her blanket tent billowing in the breeze and watched the villagers step out from the stuccoed prison walls through the entrance arch of coiled barbed wire. They crossed the moat bridge and headed out along a tree line toward the mountains. They walked slowly, stately, erect. The man with the gun went first; the sun glinted off the silver neck rings of the men and women. The coffin swung gently on its sling as the soul was carried to its rest away from the hostile valley, to the mountains where the spirit world was strong. How gently they moved, how differently from the Kamnan, who was striding toward them now like an ape in fatigues, slapping a swagger stick—really, where did he come up with that touch— slapping it at his side and yelling to the guards to herd them back to prison.

Fay watched as the beginning of the Hmong column came out from under the swaying palms bordering a terraced paddy and started the steep climb. In their way, she thought, hadn't she and Paul done right by Steve? Sure, they had fleeced him of his watch and cameras and traveler's checks and credit cards and cash and clothing, but he would have done the same. And what did it matter when he was dead? In their way, she assured herself, they did right by him. They did dump his ashes in the Ganges—that was almost sentimental—and they did send some ashes home to Lacey and to his mum. In his way, Steve did right by himself. By himself. That was all he had. No one could rip him off. A vital, inextinguishable, lonely self. Funny man.

11.

*S*nit Puaree was pleased with himself as he walked to the pond, switching against the knee of his loose fatigues the stick that the shaman had used to beat the demon, the stick that the Kamnan had expropriated to show he had the right to demand things from the Miao. Asking for the stick also showed them how little a Thai official feared their spirits. He was pleased at that, and he was pleased that everything had gone off well with the Miao ceremony. Now he could write up a report that would show his superiors that he was "innovative and correct" in his dealings with the hill tribes. But mostly he was pleased with what the Miao chief had told him: the Loi Maw syndicate in Burma would pay a thousand American dollars—$700 for the Nae Amphur and $300 for him—for the release of the Haw opium trader and for the opening up of negotiations to allow Chinese mule caravans from Burma to ford at the Mae Nam Khong and enter Thailand unmolested. This could mean a lot of money. The Nae Amphur had been looking for a deal ever since they had jailed the Haw. Now they had one. And he himself would tell the Nae

Amphur. Snit Puaree was pleased. He was young and already successful. His mother, it was true, had been only a midwife and then a cook for the district police. But his father was an "injection doctor" and had made a lot of money during the malaria epidemic that followed the work on cutting the railroad tunnel in the jungle. And with that money, his father had sent him to Chiang Mai to school, where Snit Puaree learned to speak pure Thai, not the country Lanathai of his native Amphur Mae Rim. He represented the new Thai official: *modern in technique and quick to act.* Already he had trained at Chiang Mai with the American Public Safety Officer, Mr. Connors, a policeman from Los Angeles. Snit Puaree had learned riot control and interrogation. Yes, if the Nae Amphur were behind him—as he surely would be now with this Loi Maw deal—he might even go to En Paso Texas for counterinsurgency school. Then he could really move up. The important thing was to arrange a big banquet for the Chinese syndicate. They must understand that he and the Nae Amphur were big men, that they had lots of money and power, that the $1,000 was merely a courtesy to them, a polite way of opening up discussions on bigger things.

A gust of wind skipped through the field of rustling jute sheaves tipped in cream-colored flowers. The wind caught his peanut-oiled pompadour, and puffed it up into a cock's comb. Snit Puaree paused to shift the shaman's wand to his left hand and to smooth his hair with the flat of his right. Then he switched back the wand, tapped the .45 holstered butt forward, American sheriff-style, and continued on to the pond to round up the prisoners. Yes, he was pleased with things, pleased with himself.

As Puaree reached the edge of the gardens near the pond, Fay's monkey screamed and bent the sapling to the sandy ground as it danced on its tether. The Kamnan looked up and grunted when he saw the two small boys holding bananas just out of the reach of the monkey. The monkey was nearly strangling itself and screamed again for the bananas still proffered by the two brown, solemn, and barefoot boys. Puaree joined his screech with that of the monkey and the jungle birds: "Ai ha! Koi!"

Like a mangy mutt, the sleepy old guard shook himself up, hunching his shoulders in guilt and rubbing his eyes to get his bearings. He got them and saluted with a throw of his left hand that might have passed for a swat at a fly. Forgetting his M-16 against the pillar root of the banyan, Koi shuffled toward the Kamnan.

"Mai ni, deo ni," the Kamnan ordered, pointing down to his boots as if he were calling the guard to clean them.

Koi shuffled along faster, now aware of the two boys in blue shorts who still stood silently and blankly before the leaf monkey.

"Gu bawrg hai mun, gan ay Meo aw bay," the Kamnan ranted and poked his finger toward the boys.

Under her cotton blanket lean-to, Fay propped herself on her elbow to see what was going on. And the other prisoners, playing cards in the banyan shade or, like Paul and Mai, cooling their feet off the sandbar in the jungle's mountain pond, turned their heads too.

Koi was starting up his excuse for letting the boys through the cordon. "Kamnan, ka him ay puoc Meo man bay . . ." To prove his innocence, he ran at the boys, who—quite amazingly—did not bolt but continued to stand before the monkey jumping in fits and struggling so on its branch tether that the little sapling shook and bobbed like a wild beast. As the Kamnan came over, Koi reached the kids and smacked one boy on the back of his newly shaved head and then turned to give the other a boot in the ass. "Are you crazy?" he was yelling in Thai. "Get out of here!" The boys skulked and merely dropped their bananas on the sandy shore, turning now to Fay as she, too, came up. Koi grabbed the one by his scrawny neck and shoved him toward the forest, but the other stood looking at Fay, holding his arms nearly straight down at his sides while regarding this demon witch with white eyes and red hair, and said: "Lay Si hiah." Then another furious boot in his backside knocked him away and he was running to catch up with his little friend, who was already at the edge of the jungle near the retting dam, where the valley villagers had left their jute sheaves to soak. Fay's startled "You what?" trailed after the fleeing boy. Had she heard him say "Lacey here"?

Paul said no when she told him that night back in the prison, but he was uncertain enough to warn her not to tell Mai. But just then, as the boys' blue shorts disappeared into the thicket of screw pines, no one seemed to hear the sentence but Fay. Koi was too upset with his bawling out and the boys' uncommon obstinacy to hear the three foreign syllables. And the Kamnan, with his sidearm and swagger stick, didn't notice, because suddenly, picking up the discarded bananas, he got interested in the monkey.

"You sell monkey?" he asked as Mai and Roberts arrived with quizzical looks at all the shouting.

"Me no sell monkey," Fay replied, ridiculing the Kamnan's pidgin monotone.

"*Give* it to him," hissed Roberts.

"Right," she said turning to Roberts, "and what will he do with it?"

"Gif' for Chinee frien'," the Kamnan said.

"Yeah, that's cool, Fay. A gift."

Puaree was nearly a head shorter than Fay. She regarded the lacquer of his shiny hair. "Bugger off, Paul. It's my monkey."

Roberts lunged for her, but Mai grabbed his arm, getting knocked down herself, as he swung a haymaker at Fay's head. And when Fay lunged to scratch at Roberts, Koi had to grab her from behind, holding her arms down at her sides. It was like subduing a weak, sickly child.

"Stop! Stop!" Puaree yelled and drew his .45.

They stopped. "Alright, Mr. Puaree, you can have your bloody monkey. But in return I want a free day here, with Mai."

The Kamnan drew a circle in front of her bare toes with the shaman's stick. He thought a minute and then said, "No sweat, baby." He smiled at conjuring up one of Mr. Connors's favorite phrases.

"Aw, kiss my ass." Roberts turned his back and walked toward the prison. He turned again and yelled, "Dumb cunt! You want to rot here? Maybe this guy can help us. Be nice to him. You scratch my back, I'll scratch yours. Right, Snit?"

"Right," Fay answered as she looked at the smug, greasy-haired twit in green fatigues. "You're bloody well right. So," she said, smiling at the Kamnan, "shall we three have an outing? You and me and Mai?"

The Kamnan beamed, holstered his pistol, and tapped a jaunty salute to his forehead. Then he too turned away, calling the guards from the perimeter, shouting orders for the roundup and for bringing in the BAR. With his hands on his hips, boots spread apart in the sand, he studied the Haw opium trader, whose private guard gathered up his folding chair and card table from beneath the root canopy of a pandanus tree. "Koi," Puaree called over in Thai, fists still on his hips, "give the monkey to the cook."

Lacey *was* there. Two days later, during one of Roberts's hour-long vigils on the outhouse boards—where he broke into opium sweats that would fog his glasses as he strained and waited for his sphincter to fight the opium effects and roll out a little marble of a turd that would plunk into the pond where the little fish would clash for it— he read in the newspaper that Lacey had arrived. As he reached into the Thai papers piled in the corner of the jakes, Roberts pulled off the top sheaf to discover below it an edition—actually only the single sheet that made up the first, second, and last two pages—of *Stars and Stripes*, the "Authorized Unofficial Publication Of The U.S. Armed Forces Of The Pacific Command. Thursday, August 8, 1974." The paper was a little more than a month old.

It was a miracle. For six months Roberts hadn't seen anything in English.

The main headline, over a big photo of a sour-pussed Nixon sitting between Henry Kissinger and James Schlesinger, ran: ANOTHER SET-BACK FOR NIXON: RHODES TO VOTE TO IMPEACH, and below that a smaller headline: NOT RESIGNING—PRESIDENT. On page two, two more big photos, captioned "Reps. Charles Wiggins (top) and Charles Sandman Jr. (right) join other top Republicans calling for Nixon's impeachment. (AP)" Whew! What the hell did the creep finally get caught doing? The first page and most of the second was all Nixonmania: MEANY ASKS OF NIXON—GO. "Labor leader George Meany said Monday he wishes President Nixon would 'just go away' and pledged American labor would cooperate with Vice President Gerald Ford if he became President." Ford? President?

Roberts whistled, "Holy shit!" and fished in his shirt pocket for a homeroll of Laotian tobacco that usually produced hopeful rumbles in his bowels. He read on, scanning the headlines hungrily and dipping into the stories. Even more interesting to him was a squib near the bottom of page two, THAI BARREL MURDERS ALLEGED, a UPI report that said:

> James Lake, a representative for the London-based Amnesty International, was expelled Monday from Thailand after asserting that Thai police routinely exterminated political prisoners by incinerating them in steel drums called Tang Dang, or red barrels. A spokesman for the Thai Ministry of Information, Colonel Pot Swasdi, termed the charge "a bizarre fabrication of the Communist left!"

That's what they were for!

But the real surprise, as he read on, came later—after THAI FARE-WELL FOR PHANTOMS, 7 DIE AS ROCKETS HIT PHNOM PENH, SIEGE TIGHTENS—RED TANKS SHELL DANANG, and MARTIN SAYS THIEU O.K., —for on the next-to-last page, beside a photo of the DAYTONA CURVE QUEEN, "Barbara Ann Lyons of Holly Hill, Fla.," who was smiling into the camera in her white shorts, white boots, and white halter while holding a checkered racing flag, Roberts found, just below the crossword puzzle, that his horoscope had been inked in blue:

Libra (Sept. 24 to Oct. 23) Quite unexpectedly you may be afforded the chance to do something "different," attain a surer foothold on the ladder of success. Keep alert and ready to act.

Above that, the crossword puzzle had been partially filled in: "H.O.L.D.O.N.J.L."

Roberts took a long, dizzying drag on his Lao cheroot, scuffed his bum with the Thai paper, pulled up his cutoff jeans, folded the *Stars and Stripes* into his back pocket, and walked outside into the blinding sunlight, where the air echoed with the stammering of a gas-driven pump flooding the gardens beyond the stucco wall topped with jags of glass and coils of barbed wire . . . where Lacey was waiting. Who was he with? Did he come alone? How did he find them? How would he get them out? Roberts flipflopped along in his sandals across the prison yard. A jailbreak!? Fuck-an-A, he thought. If Lacey were going to spring them legally he wouldn't need secret messages in the shit house. How did he get the newspaper in? That meant somebody inside was being used. Koi? Roberts decided he'd watch the old shit a little more closely. Maybe that was why Koi had let him carry the M-16 when they went goby hunting. How did he train those Thai kids to say "Lacey here"? Lacey spoke Vietnamese; he didn't know any Thai. So he had local help.

Roberts crossed the cracked-mud yard to the watchtower and its stack of three red barrels. The big sow, her piglets now sold or eaten, was stretched out in the shade next to the barrels. Now Roberts noticed that air vents had been drilled in the tops and cut along the sides at the bottoms. Two simple clips like those clamps on old-fashioned canning jars sealed the lids. A man could be forced into there, hunkered down and clamped in, while they poured gas through the top holes, threw a match, and whoosh. Down by the burning ghat is where it's at. Cremo A-Go-Go. Hello, Prescott. There wouldn't be much evidence left, huh? No corpse rotting in the sandy soil below some saw-toothed fan palm. "Keep alert and ready to act. . . . Hold on. J.L." Roberts figured he'd better tell Fay when Mai wasn't around, which was just about never. Poor Fay. The sand flies at the pond or something had gotten to her—maybe dengue fever. Anyway, Mai had her wrapped up in blankets and had blocked the light at the windows, because Fay shivered and sweated and winced at the slightest ray of sunlight. Her cell smelled of her vomit, and her lips and tongue were swollen with blisters. Her face and back—which had been spared by the scabies—were now covered with some kind of rash. Well, honey, he thought, you won't be getting tight with Snit. Which maybe, he thought, was too bad. Then again, maybe that didn't matter now. Lay Si hiah. They had to hold on. Christ, where had Lacey gotten the cash? Lacey didn't have any bread of his own. Was it likely Lacey'd spend his own savings on him and Fay? Shit, he had to get Fay on her feet. "Attain a surer footing on the ladder of success." Fucking Lacey. The fucker had come through.

12.

*J*ohn and Louise Lacey, looking very American in summery seer-sucker pants and white shoes and wraparound denim skirt and Villager blouse, sat at breakfast in the Ngoc Loi, the Golden Pearl Restaurant, littering their metal table with travel brochures. Five days before, after spending some time in Chiang Mai touring the Buddhist wats and chedis, they had arrived in Chiang Rai, the old northern capital on the Kok River about forty-eight miles south of Fay and Roberts's jungle prison.

Folded among their many maps from the Tourist Organization of Thailand was a 1942 map from the U.S. War Department that had been given to Lacey by Paul Grant, a former agent for U.S. Army Intelligence in Vietnam. The map, which Lacey was rereading as he poked at his oily *omelette au jambon* and sipped his black, silty *café filtre*, covered the lower section of the Southern Shan States of Burma, just north of the Thai border, and the northernmost provinces of Thailand: Chiang Mai and Chiang Rai. From the left of the map, at the fork of the North Feng and the Kok rivers, tracing your finger up and to the right, you came to a spit of the more gently sloped Thai terrain as it jutted into the steep ravines and rugged ranges of Burma. Just below that little peninsula was a large mountain, Doi Sam Sao, that seemed bisected by a small river identified as the Jan Luang, which ran out of the steep forested mountains of Burma into the more open river valleys of Thailand. And there, where the map symbols indicated a scattering of valley huts and a fort, Grant had marked a careful X to locate the prison and the Border Police station. The prison lay in the dead center of the Golden Triangle.

So Lacey had known where Roberts was even before he got to Thailand. What he still did not know was how to contact him.

Lacey looked up from his map and turned toward the waiter, a teenage boy in loose blue pants and white shirt who was whisking flies with a dish towel as he watched a tennis match just beyond the restaurant fence. Lacey called in Vietnamese, "Anh, oi. Xin cho toi hai tac kaphe nua," pointing to his and Louise's cups.

The Golden Pearl was a Vietnamese establishment, run by a family that had fled to Thailand during the chaos of the Vichy collapse, the Japanese defeat, and the subsequent clash of the Viet Minh and French forces when the latter returned to reclaim their Indochinese empire. A desk clerk at the Prince Hotel where the Laceys were staying had told them about the Pearl, but only after first challenging Lacey on Vietnam. Why, the clerk had wanted to know, hadn't the Americans used nukes on the Vietnamese. "Make soap out of them," he had suggested. Then the clerk, a young Thai from Bangkok, just to make sure that Lacey did not think that he or other Thais were racist, said that the Laceys should go have breakfast at the Golden Pearl or, as he called it, the Tennis Court Restaurant.

"We are not against the Vietnamese people," he added, "only their Communist bosses."

The well-populated Buu family had stayed on to run the restaurant next to the fenced-in tennis courts not far from the river where many of the province and municipal offices stood: tall, yellow-stuccoed affairs set back handsomely behind tamarind trees, colonial buildings with high ceilings where the river valley heat was stirred by slow ceiling fans. The restaurant was semioutdoor. It was like a big bird cage with a cement floor, because the whole dining area, including the three-sided room that backed onto the rear kitchen, was enclosed in heavy wire mesh, maybe to stop the tennis balls that were pock-pumping in serve and return just beyond the tables, but more likely, Lacey thought, remembering La Cave and other places in Saigon, to bounce back the possible hand charge thrown by a terrorist. Thai terrorists, Lacey supposed, but the Buus had said that when they built the cage it was to protect them from the Viet Minh. The Buus had stayed along with their relic of rougher times, now prettily trellised in a kind of wisteria and, over the bar where the waiters picked up their dishes, in grapevines. What with the river breeze riffling the leaves overhead and the white-clad tennis players, the place was a bit Mediterranean. A Vietnamese woman on the radio was singing "Why don't you know why you are sad?"

The tennis players were middle-echelon bureaucrats: well-fed, husky men who seemed more intent on their form than on their game, more interested in being seen playing tennis than in playing. Attending the men—along with the boy who hustled after loose balls and fetched them beers from the restaurant—was a Thai soldier leaning against a bougainvillea tree with an M-16.

Lacey liked the Pearl because he could speak Vietnamese there, and also because under this shady arbor and closed-in, but see-through, perimeter he could see whoever might enter through the wire gate. And they couldn't be overheard. Being a tourist was getting to be a drag and was using up a lot of the Roberts's estate. And they were getting nowhere. He had now what he had in New York: Grant's map and Grant's report derived from Grant's "interview" with a Lao prisoner of war. Grant had sent the report back to an organization set up to find missing journalists lost in Cambodia in 1972, when Nixon and Kissinger ordered the mad juggernaut that rent the delicate neutralism of Sihanouk and plunged Cambodia into grisly civil war. The prisoner, a Pathet Lao whom the Thai Border Police had ambushed along with a small band of Thahan Pa, had been in the same prison with Roberts and Fay. He had escaped from a truck carrying him to interrogation in Chiang Mai. There was no doubt. The guy had on him a California driver's license—Steve Prescott's driver's license—with an inscription on the back: "For Vieng, Best of Luck in Your Future, Paul Roberts."

Lacey broke off a piece of his roll of French bread, considered the jam pot that sat on the table (probably all day, he thought), and, deciding against it, ate the bread dry. He looked over at Louise as she read brochures, all bright with color photos of silk parasols, gilt Buddhas, gold war elephants, and temples: old wats crumbling in the jungle, and new ones, white-walled and roofed in gold. Above them a mynah bird wrapped its big claws around the roof mesh. The antic bird had flown off from the noisy flock that hung out in the bougain- villea, where they waited for scraps from the restaurant. The bird scratched its claws on the mesh as it bobbed its neck, cocking its head sideways to see the feast below.

"Oh, look, John." Louise had looked up at the desperate bird and laughed.

Lacey tossed up to the bird a bit of bread, which reached short and dropped to the floor where the smaller, luckier sparrows rushed it. Lacey tossed another piece and this time the mynah snatched it and flew off across the street, fearful that his brothers might find him out.

Their waiter came, sucking his teeth. "Uong kaphe, khong?"

"Da, phai," Lacey said, giving a couple of baht for a tip. As Lacey momentarily held the Thai note up to the light, he saw that an image of the young, spectacled King, in military dress, appeared as the watermark on what had seemed a blank circle on the engraving.

Lacey remembered other Asian currencies that he had spent: the Cambodian riel, which against the light revealed a watermark of a magnificent Brahma-Vishnu-Shiva head from the Bayon temples near Angkor Wat . . . and the Vietnamese 20 dong watermark, which revealed a tiger.

"Listen to this," Louise said, and she read from her travel brochures: "'Chiang Rai Province. General. Chiang Rai (also spelled Chiengrai), the northernmost province of Thailand, is in the Fifth Administrative Region. It is the fabled land of the opium trade, in the old days (and still is unfortunately known for the illicit trade which passes through the area from Burma, Laos, and China on the way to markets in Hong Kong and elsewhere). It is a breathtakingly beautiful land of mystical mountains, fertile earth, and gorgeous flowers. . . .' "

"Where the hell is he?" Lacey asked. He hadn't been listening.

"Oh, forget him for once. Listen to this: 'Another river of Chiang Rai Province, the Ing River, is unusual because it flows north instead of south, due to the layout of the mountains; after a course of 190 kilometers, the Ing River, like the Kok River, flows into the broad Mekong River. Among the natural resources of Chiang Rai are teak and tin.

" 'In 1962, Chiang Rai had 124 days of rainfall, for a total of 1,248.0 millimeters.

" 'The roads to Chiang Rai are still rather primitive and rough, so much travel to and from the province is by air. There is no railway into Chiang Rai.

" 'Expatriates from the West have been happily living in Chiang Rai for generations. Among the Americans, perhaps the best-known family is the Gordons, famous for their work with animals and hill tribes. Mr. Richard Gordon, who is probably now about forty years or so of age, is one of the foremost experts anywhere on the hill tribes of northern Thailand and the Shan States of Burma, and he has written books about them also, with beautiful pictures. Undoubtedly the most famous Englishman of Chiang Rai is the "doyen" of the foreign colony of Thailand, the inimitable Mr. W. T. S. Good, now in his active eighties. Mr. Good has been in Thailand more than sixty years and has written several books about the area. His latest one, recently published in England, is entitled *Consul in Paradise*. (He was, in his early years in Thailand, a British consular official.)'"

Lacey nodded ruefully. Mr. W. T. S. Good was no longer in his active eighties. Mr. Good, whom Grant had set up as the contact to arrange the bribes that would free Roberts and Fay, was dead. They had arrived in time for his funeral. And so far, none of their telegrams—either to Mary, Roberts's mother, who had bankrolled their mission with Roberts's own patrimony, or to their friend, Helen Petri, the wife of a missing journalist and their initial contact with Grant—so far, none of their telegrams had been answered. Probably, Lacey thought, the telegrams were still being translated by some low-level snoop in the Thai Post Office.

"Troi oi! Tai sao em lam nhu . . . Troi duc oi!" Madame Buu was hollering up a fuss in the kitchen as she did each morning, badgering her daughters, Nice, Plum Blossom, and Spring Essence, who made the yogurt and *crème caramel* and did the cooking. Soon she'd come slipslapping out in her oversize sandals to flash them her smile of gold fillings. She was a rather plain woman with dyed, curled hair crimped in a forties shoulder-length style that was almost back in fashion. She wore a great smear of red lipstick and painted both her toes and fingernails bright red. She liked Louise and would soon call her over again to the bar to have some tea *entre nous*, while she reappraised Louise's blond hair and American clothes. They spoke French together. It was hard to tell whose was worse.

" 'Amselle." Muoi, the littlest Buu, whose name meant mosquito, had been sent over. Louise looked down and took the little girl's hand, sticky with something or other, and then looked up across the restaurant to Madame Buu, who was beckoning from behind the counter with that downward flapping of her hand that seemed to Westerners to say good-bye instead of come here. With a nod to Lacey, Louise got up, scraping her metal chair on the concrete floor, to join the smiling Madame Buu.

"Bonjour, Madame Buu."

"Bonjour, ma chérie." Madame Buu eyed Louise's denim skirt and pushed a cup of tea across the countertop as she nodded for Louise to take a stool. Louise sat down, still resting her hand on the nape of Muoi's neck. Muoi, with her very black eyes and cropped hair, smiled importantly and then became engrossed with the soft blond down on Louise's other arm resting on the counter.

Lacey sipped his coffee and watched Louise getting her arm petted as she talked. He hadn't wanted her to come, but it was just as well she had, for they passed as tourists. With Mr. Good dead, and with the Bangkok police denying knowledge of Roberts or Fay, he needed time to make a new contact in Chiang Rai—or decide to go home. It was just as well, too, that Grant had advised taking along a bodyguard in case he got stiffed in the bribe or street punks harassed them. But the guy Grant suggested was off in the Philippines as the military adviser on a war film, so Lacey had come up with Carlos Romero. Where the hell was Carlos?

He remembered their meeting on a rainy night six years before in a radio shack at an encampment that Lacey had fled to during the Tet offensive. Romero, a little Chicano with oily hair and a few sprouts of a goatee, was running communications with the base's perimeters. When Lacey ducked in under the sandbagged lintel, he found Romero, a flyweight with a worried look, tapping his short-time stick on the cast of a broken leg propped up on the desk. The stick was topped with a death's head with rhinestone eyes.

"How short are you?" Lacey had asked.

Carlos stopped tapping and looked up at Lacey, whose civilian clothes were still spattered from the night rain. From a belt hook of his baggy Vietnamese pants hung a shaving kit weighted with two concussion grenades. He was carrying an old .45 greasegun.

"Hey, bro', what the fuck are you?"

"Well, I'm kinda like a medic. Civilian."

"Kinda medic. Civilian. Madre!"

Lacey offered a handshake. Carlos looked at his hand and locked his thumb around Lacey's in a soul shake.

"Bro', you look a little Spanish?"

"My mother's Italian," Lacey lied.

"Dig, you half Latino." Carlos laughed like a snake hissing. Some of his front teeth were missing.

"Yeah." Lacey sat down on an opposite desk and pointed at Carlos's stick.

"Oh, man, forget it."

"Huh?"

"Gabacho, ain't no one here's got no short-time. Bro', the whole fuckin' NVA's out there. Charlie's gonna take us tonight."

"How come? That's your main strike force out here." He was frantic. For three nights he had evaded the firefights in the nearby province capital, only to get to the base and find out he had a good chance of being killed.

"Bro'—hey, what's your name, man?"

"John Lacey."

"Well, bro'," he said, pointing then to his receiver, "listen for yourself when the berms call in. NVA. NVA everywhere. And they got cloud cover, bro'. Spooky's up there but can't see shit."

Lacey walked over to the bunker door, ducked his head out, and looked up at the night sky. The drizzle had stopped. Flares burned in brilliant pinks and floated on their parachutes under mottled clouds. The moon was casting fuzzy light through one mess of clouds.

"Could clear," he said, turning back to Carlos, who had opened a drawer and was pulling out three grenades and a Browning pistol and was laying them out next to his M-16 on the desktop.

Carlos stared back at him. "Gonna fight, bro'. Gonna fight. Gonna take some dinks with me. Didn't learn that in no fuckin' Marines, neither. My people are from Velarde up on the Rio Grande where the river's deep, you know, and they got everything in orchards. Apples. Fuckin' apricots. Hey, we fought Indians for that land. And Anglos. Now it ain't worth shit. Just some fuckin' anthill or something. Dig?"

"How'd you break your leg?"

"Leg, shit. Look at this." Carlos pulled up his green T-shirt to reveal a surgical corset cinched around his lower belly and back. He pulled his shirt back down and ran his fingers back through his hair and gave his head an I-don't-know shake. "I'm small, dig?" he explained, "so I'm like the company's Kit Carson 'cause the captain don't trust no Vietnamese to get his ass blown away. So I crawled in and out of tunnels for those mothers, got my sweet ass shot off a truck, and this time I tried to bring in this huge black dude, Quentin, my good buddy, Quentin, during this firefight and ka-pow! Zap! Quentin had been rolled over on a grenade that Brother Charles felt the need to borrow the pin from. Ya dig, bro'? I pull up Quentin and ka-boom! Zap! I'm in this hospital bed in a Navy ship off Danang. I'm a fuckin' hero, but I forgot to fill in the claim forms. Like, bro', nobody ever gave me no forms, dig? With a back like mine, you can retire. But instead they just sent me out here to rest up some, and then a fuckin' slope goes and drives a backhoe over my leg." With a throw of his hand, he slammed the drawer back into the desk.

"Look, I better go. You take care of yourself in here."

"Chíngate." Carlos laughed. "Where you goin', bro'?"

"Just take another look around."

"Hey, gabacho, take a look at this." Waving him over, Carlos took out a big K-Bar bayonet knife from its sheath. Near the hilt was a strip of electrician's tape. When he peeled it back, he showed Lacey a row of flat shiny crystals.

"What's that?"

"Window paint, bro'. Here. It's kinda speedy."

"No. Thanks. I want to keep a clear head. I plan to get out of here."

Carlos tapped a crystal with his index finger and then touched it to his tongue. "Suit yourself."

Lacey walked to the door, his shaving kit slapping against his thigh, his greasegun clanking against his back on the woven strap.

"Hey, bro'."

Lacey turned.

"Maybe you *will* get outa here. Do me a favor?"

"Sure."

"You get back, tell my mama I love her."

"What's your name?"

"Carlos, but she calls me Chinche, bedbug, 'cause when I was a kid I was always gettin' in on things. Here." He turned over a blank ops order and wrote his Albuquerque address and his full name, Carlos Romero Mondragon, in large block letters and beneath that, in grand swirls: Chinche. It was like an autograph, more than a message. "Vaya con Dios, bro'."

They shook hands.

Outside, by the light from the door of the communications bunker, Lacey wrote a note on Carlos's paper: "To Whom It May Concern: I, John Lacey, have no regrets for what I've done. I wish you well. Stop the goddamn war." Then he tried to figure out where, if he got hit, he might bleed least. The fatty tissue on his buttocks. So he put the note in his right hip pocket, hoping the VC would settle for his watch and wallet. But he figured that he wouldn't die. Only those who had to hold a perimeter, or a tower, or a barrack, or a piece of artillery, or a radio, only they might die. Lacey didn't intend to fire a shot unless he got nailed. No, he'd head out along the coils of concertina wire by the ditch along the main road. He'd hug the ditch. He'd stay clear of the field beyond the wire because it was mined with claymores.

Later that night the attack came under a barrage of mortars, the stutter and slap of small arms, and the answer of the camp's ground-leveled 105 howitzers. When it was clear that one of the perimeters had fallen, Lacey disappeared into the shadows and waded along the ditch like a muskrat. An hour later the clouds broke and the Spooky Dragonship bellowed off its banks of guns—fifty rounds a second, every fourth a tracer so that streams of fire crackled from sky to earth. Lacey put his nose to the air and smiled as he heard—between bursts of small arms, popping of trip flares, crash of mortars, slams of grenade launchers, and the animal roaring of the dragonship—the cheers of the soldiers whose lives had been saved, hooting for the deathship sweeping the battlefield with a slow, pulverizing, electric plasma of bullets that stopped the advance and forced the North Vietnamese to take the town instead. Later in the morning, he helped pull the dead off the wires. He owed the camp at least that much.

Lacey tossed a piece of bread to the sparrows hopping among the metal chairs. It was Grant who insisted on having a bodyguard for the bribe money. Aside from a gay Army doctor, Carlos was the only soldier that Lacey had known in Vietnam. Odd. Odder still, he *had* called Carlos's mother when he got back to Saigon and could use the free phone at the USO. Six years ago.

This time, Carlos hadn't been easy to find. His mother said she didn't know where he was ("No está. Está loco.") but that Lacey could call the bus company where Carlos worked. When Lacey called the bus company in Albuquerque, he was told that Romero had been fired. That was it. No good-bye. "Don't work here. He was fired." Click. Lacey called back identifying himself as an FBI agent. He could tell by the sudden cooperation that the guy hoped Romero was in big trouble. Lacey finally reached Romero at some Chicano politician's house where the ex-Marine was helping to build a swimming pool. Lacey offered him $5,000 of Roberts's estate plus expenses.

The trouble was, Lacey had learned, you couldn't just tell Romero what to do and send him off into the mountains to bring back Roberts and Fay. You had to *go* with Carlos. Generally, the guy was kind of helpless, except, Lacey supposed, at using a gun. His Vietnam experience had been just that and nothing more. Outside of running point or setting up an ambush under orders, he wasn't good at much. He got lost in airports; his dope-smuggler looks got them harassed at customs; he didn't know how to behave around stewardesses; he was inept in restaurants and hotels; and the only Thai food he liked was *satay*, peppery chicken or beef on a stick that you bought from street vendors. Romero got lost. He was probably lost right now. Hell, maybe he couldn't even manage a pedicab from the Prince to the Golden Pearl. Maybe he was walking. I bet, Lacey thought, that half of Romero's trouble at the bus company came from the fact that he had developed his few skills pursuing, trapping, and killing Vietnamese youngsters whose only developed skills were pursuing, trapping, and killing American youngsters. Would Vietnam's veterans be as fucked up as America's? Probably worse. They had over thirty years of continuous warfare; a whole generation had grown up never learning to farm or fish or work a trade. And in the South alone there were a million young men under arms. Christ, he should have let Grant find someone reliable.

Lacey lifted his wrist to check the time. He turned to regard the few other customers. Some Chinese guy sucking at a bowl of noodles. Two Thai municipal government types in white shirts, baggy tan slacks, and sandals having custard and coffee. A Vietnamese friend of the Buus working at a bowl of *pho* beef soup.

Where the hell was Carlos?

13.

"*H*ey, bro', qué pasa?" Carlos called in from the street, descending through his "hey" like a musical scale.

Lacey looked at his watch. It was 10:30 and already getting hot, even under the grapeleaf canopy. Lacey was thinking of two things as Carlos opened the wire door and entered. The first was that Madame Buu, who was showing Louise her jewelry, was an older, Oriental version of Curley's wife in *Mice and Men:* "Her face was made up and the little sausage curls were all in place." The other thing—the other thing he forgot as Romero called over to Louise.

"Hola, mama. What's happening?"

Louise smiled and waved from the counter.

"You eat yet?" Lacey asked. He pushed out a chair for Carlos and looked at the tight slacks, blocked-up shoes, Columbian Grass polo shirt, vest, and white wool cap. Maybe he picked the wrong bodyguard.

"Yeah, man, no problem. I had some of that stick food, man. And walking down here I seen this dude sellin' this chick some flat thing, you know, all wrapped up in a newspaper? and he opened it up for the chick and spread it all over with *salsa!* So I got some of that shit too, but, dig, it turned out to be some kind of weird dried-up fish, man. Tasted *terrible.* Nachos, bro.' Tha's what you want. 'Ey, bro', I need a beer." He fixed his feet on a metal rung under their table and leaned back on his chair.

Lacey ordered Carlos a beer and also a *crème caramel.* The very idea of eating hot *satay* and topping it off with dried squid smeared with red pepper paste was pretty awful.

The glass of Singha beer came with ice and a fly.

The ice bothered Carlos more than the fly did. "What's this ice shit, man?" he asked as he plucked out the fly and tossed it wet and wiggly onto the concrete floor. Then he noticed the custard. "Okay, man. Flan. So what's doing today?"

"We're going to see a missionary."

"A missionary?"

"Who works up in the hills north of here. With a tribe that was discovered only about ten years ago. The Mrabri."

"What you sayin' he 'works' with 'em? What this dude do, plant potatoes an' shit?"

"No, he lives with them to learn their language and to write it down for—"

A tennis ball banged the courtside fence behind Lacey's head. The kid came running over to catch it on the rebound.

"That's cool, bro'. Then these Indians can read the *Jungle Times* when they get home from chasin' monkeys all day. Far out."

"No, he's learning their language so he can teach them to read, so they can have Bibles printed in their language."

Carlos considered this as he spooned up the caramel juice from his dish. "How long he's been at it?"

"I don't know. *Years,* probably. Anyway," Lacey lowered his voice and looked at the two Thais who were getting up to leave, one of them shoving a toothpick in his mouth and giving them a look, "anyway, these Mrabri come from the area we're interested in. Maybe we can find out how to make contact."

"Dig, bro', but I gotta have a gun. How am I going to guard anybody with no gun?"

"Yeah, if we go into those mountains we'll get you a gun. Like what?"

"I donno, bro'. Something small. Maybe a .45, so you can stick it under your shirt, you dig? Or some police number. A .38. You know, a snubnose? But something."

"Right." Then Lacey said, "But, Carlos, don't let Louise know you have it, okay?"

"Okay, but you know where to get one?"

"Yeah." Grant had given him the name of an Indian silk merchant in Chiang Rai who dealt in stolen and smuggled goods and who could be trusted. Anyone else, Grant had warned, might be working for Thai security. Nearly everybody, he had added, worked for Thai security. Or for the Chaozhou syndicate from Hong Kong, which ran the heroin labs in Thailand. Or for the Loi Maw syndicate, those remnants of the Kuomintang army that had fled to Burma after Chang Kai-shek's defeat, now just a band of Chinese thugs who moved the opium out of the mountains in competition with the Shans. Or for the Shans. Or for the Thai Communists. There were even Vietnamese agents. Grant neglected to mention the CIA or the U.S. Narcotics Suppression Team. But the point was: you had to be careful. You could get almost anything you wanted in the Golden Triangle, but somebody was always watching and figuring out how you got it and how to get you. At the railway station in Chiang Mai, you could buy children for about $45 a head. Mostly they were sold as slave labor in textile factories. So buying a gun was no big deal. You just had to be careful who you dealt with. The Indian silk merchant was okay.

The beer-glass fly was still wriggling around with its wet wings gummed to the floor. Carlos drained his glass and held it up for the waiter to refill.

"Carlos, you want to hear a story?"

Carlos grinned and showed his yellow teeth, one of them capped in silver. He still sported a wispy patch of hair below his lower lip and a broad mustache. "Tell me a story, bro'."

"When a person first gets to Asia and he orders a beer and it comes with a fly in it, do you know what he does?"

"No sé. You tell me."

"He complains and sends it back."

"Fantástico."

"Now, a year later when he gets a fly in his beer, do you know what he does?"

Carlos merely shrugged in reply and used the returning waiter as his excuse for turning away to look over Louise at the counter.

"He drinks it," Lacey continued.

"Grande." Carlos was still looking Louise over.

"And the third year in Asia when he gets a beer and *doesn't see* a fly in it, what's he do?"

"Beats me, bro'."

"He complains to the waiter and demands to have a fly put—"

A muffled explosion followed by a series of shots that sounded like a kid slapping a stick on a wooden fence ended Lacey's story. In a second Carlos had knocked over the round table and was on the floor behind it lying belly down next to Lacey, who was still sitting in his chair, mouth open, waiting to deliver the end of his punchline. Louise, Lacey could see, was still at the counter, also a bit agape as she and Madame Buu stared through the mesh across the tennis courts toward the province prison. The two tennis players, frozen for a moment in serve and receive poses, now scuttled over to crouch behind the bougainvillea tree along with their guard, who leaned forward in front of them with his M-16 kept out of sight. They too were staring at the prison where shouts, or rather one voice shouting, could be heard from behind its walls. A man in uniform was lying in the gravel near the sentry box before the main gate, either shot or made to lie still.

"Get *down*, man. They're shootin'."

"Not at us, Carlos." Lacey was reminded once again of how different their experiences had been in Vietnam: in Saigon or Hue or any southern city, shots could mean anything—a soldier shooting a rat, a family feud, a bridge guard popping off at some suspicious debris floating toward him—anything; so usually, nothing. But for a Marine in the country, shots were usually personal.

Carlos got up in a crouch and looked where Lacey was pointing. The other customers, the Chinese guy and the Vietnamese, had put down their chopsticks and were looking too. Slowly, the Buu children came out from the kitchen to stand behind the counter. Muoi had shuffled herself between Louise's knees.

They could see a group of armed men, maybe seven or eight, leaving through the main gate. The men wore loose, homemade cotton trousers. And sandals. Some had turbans, others big bandannas. One—who just now kicked and shouted at the man lying in the gravel—had a long, black-and-white checkered cotton scarf that was wrapped around his neck and fell to about his belt. He also wore a baseball cap pulled to one side of his head. Some of the men had machetes flopping at the backs of their belts. Two of the men were supporting a third who was doubled over, trying to straighten himself, trying to walk. He fell. They picked him up. Lacey could see that shackles—the leg links broken—still rattled at the guy's skinny ankles. The guy in the scarf and baseball cap, who maybe had a greasegun—Lacey couldn't tell from where he was—was gesturing with his free hand toward the river. The two men holding up the disabled man each took one of his arms around their shoulders and started to run with him. The guy in the scarf and cap waved one man to position himself across the street, just behind a soup stand whose owner had disappeared. Then cap-and-scarf fled down the street after the two carrying off the injured man.

A few moments later the prison guards came to the gate. They were standing behind it and peering out cautiously when the guy at the soup stand opened up, spraying the grill of the iron gate. The slugs rang it like a primitive bell, and the ricochets zinged off into the stucco wall, zipping through the foliage overhead, slapping against the heavy trunks of the tamarinds, jabbing into the ground. The man lying on the gravel was howling and bellowing. The prison people took cover away from the gate, but some guy in a tower started popping at the soup-stand man, who ran off, jogging past the tennis courts and doglegging toward the river.

"C'mon," Lacey said and started for the door.

"Qué?"

"C'mon, man. We're going after them."

"You crazy, bro'?"

"Hurry up!"

Carlos got up to follow, pushing his wool cap back off his forehead and throwing Louise a you-know-this-guy-talk-to-him look.

"John," she began.

"Stay here," Lacey called as he passed through the gate. "We'll be back." He sprinted toward the river as a siren sounded from a prison tower, and the man lying in the gravel got up and, in the blare of the siren, began gesticulating furiously to the assembled guards. Carlos, shaking his head but starting to hustle, followed Lacey down the street.

Madame Buu, who didn't know where they were headed or why, clucked with amusement, nodding her head at Carlos. "Ong ca loc," she said. Mr. Catfish.

Louise was aghast. John and Romero, who had shown himself a macho jerk and a useless one, who was always throwing her sneaky, passionate glances—John and this jerk were chasing after some thugs who had just shot up the province jail. Well, she thought, as she exhaled a great puff of exasperation and raised her eyebrows at Madame Buu, inviting her sympathy— well, probably they wouldn't catch up with them.

With Lacey ahead, they ran down to the river and the central market, past the boulevard where an elaborate fountain had been sandbagged years ago into a machine-gun nest, now abandoned. They ran down a fairly uncrowded, shady, narrow street where fortune-tellers spread their charts out on the sidewalks. Suddenly they were among stinking fish stalls, where the fish lay in baskets or spread out on fans of palm leaf while kerchiefed women, crouched over cutting boards, slapped at the fish heads with cleavers.

"Cabrón!" Carlos yelled as he tripped over a mangy cur cruising for scraps. He skidded to a stop in his elevator shoes and kicked at the dog.

"C'mon!" Lacey called back, waving Carlos forward into the main market area. He had to find out who those men were. He wasn't sure where they were going, and now the crowd was getting thick . . . women mostly, women in loose scarf turbans, women carrying pans of live eels, women in sarongs peering down at little piles of saffron and seeds and spices spread out on plastic sheets or tarps. They were in the central market; it was packed with hawkers, cramped together, sitting behind their wares on little wooden stools, some shaded by ponchos fixed on poles overhead. Lacey bumped into a man shouldering a pole tied full of tin basins and brightly colored plastic pots. Carlos caught up with Lacey. They slowed to a walk. A woman in huge black drawers and a bamboo hat inched past them, a yoke across her shoulders from which were balanced two enormous brass containers of steaming soup.

The place was dazzling, dizzying, deafening. They passed stalls fronted by bins of brilliant tiny silver fish; passed a man whose neck was coiled in live snakes; passed a stall fuming with incense and hung with bright red paper cutouts of animals and Buddhist deities. A child was screaming. Mynahs were screaming in split-bamboo cages. Lacey and Carlos kept moving toward the river in the direction of the breeze that rippled the rags and ponchos and tarps tied overhead. Out of breath, they kept moving, slowly now because of the crowd, past quarrelsome dogs, past hawkers chanting songs or tapping out rhythms on wooden sticks, past huge tubs of marigolds and thin, pale green lilies, past the whine of knife sharpeners and sewing machines, past butcher stalls where the posts were hung with hunks of mushy pork and beef orbited by skims of green flies. They finally reached dockside, both of them winded, puffing hard, sucking in air. Carlos was grimacing and pressing his palms into the small of his back; Lacey limped. Lord, it was a bitch to face your thirties, but, Lord, Lacey thought as he wheezed and sweated and scanned the boats, this was fun. He had been plucked from his purgatory, from a gray limbo of desks and blackboards and witless students and fat-ass colleagues. In a way he owed it to Prescott. It all began with Prescott, a trip that had led to San Francisco, to London, to here—this resplendent riverside halfway around the world.

As they stood there a man with a bag of pipes and cigarette holders carved from roots of forest trees went into his hard sell.

"Qué haciendo, man? Chinga tu madre. Beat it, papasan." Carlos pushed him away, but the guy came back mumbling at them, holding up a pipe he had carved from a small gourd.

They ignored him and instead scanned the motley fleet of junks tied up and bobbing in the river water, knocking against the truck tires nailed to the docksides at the ends of walkways slippery with glittery fish scales and guts and crushed fruit.

Then they spotted their men, four of them in one boat, driven by a slow put-puttering engine that sounded like an old Citroën *deux-chevaux*. They were already in midriver among little, marshy, half-submerged islands, where white egrets stalked or flapped up over the river in slow lift-offs. Another bunch were still tied up at the wharf. The man in the baseball cap and checkered scarf was standing in the boat looking back at the crowd, staring straight at Lacey and Romero. Lacey waved. Carlos hissed "Leche." And the man in the cap, without acknowledging them, reached down and put a walkie-talkie to his face.

At the same moment, the last man showed up. The guy who had been left behind to shoot up the prison gate was walking out of the market crowd and along a catwalk to the boat. His rifle was hidden in a burlap sack that he held under his arm.

Lacey waved again and started for the boat.

Carlos lagged behind. "Be cool, man. These dudes don't know shit about us."

"C'mon, bodyguard. Did you see them kill anybody back there?"

"No, man, but that don't mean they won't kill us right here."

Lacey hesitated. And as he hesitated at the edge of the milling market crowd, as the prison siren still rose in a drone and died behind them, the man in the baseball cap gave a quick wave of his hand as if warding them off and, almost simultaneously, a huge, six-foot, barrel-chested black man in a U.S. Air Force summer uniform— with bare arms as thick as Carlos's midsection bulging below sergeant's stripes and an Air Police band—stepped in front of them. He had a gun.

"'Ey, bro'!" Carlos began. "No problem. We ain't military, man."

"Move yo' white asses, I shoot."

Lacey looked at the gun. The guy wasn't pointing a mere Colt .45, the standard sidearm for military police. In both hands he held a small submachine gun of pressed steel, its dull gray metal in ugly contrast to the man's black sweaty hands and light-skinned fingers curved around its rectangular magazine and trigger. The gun was only about ten inches long, including the little stub of a barrel—an Ingram. The Special Forces sometimes carried them in Vietnam. He could put a dozen slugs in each of them in less than a second.

Lacey slowly looked around. Some men walking burlap sacks down a plank to their boat paused for a moment to watch; some women behind them laughed nervously and hustled out of the way. Nobody paid that much attention. This was an American problem. GIs from the U.S. bases to the south, either on R-and-R or AWOL, often had to be herded up by military police.

You see a lot in a moment of crisis. The guy's shoes, Lacey noticed . . . they were all scuffed and muddy. His light tan uniform was sweat-stained and rumpled. No name tag over the right pocket. And where was his buddy? And the jeep!? These guys never worked alone.

The sixth second of their encounter was broken by a burst of static from the walkie-talkie clipped to the guy's belt. A parrot voice squawked: "Bring them over, Beta."

"Beta?" Lacey said, noticing the braised red scar, a Greek *B*, on the soldier's right bicep. "Beta, we just—"

"Move, jive-ass." Beta motioned toward the river with his gun.

Carlos, pressing both his hands against his chest in a gesture of sincerity, tried again: "'Ey, soul brother, we ain't military. Check our ID."

"Carlos," Lacey said shaking his head, "he isn't military either."

Carlos looked at Lacey like he had flipped. "Say what?"

Then Lacey added, "It's okay. He's taking us where we want to go."

"*I* said *move* it."

"Pendejo," muttered Carlos, falling in behind Lacey as the black soldier from the Air Police herded them toward the river.

They stepped onto a boardwalk driven out over the river on pylons of concrete, and then, farther out, on palm logs. Small boats were docked here, family affairs: unpainted wooden junks whose prows were decorated with large eyes or with Garudas, the sunbirds of Thai and Hindu mythology, whose great beaks formed the prows. Some of the smaller boats were open, like the one that had carried off the four other jailbreakers, and these open, smaller boats had their propellers dropped off their sterns at the ends of long metal poles that could be swept left and right as rudders.

Others were enclosed, with wooden canopies roofed in tin for stowing market stuffs—wire baskets of chickens and ducks and burlap bundles of farm produce. The man in the baseball cap—the Atlanta Braves, Lacey now noticed—was waiting in one of these enclosed boats, leaning against the roof canopy cluttered with reed and bamboo baskets as well as a squealing and trussed pig. He studied them closely as they came down the slippery dock steps to the boat. As each of them stepped on board, the boat listed and rocked in the water, lurching out ripples against a bloated, drowned cat and a long branch of bananas floating alongside. "Who ah you?" he asked. Lacey and Romero faced him in the hard sunlight, and Beta moved behind him, stooping out of sight in the shadows under the canopy. The siren, which no one seemed to notice, droned on.

"My name is John Lacey." Lacey looked at him carefully. The guy was young, thin, with pronounced cheekbones. Beneath his cap, his straight black hair was cut below his ears.

"What you do, Mista' 'Acey?"

"I teach English." Lacey paused. "I'm a poet."

"A poet?"

Lacey nodded.

"An' you?" The man turned to Carlos.

"He's my bodyguard."

With that, the man in the cap motioned to a man stationed on the jetty steps to block any escape to come over and frisk them. No guns—but he took their wallets and passports and gave them over to their interrogator.

"Why does a poet nee' bodyguar'?"

"We're here to get a friend out of jail."

"Oh, I see." The man smiled and, wiping his face briefly with his scarf, called to the men inside the boat. They laughed. Lacey couldn't place the language.

Lacey peered into the shadows. He could make out the man they had taken from the prison lying propped up on some burlap sacks.

He was sipping from a cup and munching slowly on something. He looked tired, perhaps sick. The shackles were still on his ankles.

"So, that's why you follow us?"

"Yes, I want to hire you to get our friend out of jail."

The guy didn't laugh or translate this for his friends below, but called in English, "Beta, what do you thin'?"

"Maybe narcs."

"Maybe." He turned to Carlos. "Do you speak English?"

"Fucking right, bro'. I'm Spanish-American. I speak Anglo."

"What do you do?"

"He told you, man. I'm his bodyguard."

"An' no gun?"

Carlos looked at Lacey in embarrassment.

"My friend was a Marine in Vietnam. He knows guns. We didn't see a need to have one."

Beta called up from below, "Marine, huh. Where you at in 'Nam?"

"Up north, bro'. Hue. Danang. Quang Tri."

"Uh-huh."

"How come, bro'? You in 'Nam?"

"Was. With the Ninth. In the Delta."

"The Ninth Division pulled out two years ago," Lacey said.

"Do tell." Beta laughed huskily in the shadows.

While their interrogator studied their driver's licenses, Lacey's credit cards, and the photos of Carlos's girlfriends, Lacey tried to spot a place to jump. The catwalk was out of the question. There was the guard, and Beta could blow them right off. The river was a possibility if you could make it under the boat and then under the next. Once they started shooting, they'd attract the cops who, Lacey figured, must be combing the market by now. Jesus, Lacey thought, if he had been able to find them, surely the Thais could.

He looked around some more. Beyond their stern was a point of land that jutted into the river from behind some official residence with a formal garden extending to the river's edge. The garden ended in a private jetty, some gardenia trees, and a grove of tall coconut palms, whose upper branches were threshing in the breeze. Under the palms were two armored personnel carriers. Those APCs would use their guns if there was any shooting here.

"Mista' 'Acey." The guy was handing back their stuff. The siren was still rising and dying on the prison tower. "We happy to have you with us. No matta if you narcs, or CIA, or poets. I fee' safah with you an' frien' along."

"Hey, man. They gonna blow us out of the fuckin' water."

"Who?"

"I don't know who, bro', but they got gunships, helicopters, man, and they got boats of their own, bro', so what's gonna save our ass?"

"No prob'em, rea'y. You Americans will stay up front, so our police can see you when we pass the poin'. But don' worry. The prison warden, who you can see lying in the dirt today, know if he pursue us, his little boy and his private car blow up. No prob'em. No 'hot pursuit.' So relax." He turned and called down into the boat. Up came two bottles of Singha beer, which he offered to Lacey and Romero. "Have a seat, and a beer. The sun hot today."

An hour later they set out from the dock, after firing up the old tractor engine that sat in an oil slick in the middle of the boat, an ancient John Deere that turned the prop through a pipe running along the keel beam to the stern. Then one of Chom's men—Lacey had finally heard his captor's name—jumped chest deep into the river, while another hauled a line from the catwalk and, together, they turned the boat around. Moments later, when the boat pulled past where the APCs were parked under the palms, Lacey and Romero and Beta were sitting on the little deck up front. Lacey could see the soldiers: some drying clothes they had strung on lines between the trees; others bathing in the river along with their young sons—lathering up, scrubbing scalps, frisking. The machine guns on the half-tracks were pointed at the river. Lacey could smell the gardenias from behind the house. He was scared. Louise would never even know what had happened to him. It was 12:15. Was she still waiting at the Pearl being soothed by Madame Buu?

Carlos seemed okay. He and Beta were talking shop and drinking beer. Ingrams versus the M-16s, firepower versus accuracy. Did Carlos think they were going to die?

A big turtle rummaged across the mucky shallows by the soldiers' jetty. As it tumbled across a basket rotting in the mud, Lacey felt himself submerged in another world, one darker and stranger. But once they got to the little islands in midriver and the boat swept past rushes and bamboo brakes where herons and egrets were stalking frogs or standing quietly folded up on one leg, he took heart. Two blue magpies took off before their prow. The smell of the slapping river and the shakes of brilliant light through the branches were exhilarating. Lacey recalled a long Mekong trip that he had taken to Sa Dec with a CIA agent from Cao Lanh. At first he had felt only the terror of being strafed from the banks by guns hidden in the low palms and scrub . . . and then came the rapture of the open river and remote villages perched on coconut pylons, villages where the river came lapping up under the floorboards, villages that had been there for centuries, villages that no white man had ever entered. Lacey remembered the thrill of seeing the mouths of tributaries open up momentarily in a sea of sugarcane and reeds. Where did they lead to? Who lived up those backwaters?

He leaned back and felt the sun on his face and the wind whipping at his hair while the John Deere barked and coughed and putted them upstream.

Some minutes later, when the sky began to cloud over, Chom came up to ask how he felt. Lacey replied, "Happy. Intensely happy." Chom searched Lacey's face for irony and found none. Lacey had meant it. Dying here, if indeed that was what lay in store, would bring with it a certain bliss. Alive. He once had seen a corpse hanging on the perimeter wire at the Can Tho airfield. Some GIs were potshotting at it, going for the head and the crotch. The VC had been dead all night, yet his body lifted and flinched with each shot that grisly morning. Lacey did not want to die like that. He wanted to be alive when he died. He had escaped from the Land of the Dead. Escaped from the company of colleagues whose entire pallid lives were spent like potted plants on dusty, office window-sills, whose life-forming experiences had occurred in schools: high schools, then colleges, then graduate schools, then teaching. Whose '60s Ph.Ds had devalued like *liras* and *pesos*. Whose humane erudition was just genteel smuggery. Whatever was now happening to Lacey, it was exhilarating and *not that*. He remembered the shrink he had once sought out of depression. ("You're bored, Mr. Lacey. You'll die without danger." —"How do you know that?" he had asked. —"Your eyes, Mr. Lacey. Whenever you talk about Vietnam, your pupils dilate with those little squirts of adrenalin your brain calls into your blood. Otherwise, they're dead.") Now they must be sparkling, he thought. Here on an open river wheeling with egrets, here riding with these thugs, here on a junk scudding along in the echoes of birds—here was the Land of the Living. Here the poetry was not in print but as palpable as that turtle off the jetty in Chiang Rai.

14.

*W*hen Louise got back to the hotel that evening, it was raining. Although the southwest monsoon season was over, a little freak storm had squalled into the city as if to provide a gloomy backdrop for her fears. All afternoon she had sat in the Golden Pearl, watching the rabbit-wire door and listening to the gunshots of the morning echo in her head. Across the tennis courts, dotted once more with chubby men in white outfits, the prison gate had quieted down again after the guy had picked himself up from the gravel and started shouting orders. A half hour later, they cut the siren. So all afternoon Louise had watched and waited and played pat-a-cake, stone-paper-scissors, and one-potato-two-potato with little Muoi. For a while Louise talked with Madame Buu, who was little help. Without much conviction, Madame Buu implied that John and Carlos were probably drinking at one of the girly joints set out on posts over the river. But she too had shown her worry by sending a waiter over to the prison to ask if any "American tourists" had been hurt in the fracas. The mystified cops said no. After hearing that—and after helping Co Mai pour milk into the yogurt pans for the next day's menu—Louise had given up her vigil at afternoon's end and taken a pedicab back to the Prince. By then, it was raining.

When Louise got into the pedicab and sat back in the cushioned seat, Madame Buu, shielding her head with a bamboo-leaf hat, had yelled instructions to the driver through the restaurant's mesh enclosure: the Prince Hotel via the river market. The driver, intent on fastening the canvas curtains of the flimsy cab before Louise and his upholstery got soaked, nodded that he understood. Under his pith helmet—perhaps a Viet Minh or Lao Issara relic—a big wet cigarette dangled from his lips. And under his cheap, see-through plastic raincoat he was wearing only shorts and a cotton shirt. He was an old man; his brown legs were ropily muscled; his bare feet, calloused and scraped. The rain drummed the awning above Louise and sizzled on the tin roof of the kitchen. As they wheeled off she noticed a morose waiter whipping the red-and-white checked cloths off the tables where the salt and pepper dishes were filling up with rain. Curtained in her dark and dry compartment, with only a crack of light showing a sliver of the rainy street, Louise began to cry.

The market was almost empty by the time they wheeled through it to the sound of growling gutters and the smooth swish of the tricycle's tall skinny tires cutting the flooded street. Louise pinched back the front curtain. Shopkeepers with soppy turbans or broken straw hats hurried about with plastic sheeting to cover their goods until the rain stopped and they could pack up for the day. The rain had caught everyone by surprise, but some of them were already finished and now stood quietly, smoking or chatting in their stalls while the rain bellied the tarps over their heads and shot rivulets spattering to the ground. By the butcher stalls, Louise saw two men hefting a partially hacked and bloody pig carcass by its feet into a bicycle cart not much bigger than the one she rode in. The rain drummed on what was left of the upturned ribs and flooded out of the chest cavity where the pig bent as they lifted it up and set it down in the tin-covered box at front of the bike. Christ, she thought, I don't need this.

The driver let her off under the rickety aluminum porte cochere of the hotel, unfastening the curtain snaps and helping her out. Despite his helmet and raincoat, he was drenched down his chest and back, and his feet and calves were splattered with grime, including a few shiny fish scales. He had a fearsome left eye cataracted in a milky cloud, but he seemed nice. His gestures were slow and methodical, and he didn't shout pidgin at her. In fact he said almost nothing, except when she handed him five baht. He looked at the money and said "Too ma' " and took off his pith helmet to pluck out three baht from the liner.

Louise saw that his hair was mostly white, but thick and in the crew cut that older men, especially workers, preferred. "Thank you," she said with a startled smile and took the change.

He smiled a leathery smile and turned his three-wheeler around. Hopping on the lower pedal, he threw a leg over to catch the other, and stood on the pedals, leaning down hard to get the thing going. He disappeared down the gravel path into the storm with slow, calm pedaling.

The room was damp and cold and horribly empty. A pair of John's khaki trousers were slung over a chair; his Japanese straw sandals were lying beneath them. When she shut the thin, louvered door and put her hand to the stuccoed cinder-block wall, it felt cold and clammy. Louise shivered and started to cry again. She stopped herself. She had to keep a clear head. If John did not come back that night, she'd have to go to the police and then to the American consulate in Chiang Mai and tell them what had happened. She'd give it until tomorrow, and until she had done those things, she didn't dare start falling apart. She first looked in her suitcase for a sweater but then decided that a hot shower might make her feel a lot better.

She pulled the batik curtains of the room's one window that

looked out on the distant waterfront and the Kok River. Stripping quickly because of the chill, she hurried into the bathroom, shut the door, and started the shower to warm up the dank room. While the hot water chugged into the drain, steam began to cloud the mirror. She stood before it and turned sideways, laying a hand on her flattened stomach and regarding her profile as she always did before showering. She had no tummy. Her ribs stood out when she held her back straight, and her breasts were full and prettily cupped. Absently pleased with this, even in her current misery, she stepped into the shower and shampooed her hair, working the lotion into her scalp and pulling it down through her long blond hair. Her hair was especially light and fine, and she realized that it would never dry on a day like this. She'd have to wear it up in a wet bun at dinner in the hotel restaurant.

The hot water relaxed her. She closed her eyes against the soap suds on her face. She felt a light tickling on the back of her leg. And then on her back. With her eyes still shut, she turned her back into the hot stream to rinse off what she thought were blobs of soap suds. And then she felt tickling over her feet and on her shoulder and neck. Louise brushed her neck with a soapy hand and her fingers felt something large and alive.

She squinted through the soap and screamed.

All about her—pouring up out of the drain, crawling over her feet and trying to climb up her and the slippery walls—huge, four-inch cockroaches were scuttling about the shower stall. Living in the drains and sewage pipes of the low-lying hotel, they too had been surprised by the rain and forced to scramble up the drains as the city gutters filled and the sewage backed up from the river. They were already clustered in the dark bubble of air underneath the shower when Louise had flooded them with hot soapy water. Hundreds of them, little leggy matchsticks and gross granddads, were now scrambling out of the drain to escape drowning in hot soapy water. Louise screamed again, slapping them off her legs, grunting in terror as she tried to get them off her back, and running out into the other room. She screamed again as she batted them out of her wet hair.

As she shook and flailed, the outside door was bashed open, splintering the wood about the little lock. Two men burst in. One, a young man with long hair, was pointing a machine pistol. The other man was her cloudy-eyed pedicab driver. Both looked bewildered, and then they started to laugh. They had burst in to rescue a screaming Louise from her assailant and now they saw herds of big bugs scurrying across the floors and clumsily leaping off the walls of the bathroom. They looked at Louise, naked and terrified and beautiful, and their smiles disappeared. She pulled the bedspread off the bed and covered herself. The young man replaced his gun in his belt under his shirt and turned to look at the driver, who nodded and extracted an envelope from his pith helmet and placed it on the bed.

"From Mister," he said, rubbing his hand across his crew cut and putting his helmet back on. "We wai' ou'si'." Pulling the door shut on its jarred hinges, they left her there—the soap still in her hair and roaches milling about, still emerging from the drain and dropping off the walls onto their backs and wiggling their legs obscenely. Wrapped in the bedspread, Louise reached for the envelope.

"I'm O.K." it began. It was John's handwriting.

> *Don't be frightened by these men. They are part of a group that will get Paul and Fay out. Don't worry. I trust them. This morning they took me and Carlos to a place upriver. I just hope you get this tonight and that you haven't gone to the police because that could queer everything. Tomorrow go to the bank and cash $2,000 of the traveler's checks into U.S. dollars. Give it to these men. That's their fee. They understand everything. One of them was radioed earlier in the day to watch you. Apparently everyone in the town has been keeping an eye on us since we came. As soon as you give them their money, take all the rest and all of our stuff and Carlos's and fly immediately to Bangkok.*

Then get out of the country and go to Penang. Stay at the Lone Pine Inn on the north shore. If I am not there in three weeks, go to the American embassy in Kuala Lumpur and ask to see the consul. If he won't help, call Mary Roberts to get things going from Washington. Tell the consul that I have been missing since trying to bribe our friends out of prison. Repeat everything that we told the embassy in Bangkok. This time they will have to accept that at least the two of us are missing. Go to Bangkok yourself only if you are sure you have the support of the embassy at Kuala Lumpur. The Thais can't be trusted, as we already know. They want to cover this up. But don't worry. I'll be with you in Penang in three weeks, some enchanted evening. I love you. John.

Penang. Some enchanted evening. Louise and John had once vacationed at the Lone Pine Inn, a colonial British stage set erected on the desolate north shore of the big Malayan island. Each morning they were served coffee and hot porridge and then fish—usually creamed finnan haddie—and then bacon and eggs and toast and, God, they thought they'd split their guts and so they'd take a walk along the beach onto the cliffs where large iguanas (the bald blink of their eyes made her shudder) sunned themselves on the sea ledges. Somehow John saw the whole setting as very *South Pacific* and the iguanas as the cast, sailors in drag. He had imitated one in deep male, romantic timbre singing "Some Enchanted Evening" like Ezio Pinza. He must be okay if he could bring up that.

Louise pulled the bedspread around her, tighter like a sarong, and peeked out to see if the two men were there. They were. Standing under the porte cochere and flicking their cigarette ashes into the topiary hedge, they looked up immediately when she waved. They looked about, and walked slowly over.

The old man smiled and held out a key—number 31. Louise regarded it from behind the cracked door. The number dangled from the key on a yellow plastic tag. 31—that was Carlos's room.

"You wash other pla'," the old man said. "We fix up here. Okay."

Louise looked at him. Behind him the kid with the gun hidden in his belt was smiling and nodding reassurances.

"No sweat, lady," the old man continued. "Too ma' bug here. You make too ma' water. My frien' hotel give me key other man. You go, but make little water now. Okay. You want me, ask hotel man for Phau. My name Phau. We come here early 'morrow. Go bank. Okay. Police come, you tell hotel man." He smiled again, and Louise thought he might be laughing at her, but good-naturedly, paternally.

"Okay," Louise said. "Okay." She shut the broken door and turned to gather her clothing, comb, and brush. She stepped on a roach and heard the crunch. Her tears were brimming once more: from the long dread of the afternoon, from the horror of the roaches, from the shock of the two men breaking in the door, and finally from the relief. John was alive. She blew air through her mouth to keep from crying. Okay, she repeated to herself as she opened the door to let the two men in.

"Never mind about the roaches," she said. "I am leaving tomorrow." She slowed down her English to be sure the old man understood. "I stay tonight in other room." She held up Carlos's key.

The old man smiled and nodded. The bugs would go back down the drain eventually, no need to go chasing after them with brooms. "Okay," he said, "we bring things other pla'."

"Okay," Louise said.

15.

*T*he river narrowed and the water cleared as they shunted along, their bow rolling out gentle furrows on either side. In the shallow channels, choked by tangles of bulbous water plants, they scraped through marshy islands, past bamboo thickets filled with birds, some of which Lacey knew from Vietnam, from those long months, over three years, during which he and Prescott had been in the burned-baby business: squadrons of quarrelsome scarlet flowerpeckers, tinier than sparrows. And below these, the water birds: a little green heron perched morosely on a dead branch twisted up and out of the water, an adjutant stork that clacked its beak at them, and egrets frozen in the reeds. Some of the birds would shriek and flap off under the darkening clouds when they heard the boat approach. Others stood and stared with beady blinks, as flattish turtles dropped off muddy logs and river snakes curved away in dignified glides.

The beginning rain soon hushed the jungle racket. Shortly after the drizzle muffled the bird cries from the islands and the riverbanks, they drew up to a small dock sunk on cement pylons. A bright new speedboat bobbed at its mooring. A wet red-cross flag hung limply at the bow. The dock was trimly whitewashed and stood out from the dark green shadows of the riverbank. Above the cement steps, now washing in the ripples of their wake, Lacey noted a welded archway, also painted white, topped with a Christian cross and below the cross a simply cut metal sign that spanned the arch: Ban Phing Paung Leprosarium—The Reborn Minority Mission.

"Qué haciendo? Hey, man," Carlos, sitting inside next to Beta, flicked a finger against Beta's knee, "what's happenin'?"

But Beta had turned silent and paid Carlos no attention; instead he stood up in the bow, now misting with rain, and stared down the glistening sandy path lined by white posts and coconut trees to where a native, dressed in Western pants and shirt, was running toward them, shielding himself from the rain with a strip of cardboard. Clouds of sand flies and mosquitoes seesawed under the dock as their boat rocked against the tires lashed to the pylons. Beta ignored the native too.

Carlos was perplexed. He and Beta had hit it off right away. Now he looked up to the big black man for a reply and got none. "Chíngate, maiate," he mumbled and turned to Chom. "Hey, Chum, why we stoppin' here?"

"We free another frien'." His tone was hollow, and he grinned stiffly at Lacey as he said this.

"Qué?"

"You see."

The native from the leprosarium was firing a lot of questions down from the dock. Chom answered him in a calming voice. When Beta reached back in, to pull his Ingram out from under the wooden bench that ran along the inside, the man shut up, looked at them angrily for a moment, and then, still holding his makeshift umbrella, turned and sprinted down the pathway. The pink soles of his sneakers lifted out of their line of view as he neared a large teak structure half-hidden behind palmyras, coconuts, and lush banana trees whose tattered leaves were dripping rain.

Without looking behind to see if the others were following, Beta, clutching his small machine gun, moved slowly and heavily up the dock steps onto the landing. Chom followed with the two other men. Chom was unarmed. But one companion, in baggy pajamas trousers and T-shirt, carried an old carbine with a banana-clip magazine, and a machete scabbard dangled from the back of his belt. The other was a young man whose head was turbaned with a checkered scarf like the one Chom draped around his neck; he carried an M-16. He puffed on a small homemade pipe. No one seemed very excited. They walked heavily as if carrying out a chore. They had left the sick man with the broken shackles sleeping on a pile of jute bags.

As they followed along the neatly swept path, Carlos looked at Lacey, but said nothing.

Lacey shrugged his shoulders. "I don't know," he said. "Maybe there's a doctor here for their friend."

"Bro'," Carlos whispered, "wanta make a run for it?"

"No."

"They ain't payin' shit to us now, man."

"No. These guys won't hurt us."

"You sure, man?"

"Pretty sure."

" 'Ey, gabacho. 'Pretty sure.' " Carlos pushed his woolen cap around his head and sucked air between his lower lip and teeth.

They tracked Beta through the drizzle. Lacey's white canvas shoes were squishy in the toes and his short-sleeved shirt was beginning to stick to his back and chest. A white man and woman stood under umbrellas at the end of the path. The man with the cardboard was gesturing toward the armed group.

In a firmly polite voice, the woman greeted them first. "Hello,

Chom. Hello, Beta," she said and looked suspiciously at Lacey and Carlos.

"Mrs. Crane. Rever' Crane."

Beta nodded sullenly and looked off at the buildings.

"How is James?" Chom asked.

"Much the same, I'm afraid, Chom," the woman said, smiling at Lacey, who, in his seersucker pants, didn't look the type to be traveling with Lawa bandits and their Negro renegade.

The Reverend Crane nodded concurrence. "Much the same," he said. He looked grayer than Mrs. Crane and more distant.

"Please meet Dr. Lacey and his assistant," Chom said.

"Oh," said Mrs. Crane, "but let's get out of this rain. You'll be soaked.'

They moved under the eave of the nearest building, a barrackslike ward where a man with no nose stared at them from a screened window. Behind him, Lacey could make out two men playing cards on an army cot. They held the cards between stubbed knuckles where their fingers ended in whitish scabs. They smoked their cheroots in the same way and ignored the visitors just outside their dormitory.

Lacey shook hands with the Reverend Crane. Carlos, disconcerted by the noseless man at the window, shook hands too and then wiped his hands on his wool cap, pretending to adjust it.

"A doctor?" asked Mrs. Crane.

"Not really . . . ," Lacey began.

"He's the new public health officer for AID," Chom said.

Mrs. Crane looked at Chom in disbelief. Why would the AID health officer travel upriver with *them*? She stared again at Lacey, who did not appear to be distressed, or kidnapped, or whatever. "I see," she said. "How nice of you to visit our mission."

Lacey smiled back, not knowing what to say.

"Could we see James?" Chom asked.

"Of course. Of course. Wilfred, you show them the way. I'll fix some Kool-Aid. Can you stay for refreshment, Dr. . . . Mr. Lacey?"

"That would be nice."

"And, Chom," she continued, "oh, you know: no nasty guns in the house. 'Thou shalt not kill.' " She sounded almost girlish.

Chom smiled, nodded, and turned to follow Beta and the Reverend Crane to a cluster of barracks—maybe ten in all, some of them two-story affairs that looked like Carolina tobacco sheds.

"Holy shit," Carlos said. He stopped.

With a grimace that might have indicated embarrassment, the Reverend Crane stopped too and pointed up to where Carlos was looking: to the second story of one of the teak buildings where a large, emaciated black man sat on the sill above their heads, his legs and arms hanging limply through the bars, his head pressed against the bars as he stared into space.

"I'm afraid he's worse." The Reverend Crane coughed and winced a quick smile to no one in particular. "Olivia prays for him daily, of course, but it's no good now . . . although who knows?"

Beta, so tall that he could almost reach up and touch the man's dangling feet, stood below and called up loudly, "James!" "James!" he called again, and then, when no response came from the wasted man, naked except for his green military shorts, Beta said, much more softly, "Jimmy."

"What's wrong with him?" Lacey asked.

"Schistosomiasis."

"Snail fever?"

"Lacey, you know this?" Chom asked.

"Yeah. You get it from bathing in rivers. It's a blood disease. Snails sometimes carry these little worms . . ."

"Yes," said the Reverend Crane. "Trematodes. Most of it is no worse than swimmer's itch, but James has the most severe form, *japonicum*. The worm eggs are growing in his lungs, his spleen, his heart, and lungs. He's anemic, fibrotic. You might say he's being eaten alive."

"Can he live?" asked Lacey.

"Oh, dear, I doubt it. Besides, he's insane now. When we put him in there, he was thrashing about despite his weakness. Now he just leans against the window."

"Shit, man," Carlos said, "why don't you get him out of here? Medevac him?"

"I'm afraid it's too late," Crane said softly. "Olivia thought we could treat him here. At first, it seemed to be only malaria or dengue. The symptoms are so much the same. And going to a hospital meant jail." He paused and turned to Lacey. "He's like Beta, you know, AWOL from Vietnam. We pray for him, Carlos. We pray for them both."

"Fantástico."

"Rever'," Chom said, "Beta want finish this."

"Beg your pardon?"

"Beta now shoot James," Chom explained.

"Oh, you can't do that. It's . . . a sin. Olivia wouldn't permit . . ." His tired blue eyes were troubled.

But Beta had already raised his Ingram toward the verminous chest of his friend, and Chom was guiding the minister around the corner of the building away from possible ricochets off the iron bars. Lacey and Carlos looked at each other and walked over to the two other men standing behind Beta. "Please, let's talk to Olivia," they could hear the preacher protesting as the compound rang with the automatic's burst. When Lacey looked up again at the window, he saw only the pink soles of James's feet as his legs stuck out above the sill. He had been thrown back. Beta was still standing in front of the window, head bowed, staring at the ground, his gun pointed at the ground. The two Lawa were already climbing the narrow, high steps to see if James was dead. He was. Soon his feet disappeared from the sill, and the two small men were dragging him, folded up in a cotton blanket, down the stairs. Lacey thought of Horowitz, the Johnny Appleseed of the Mekong Delta. When they lifted Horowitz onto the chopper, he too was wrapped in a thin cotton blanket, sopping with his blood and with the river water that had soaked into his clothes and gunshot wounds. Lacey had gripped him under his cold wet arms. Horowitz's head fell back against Lacey's knees when they stopped to raise him up. Lacey's hands, his knees, and his pants were wet with blood.

As the two men half carried, half dragged the body toward the dock, Lacey turned and walked ahead. Together under the minister's umbrella, he saw Chom walking the Reverend Crane back toward the house. The minister was shaking his head. The drizzle had let up, but they were all wet and chilled. Behind him, Lacey could hear Carlos say "shit, man" through chattering teeth, and behind that, the sound of the body being dragged over the sand-and-gravel path. Somewhere behind was Beta.

A few minutes later, when they were on the dock about to board, Olivia Crane came hurtling down the path. James, still trussed in his cotton shroud, had been roped to the bow deck. "Oh, sinners," she declaimed, "*how* will you repent? Who *are* you?" she demanded of Lacey.

They just looked at her and boarded the rocking boat. The two Lawa, who spoke no English, were nonetheless grinning broadly. Beta collapsed back on the wooden bench, creaking the boards with his weight. And, after checking the man still asleep on his jute-bag bed at the back, Chom signaled them to move the boat out. Olivia Crane glared at them with crossed arms. When they reached mid-stream, they heard her yell "Sinners" once again.

"Hey, Chum," Carlos asked, "you said you was going to *free* a friend. Por qué?"

"I was being poetic." Chom smiled wearily at Lacey.

"Dig." Carlos then turned to Beta who sat next to him with his knees splayed as he studied his palms. " 'Ey, man," Carlos said, "you done the right thing."

"Little man, what do you know—"

"Okay, man—"

"—what do *any*body know? You know that dude?" he pointed to the bloodied shape draping the bow.

"He's your friend, man. A soul brother, right?"

Beta looked at Carlos and smirked. "Huh," he said. "See that?" he asked and pointed to the *B* branded on his upper arm. "Johnson gave me that. He was my *fraternity* brother. Shit, I'll tell you about it sometime."

Carlos looked bewildered.

" 'Nother thing," Beta continued, "don't let me hear no 'maiate' again."

Carlos stroked his chin to conceal a foolish grin. "I gotcha, bro'."

Lacey looked at Beta. "Lincoln or Cheyney?" he asked.

"Cheyney."

Of the three likely black schools, Lacey didn't think that Howard, in D.C., still allowed its fraternities to *brand* initiates. At Lincoln and Cheyney, two Pennsylvania schools just north of the Mason-Dixon, they still beat the shit out of rushers. To be willing to go through some of the initiations, you really had to want to be a brother. Christ, besides the pain, you could get blood poisoning from branding.

"Johnson was a classics major, you understand."

"Bro', you saying you went to college?"

"Tha's right."

"You don't sound it, man."

"Tha's right." Beta turned back to Lacey. "He knew Latin and Greek better'n I know English. He done all the brothers' language work: French and Spanish and German. Tell us all how to answer, you know. He done that, you see, 'cause he like to party. I worked in the refectory and ah'd steal some pork chops or somethin' like that and take 'em back to Jimmy's room where all the brothers be hangin' round. Big, flat-footed Willie in his raincoat dancin' by hisself in the corner. Michael Manns, no bigger than Carlos there.

We'd put the chops in a pan on the radiator and turn the heat up — steam the room wit' the smell of pork—and we'd sip our Mad Dog and go to work, askin' Jimmy when we got stuck. 'That'll git over on ol' Bloom?' they ask. Bloom was the old grayboy who run the show at Cheyney: the mojo with the sayso. That old Jew loved Jimmy, 'cause Jimmy always knew his stuff. He recite the *Ilias* an' all by heart, you see. 'Jus' write it down like I said,' he'd say. At nine o'clock or so we was on the way to the canteen, *together,* you know. He kep' us together. James Johnson. The jukebox be wailin' and it was all boogie-joogie with the girls. Jimmy loved the African chicks. He knew a dude named Shittu—Ahmad Acboola Shittu— who introduced him around the African chicks. Cheyney was like what-may-I-say, *Nigeria.*"

"How did you end up in Vietnam . . . the two of you?" A gibbon screamed in the trees by the bank as they slipped past. It was late afternoon, about two hours until sunset.

"In LBJ. Yas, in Long Binh Jail. Two years outa Cheyney. I was busted for junk and he—"

"Chiva, bro'? You did heroin?"

"Yeah, heroin. And man, James, he was in for organizing a sit-in at the PX and post office in Cholon. Anniversary of Martin Luther King. The day that cracker shot him." Beta paused to look at Carlos as if wondering about him, wondering why Carlos had joined the Marines. "It was the grayboy's war, man. I lost interest. We'd sweep through them villages looked like Georgia an' some ofay say to me, 'Beta, look at them huts. They're livin' on *dirt floors'.* Me, like some Moses, say 'Yes, isn't it awful? We must save them from Communism.' What was I thinkin'? Aunt Hagar always lived on a dirt floor."

Chom laughed at this. He had never heard the story of Beta's disaffection in quite this way.

"Tha's right, man. Man, one day I was on a helicopter pad with the Ninth in the Delta. We was under fire and *we was the support unit.* An' this chopper comes from the field with body bags. Dasn't ever land, you see, just hovers and drops 'em out and then we throw on the ammo cases. Blades whoopin' and beatin' up the dust. Then I seen this body bag all broke open, you understand, and about all I could tell about what or who was inside was the dude was black, man. It was like . . . what may I say . . . a *sign,* you understand."

Overhead, on the tin-covered roof, they could hear the chickens flapping around in their baskets and the pig working its sharp, trussed hooves on the tin sheeting. Outside, the sky was clearing, and the river birds were starting to call from bank to bank. Standing on the bow just behind Johnson's body, the kid with the checkered turban called something back to Chom inside.

"An' the smack," Beta continued, "was jus' the natural thing to do. Smokin' it, then shootin'. Mosta platoon got sent to LBJ. The MPs showed up one mornin', shook us up off the cots, and took us to some medical tent where they watched us until we all piss in a jar. And at Long Binh, Johnson said he just wouldn't fight the grayboy's war. You know Thucydides or some Greek dude say they have made a desert and they called it peace. That war's jus' white folks' boogie-joogie. But this time they fool themselves because Charlie's goin' to win. An' when I met Johnson in the stockade, he was findin' and provin' with the brothers. Jus' like at Cheyney. Shootin' and cuttin'. Tellin' 'em not to fight no honky war. I fought too much of it already."

"How did you get to Thailand?"

"When they let us out, Jimmy was waitin' already, you see, and we went AWOL." Beta paused and looked out the window into the jungle wall. "Now, I'd say there be uka brothers walkin' round Saigon or Cholon tryin' to figure out how to get home. In Saigon we paid some Vietnamese dude to put us on a boat out of Rach Gia. The big thing was the Navy patrols, you know, but we wasn't the first niggers to run north, so we took the chance. That was feet to the fire, but once we cleared Phu Quoc Island, we was home free. He dropped us off at U Taphao near Bangkok. The res' was easy.

An Army brother in Bangkok give us the lay of the land, so to speak, an' we headed up to Chiang Mai to move dope and make some bread. Met Chom. He took care of us. Ain't that right?"

"No, Beta, you an' James take care of me."

Lacey turned to Chom. "Is that where you learned English?"

"No, tha's how I get baseball cap. I know English from missionary school."

"Chum, you a Christian?"

"No, baby, I'm a bandit."

"Qué suave, man." Carlos was smiling.

"Yes," Lacey said, "but *why* are you a bandit?"

"Tha's long story. Some other time. Right now, look up river. Chert says people fishing."

"Well, what are you, bro'? A Buddhist or something?"

"A Lawa." He pointed outside. "These people once Buddhist. We built the old chedis in Chiang Mai, but Thais came and driving us off land into mountains." Over the noise of the pistons, Chom signaled the man in the baggy pajamas to cut the engine. The boat drifted forward against the current and then back, wallowing slowly toward the left bank. On the opposite bank, about thirty villagers were turned out to fish where a large canal ran into the river. The canal had been loosely dammed with a bamboo weir and along both banks about a dozen men were poised—standing on small, makeshift wooden platforms pounded into the bank—and holding large throw nets draped over their arms, the ring weights hanging down. A couple of the men waved at Chert in the bow who, like some of them, was puffing on his little gourd pipe. Then, at one of their yells, they all threw their nets, which zigzagged out first into opening parabolas and then into hovering circles that fell with splashes into the canal. With loud shouts, they hauled in.

Chom had not cut his engine for them but for the women, waist-deep in the river, who were fishing the far bank near the dammed canal. Instead of throw nets, the women fished with huge dig nets, which they worked like puppeteers from pliant bamboo cross-splints. As they waded in a group toward the bank—perhaps twenty or so girls and older women—they held their nets high out over the water on light poles. Once out of the deep water, their sarongs stuck to their backsides and hips. They had been in up to their breasts, and their coarse baggy shirts clung to their torsos. Near them, young boys, dressed only in cotton shorts, were pointing long, wire-pronged spears at the water, waiting on the bank to jab any big fish that might rise and run before the women. Some of the women wore straw hats with scarves draped at the back and some just wore scarves wrapped up in loose Aunt Jemima turbans. Suddenly the women dropped their poles. All the nets billowed down into the water, and some of the boys lunged on their spears. When the nets came up, most of them were bellied with leaping, sparkling, sardine-like fish. One boy had speared something big and had swept it flapping onto the bank as the other kids ran over. Chom, standing now in the bow with Chert and the three Americans, signaled their pilot to rev the engine and bring the boat to dock above the women. When the boat passed by, the women turned, and the men looked up from sorting their catches. They waved again, and then they saw the body in a blanket lying at the feet of the men—and the men! A white one and one with whiskers like a catfish. The women turned to each other in whispered speculation. In the growing dusk, Chom called out across the water and pointed to the pig tied on the upper deck. Laughter rippled back across the water.

16.

*T*hat night they talked business. Earlier in the day, at the market wharf in Chiang Rai when Lacey had agreed to the $2,000 to spring Roberts and Fay, he was only committing a portion of the bribe money that had been budgeted by Roberts's stepmother and their spook adviser, Grant. Lacey had agreed with no hesitation, mindful of the possibility that he was only putting up ransom for himself and Carlos. He knew damn little about Chom and Beta when he wrote the note to Louise and, of course, if they grabbed her after the trip to the bank, they were all finished. Louise, too. Purest impulse had led him on his chase after the jailbreakers, and impulse still told him he was dealing with honorable crooks. But now he had dragged Louise into this too. Horrible as the thought was—his wife killed by Lawa bandits that he had sent to her address—it did not seem likely. While these men would kill, they were not killers. That was what he had told Carlos, and in a fix like his, it was an important distinction. As he weighed things, quite simply, Roberts's and Fay's lives were not worth his and Louise's. So he had asked Chom to set his price, and then readily agreed. There was nothing else they could get out of him. There was no reason, just *no* reason to hurt them. *But what did he know?* That was the nagging thing. He was an academic and a sometimes poet who by chance had witnessed a war. How good was his judgment of people like Chom and Beta? He felt he might as well have been judging Martians.

And now, in a mountain village on a ridge four thousand feet above the river, the night air keening with crickets and tree frogs and giant katydids from the surrounding forest, Lacey, Carlos, and Chom were sitting cross-legged on a grass mat around a kerosene lamp. Moths circling the glass sent shadows fluttering across their faces as they sipped smoky-colored rice whiskey and talked.

"These your people, man?" Carlos was looking at the middle-aged woman, whose black hair was rolled in a neat chignon, standing before a large cooking counter: a cast-iron tray filled with sand and fitted with tripods, crudely forged pothooks, and angle irons that came out from a wall beam or hung down from a rafter. The roof was thatch; the floor, smooth shiny planks. The house, actually only two rooms—a kitchen separated by a rattan partition from the sleeping and sitting area—was raised about six feet off the ground. Below the floorboards were two tethered water buffalo and a pig pen. The smoke from the cooking mingled sharply with the stench from the animals. The woman was preparing a hind leg of the pig that the village had slaughtered to celebrate Pae's return from prison. Pae, revived somewhat by the fermented tea his aunt had brewed him, was sitting up in a corner. His shackles had been sawed off, and he was rubbing the infected ankle rash.

"Some Lawa," Chom replied, "some Skaw Karen come with us. Most Lawa live wes', wes' of Chiang Mai, wes' of Ping Riva'."

Except for his final *r*'s and *t*'s and his failure to apply an article here and there, Chom's English was pretty amazing. Silly, isn't it? Lacey thought; maybe he trusted Chom only because of that. How primitive. To think a man is smart because he can speak our language. How often had Lacey heard Americans in Vietnam *shouting* on the principle that volume aided understanding. And the dinks that they dismissed as idiots probably had plotted the Tet offensive. Maybe Chom was a genius; maybe he was a cretin with a gift for learning languages. "Why did you move here?" Lacey asked.

"Because no more lan'. Once Lawa big people. For hundreds years, we give gif' to Prince of Chiang Mai and he give us much lan'. The Karens come from Burma and pay us let them use lan' and we have elepha's and silk and much rice. Now, the las' Prince of Chiang Mai is dead. In 1932, the Thais come from South and kick him out. They take our lan', say if we not use lan', the lan' is public and belong to Thailan'. We use lan' only every nine years. If use more, it die."

The Lawas, like most of the mountain peoples, were swiddeners. Their land had to lie fallow for years or the slash-and-burn farming would quickly deplete it. The Thais were perpetrating a fraud by taking away their "unused" land. It was simple robbery—the same way the Vietnamese had robbed the mountain peoples of the Central Highlands.

A huge palmetto bug, a kind of roach but even bigger, scuttled out from under a grass mat and tried to escape across the floor. Chom quickly snared it in his hand and then let it out to run into his other hand, capturing it and recapturing it in hand-over-hand fashion. As he did this, he seemed hardly even to consider the huge bug threading his hands with swimming legs. Chom was thinking; playing with the bug was just a boyhood reflex. The day told on him —as did the whiskey. His cheeks were flushed, and he was lost so in thought that he did not even pay attention to Carlos, who got up to peek in the Dutch oven where the pork was cooking. Pae's aunt was amused by this and held the lid open for Carlos to sniff the sizzling pork. "Far out, mama," he said, but he was a little taken aback when the woman smiled. She had been chewing betel and her teeth and gums were bloody. "Far out," he muttered again and sat back down to have another drink.

Chom finally let the bug loose and continued his story. His father had been a *samang* or lineage leader; he had died in the influenza epidemic of 1942. When Chom was little, livestock was scarce because the Japanese were in the valleys, taking whatever they could find. So the Lawa loss of wealth, put into motion by the Thai overthrow of the Prince of Chiang Mai a decade earlier, continued during the war and after, when Thais and Karens returned to take away their deedless lands. After the war, other hill tribes—Akha, Lisu, Lahu, and the new surge of Miao—started growing opium in big cash crops, and with that money they could buy new land, often Lawa land. And then the Thais returned in force with a new government that taxed everything and returned nothing. They taxed liquor, firearms, livestock, and even the butchering of livestock. Chom's uncle, who had sent him to missionary school to learn English and Thai, turned out no good as *samang*. As a protector of a Lawa lineage, the times proved too much for him. He started smoking opium, and with that came the inevitable mortgaging and then selling off of family lands to feed his addiction. Landless, although he would someday be head of the lineage, Chom worked for a Thai lumber company that was hauling teak and then, later, on a government road operation near Mai Hong Son. As a disenfranchised laborer, he often saw the Loi Maw troops from Burma guarding the mule caravans moving the raw opium that the hill tribes had sold to the Haw middlemen. Opium. Money. Guns. Independence. Chom put it together, and with his sixty followers was in the game. They were little fry swimming around the big fish and taking care to keep out of their way. The big fish ate the little ones. The big caravans were owned by Khan Su, alias Chin Shan-fu, a Shan Chinese from Burma who used opium to fund his Shan United Army. There was also a Burma-based Shan State Army that was more genuinely a liberation movement. Khan Su, with eight hundred men under arms—sophisticated arms: machine guns, mortars, grenade launchers, recoilless rifles—ran the biggest operation and had only one serious rival, General Li Wen Huan, who claimed to be a jade collector but who ran the remnants of the Third Kuomintang Army left behind when Chiang Kai-shek fled to Taiwan in 1949. Another Kuomintang leftover, General Duan Shiwen, commanded a five-hundred-man remnant of the Fifth KMT. Driven out of China along with a large rabble of bandits and other scum, they had settled in the wilds of western Burma where no force was strong enough to evict them.

As a little fish, Chom had to be nimble and know the currents. His sense of history and his hill-tribe origins were the basis for his wise immediate and long-range views. His meeting up with Beta and James Johnson proved a real piece of luck, and his Karen associates —boyhood friends from his home village of Baw Luang—also had their special uses. But, oddly enough, it had been a missionary who first opened his eyes to new possibilities. ("Carlos, you aren't the fir' Spaniar' in these mountains," he said. "How's that, bro'?" "Well," Chom said, "we had the Duke of Albuquerque in 1511. But even Jesuits couldn't make sense of this place.") But the other missionary, the Reverend Thompson, a linguist with the Wycliffe Bible Foundation, *had* untangled some of the mess for Chom: from a linguistic point of view the hundreds of tribes in the mountains and valleys of Southeast Asia were not a matter of superior and inferior races but of common sources from which some groups entered the mainstream of Asian history while others remained in the rural backwaters. Reverend Thompson had shown Chom how the Thais, like the Vietnamese who were top dogs across the Mekong, were just like the Lawa and the other little tribes, no better. Maybe luckier. For thousands of years, people like the Lawa had been moving south through the mountain valleys, driven by the need for new land and by the pressure of Chinese expansion. The valley people, like the Thais and the Vietnamese, had organized on Indian or Chinese models, while their country cousins, like the Shan or the Muong, were bypassed in the high mountains.

So Chom was carving out a territory, in defiance of various Shan and Chinese competitors, in defiance of the Thai and Burmese governments, and in defiance of the Americans, who supplied arms and helicopters to stop the opium trade. The Thai, Burmese, and Lao Communist forces left him alone, although he had to entertain their propagandists. He saw through their game of trying to win Lawa and other tribal sympathies. The results were okay. He didn't reject the Communists, although Reverend Thompson seemed to think they were the most serious threat. With about sixty armed men—thirty-five with him in a camp near the village, fifteen in a jungle camp north near Mong Hsat in Burma, and ten in the west at Mae Hong Son—and through occasional deals with the Burmese and Thai police, he could move small caravans of opium quite successfully. He gathered raw opium bricks from the hill tribes, and he sold it to the Chaozhou overseas Chinese, wide-ranging racketeers who had formed a chain of opium dens for the British and who from their Shanghai base had monopolized the drug trade from all angles in the 1920s, even marketing a red pill (containing heroin) as a cure for opium addiction. Now the Chaozhou operated out of Hong Kong, with syndicates and heroin labs wherever they could melt into the populations of other overseas Chinese: in Bangkok, Cholon, Singapore, Rangoon, Kuala Lumpur, Penang.

The trick was to get the raw or cooked opium to these centers despite the interdiction of the Thai and Burmese militias, who were sometimes assisted by the U.S. Air Force flying short-range bombers and helicopter gunships. In the past few years that had meant a lot of setbacks for the bigger operators. Khan Su, with a big price on his head, had to flee Thailand for the more difficult terrain of Burma, where Wa tribesmen subsequently sacked and burned some of his labs. General Duan was lying low in his fortress at Mae Salong. The Shan State Army was busy skirmishing with the regular Burmese Army. The squeeze was on, and only a clever little fish like Chom could swim through the big net. Through the rivers running west out of Mae Hong Son and Mae Sariang, near his hometown, Chom used Karens to ship raw opium across the Burmese border into the vast Salween River, which flowed into the Gulf of Martaban a hundred miles or so downriver. There, at Moulmein, the Chaozhou labs refined the stuff into No. 3 heroin or shipped it west to Rangoon or south through the Andaman Sea to the Malayan island of Penang where more sophisticated labs converted it into the purer and more valuable No. 4. Or, he had simply to get Beta and Johnson, dressed either as GIs or tourists, safely to Chiang Mai, where they would board a train for Bangkok and deliver the stuff directly to labs in the capital. In the mountains a kilogram of "cooked" opium was worth about $100; in Bangkok, $1,000. Refined to No. 4 pure heroin, it was worth $10,000.

Chom had a plan to break into these bigger profits. Through Beta and Johnson he had established contacts with U.S. military traffickers. If he could set up a lab, he could sell directly to European racketeers—no Chinese gangs—at world-market prices for pure heroin. His contacts were ready to fly it out on U.S. transports. Johnson was smooth and clever, but now he was dead. Beta was too rough to handle it alone. "What do you thin'," Chom now asked Lacey, "of being my partne'? No' forever—may' you don' like the Lawa mountains—but say, for three, maybe five year. Just to get thing' started?"

Lacey laughed. That was one surefire way out of a life of boredom, petty altercations, seeping hatreds, and ineffectual noodles who couldn't fix a flat tire, let alone a drug deal. He'd be rich, he'd be moving and using his wits. He'd also probably be dead within two years, executed by a Thai firing squad or gunned down by the Loi Maw. Lacey shook his head. "I'll think about it," he said.

"Shit, Chum," Carlos said, "I don't need no thinking about it, man. You cut me in and I'll move your smack."

"You no *use* it, Carlos," Chom warned. "It kill you like my uncle."

"But, hey, what about my man Beta?"

"Beta stop. Johnson made him." Chom poured some rice whiskey into an earthenware cup and leaned back to give it to Pae. "Good," he said when he turned back to them. "We see. You think about it. After we get your frien' out, you tell me for sure." Outside, in the night forest, the katydids were spinning their ratchets in the trees. The night sang with cricket trills and the whines of millions of wings.

"Chom!" Beta called up through the floor boards. "We's ready."

The three of them got up and walked out onto the creaky porch under the awning of bamboo leaves. Beta was down below. Beside him was a pretty twenty-year-old with pouty lips, very white teeth, and a crooked smile that drew down at one corner of her mouth. Her large breasts pushed out against her loose poncho blouse. Beneath her Thai sarong, her rough feet were bare. Her head was bare, too, the shiny black hair parted in the middle and tied back.

"Who's the chick, man?" Carlos whispered to Chom.

"She James' wife."

"Oh, dig." Carlos pushed his wool cap back on his head and smiled at the girl.

Behind them were two young guys. One carried a small army shovel; the other held a torch of pitch-dipped rags wrapped around a pole.

"Where is he?" asked Chom.

"In the clearin', near the ledge." Beta turned and they all followed the guy with the torch out of the village. Most of the houses were dark or lit by the faint glows of small kerosene lamps. All the houses were raised on stilts and, as they passed through the village, momentary bright dots of fire indicated men and women smoking and sitting quietly high up on their porch steps. Some of the villagers could be heard mumbling and shuffling down the steps to join the group. Soon, guided by wavering torches, maybe twenty people were walking single file out into the hillside fields. Nighthawks circled them, whistling after the moths stirred up by their flames. Off in the forest a bird repeated a mad giggle. The group stopped at a rocky spot near a cliff face beyond the last field. Near a tangle of skinny trees and sprays of bamboo, another torch had been staked into the hard ground, and two other men were standing by an open grave, heaped earth, and the hollowed-out log into which Johnson had been laid. His hands were folded across his shattered chest. The blanket had been pulled down to show his face. One eye was shut; the other was open and glazed over. Beside the Lawa-style coffin lay about a half dozen books. Beta scooped them up in his big hands and gave them to Lacey.

"You read somethin', man. I'd 'preciate it. The Latin. Jimmy'd like that."

Lacey took the books uncertainly and looked at them in the torchlight: Marcus Garvey; the *koine* version of the New Testament; a textbook, *Latin and Greek in English Usage;* a battered issue of *Language* that contained a monograph on the Phaistos disc of Crete; the *Selected Poems* of Langston Hughes; and a bilingual *Aeneid.*

Chom took off his Atlanta Braves cap and motioned to one of his men to remove his floppy, wide-brimmed camouflage hat. Carlos took off his cap and shoved it into his belt.

"Read it in Latin and English." Somehow Beta had decided that Lacey could read Latin. Lacey panicked and wondered what to read. He considered Book IV and Dido's funeral . . . there was a good line there about being terrified by the empty vault of heaven, but Johnson didn't sound terrified by much, so Lacey flipped on to Book VI . . . the Sibyl at Cumae . . . the Golden Bough . . . and then he stumbled on the funeral for Misenus, the comrade lost at sea. As he whispered the passage to himself to see if he could do it, the jungle chattered all about them and, every now and then, an insect would fly into a torch and pop.

He heard Chom say softly to encourage him, "We have no *lam* here. We are mixed—Karens, Lawa, Christians. But we need to do this right. He died bad, with a bad ghost, maybe. My people need to think that you keep his ghost away."

"Okay," Lacey said. He moved closer to the light and read

> ". . . corpusque lavant frigentis et unguunt.
> Fit gemitus. Tum membra toro defleta reponunt,
> purpureasque super vestis, velamina nota,
> coniciunt."

Carlos crossed himself.

"Now, what's that say?" Beta almost whispered.

". . . They washed and anointed the body of their friend so cold in death. All wept. And when they cried for him, they covered the body with purple robes and the dead man's own clothing, and laid it on the bier."

"Yeah. Now read it again in Latin."

Lacey read the passage again. Johnson's wife, whose face had been warped in an odd grin, now began to sob. Beta took the book out of Lacey's hands and gathered up the others and lined them inside the coffin by the body. He put the *Aeneid* into Johnson's folded hands and, leaning over the coffin, said quietly, "Yeah, Jimmy, tha's just *right*, wasn't it."

17.

Thanu 3 4 — 1 — Mangkau-n 6 8

8 — Àthàko-hà อุตุกโกห — 7

Phrom wจ/ม 2 3 — 6 — Rà-dchasi 5 2 รจน์

Koi had brought them another diversion: an astrologer's chart. The old guy, holding the tattered horoscope, peeped into Fay's cell, grinning and looking like old Shep ready for reward. Shit, Roberts thought, if this dumb fart is Lacey's go-between, he's got everybody fooled. Roberts turned to Fay and Mai and pointed at Koi. "One thing's for sure," he said, "this guy's going to be a dog in his next life or he *was* one in his last."

Fay was stretched out on bombax pillows. Mai sat before her, pulling the aches out of Fay's calves with long ripples of her thumbs. When Mai translated, Koi grinned all the wider and almost wagged with self-approval.

Roberts coughed and looked at Koi's yellowed chart, studying the roman transliteration for a coded message; he found none. His horoscope in *Stars and Stripes* had said, "Quite unexpectedly you may be afforded the chance to do something different. Keep alert and ready to act." He had. The wait was awful. A week had passed since their outing at the pond, since the kids had said "Lay Si hiah." It was hard to be diverted by anything except speculating on the possible avenue of escape. He handed the chart to Mai. No, he was just too edgy to take an interest. He was worried that Mai had detected a change: in him; not Fay. Mai's usual ministrations of scabies salves, massages, and sex held no absorption for him now. He couldn't fake it. Fay didn't have to. Her thoughts—if she could have gathered them—were camouflaged by a fever that had subsided only in the last few days, leaving her weak, her lips swollen in burst, crusty blisters, and her eyes ringed by blue shadow. At first, after their fight, Roberts was pleased at her discomforts. Her monkey was gone, and she and Snit never had their picnic by the pond—served her right. But then Roberts got scared when throughout the second day Fay continued to dry heave and shake and scream with pain whenever light broke into the curtained cell. When her lips blistered and she could no longer stand, he had gone to Snit and demanded a doctor. Snit sat in the sun in a chair, tapping his boot with his new swagger stick. The sun glistened on his oily hair and he smelled like a shelled peanut. Snit's reply was a contemptuous smile and about two fingers of Mekong whiskey, which he told Roberts he could take back to Fay.

What did she fucking have? Dengue? Blackfly fever? There had been lots of sand flies on the mud flats by the pond. An amoeba? Malaria? Sprue? Roberts knew the names but not the epidemiologies. Whatever it was, it seemed to have burned itself out for the time being. But Fay was too weak to stand, let alone run, and that scared Roberts. How did the Montagnards survive this shit? Roberts figured they must be the toughest bastards on the planet. A fucking

A-bomb would do the Golden Triangle good: cut down on the insects a bit, kill the Chinese and everyone else, and give the 'yards some elbow room.

Did anyone suspect? Koi seemed to be suspicious, but of course he *would* notice if indeed he was Lacey's man. But Koi *had* looked annoyed in the last few days when he caught Roberts trying to do push-ups, especially annoyed when Roberts told him not to buy them any more opium. Maybe Koi was just sore; but Mai told Roberts that Koi had said to her that he was behaving like someone about to get out of jail.

But stopping the opium—and trying to sinew a body depleted by months of lassitude, by scabies, by Mai's scabies cures, by sickness, and by flights with the Black Phantom—only made him sicker. The withdrawal was a bitch: stomach cramps, backaches, dizzying headaches, nausea, chills, and bone-wrenching spasms in his limbs. Roberts had a hard time keeping food down. Shuffling outside in the shattering sunlight of the prison's triangular courtyard, he would sometimes spike a fever and break into a sweat; inside the darkened cell—as now, sitting on the platform bed with the others—he had to wrap himself in a cotton blanket while his teeth chattered and Mai steeped him a bitter brew of monkey shit and jungle roots that would drive his tongue clacking in his mouth, steam his upper lip with sweat, and snap in his gut like a trip flare.

Mai, scabbed badly only along the insides of her fingers and the creases of her buttocks, suffered from no secondary infections. She seemed on top of it all. And when Roberts handed her Koi's fortune-teller's chart, she paused from stroking Fay's legs to study it. Neither Koi nor Mai could read well, but Mai could at least pick her way through the newspaper, stumbling usually through the news of government, brightening up when some man was arrested for butchering his unfaithful wife or vice versa. The old guard sat down next to them on the edge of the bed, propping his M-16 between his knees. Already Mai was excited for Fay and Paul, at this wonderful opportunity to play a new game together.

"You know, jelly bean," Roberts said, "you remind me of the ladies who run games on Caribbean cruises."

Without the slightest idea of what a cruise was or where the Caribbean might be, Mai giggled. "Zis is call Athakoha and mean tell you what you do," she explained seriously. "You star' numa one and coun' how many year old you have. Girl coun' lef'; man he coun' ri'." She pushed a kerosene-stinking finger counterclockwise and clockwise to demonstrate.

Fay went first, or rather Mai asked Fay her age (which she already knew, but it was part of the game to declare your age out loud), and then Mai counted out for her. It wasn't clear whether to start with the next square or triangle as one or two, but Mai declared that one should be counted as one. Fay was thirty-two; Mai's finger went around the chart a few times and finally stopped on five in the Râd-chasi corner. They consulted the table printed on the reverse. "Fortune: You leave your house; you get in quarrel; you be sick; you lose four-leg an' two-leg animals."

"I should hope that it is this house I lose," she said slowly, with effort, from a puffy smile.

"Zis too true, baby, 'cause you already sick."

"Yeah, and you already lost the two-legged animal. Ouch!" Roberts slapped off an earwig that was pinching at a sore between his toes. "Wonder who the four-legged animal is? Koi?"

"Wai'," Mai said, "I rea' what you must do."

This part translated with some difficulty, involving an awful lot of prepositions and things for Mai's small command of English: "Countermeasures: Offer nineteen big (three-tail') flags; can'les with whi' wicks, with yellow wicks"—here Mai imitated a wick by poking a finger through a circle made by her other index finger and thumb; she laughed at the possible obscene interpretation—"an' with red wicks; one yellow flag. Set free turtle. Move to differen' home."

They weren't sure what three-tailed flags were, but Koi said that meant temple flags and that if they wanted, he could get them all the paraphernalia.

"And what about the new house?" Fay asked pointedly.

Mai translated; Koi laughed and wiped his greasy, pitted face with a dirty hand. He said he'd make a spirit house for her to get well. Maybe her bad spirit was to go live there.

Roberts stared at Koi closely. Was this fucker putting them on? Anyway, Roberts was next. He was thirty-seven; his finger brought him back to number one: "Cows and buffaloes get in trouble. It is not good to go west to jungle. Blood flow from mouth; you lose things."

Koi scowled. He didn't like the fortune any more than did Roberts, who repeated thoughtfully, "Blood will flow from my mouth? O-oh, shit. What's west of here, Koi?"

"He say Burma and Salween River. He say this not good fortune."

"No shit. Okay, what's the countermeasure?"

"You give four trays rice an' foo'; six can—"

"Candles."

"—six can'les with red wicks. Let go captive birds."

"Oh, yes, the captive birds." He grabbed Fay's knee and Mai's. "Okay, Mai. Your turn."

Twenty-one years old, their upbeat Laotian whore, girlfriend, nurse, and go-between with the creeps who ran their jungle prison, landed on number two, in the Râd-chasǐ corner, right next to Fay's number five. Hopeful at first and delighted at landing next to Fay, who probably was the loveliest friend she'd ever had, Mai was quickly downcast, turning her thick lips into a pout as she translated: "It say I fight with woman and get angry 'cause I los' something I love. Oh, that too sad." The countermeasure was more flags and candles and to release one white fish. That intrigued her. She asked Koi which kind of fish, but Koi was already counting out his forty-nine years, landing with a laugh, and then a frown, right back on number one, with Roberts. Lost cattle. The western jungle. Blood from the mouth. Losing things. The old guard sucked his teeth in disgust and got up.

Mai followed him out with her customary requests for herbs and things, and Koi, at the door, said something to Mai that changed her business-as-usual tone to something more excited. She asked him some questions. He shrugged and walked out.

"What was that, love?"

"He say we mus' go party tonigh' at Kamnan. Many big people coming tonigh'. He say Fay and Mai look pretty. I say Fay sick, what he want. He no answer."

Fay sat up farther and looked at Roberts.

"What about me?" he asked.

"He no say about you. Just me and Fay." Mai was worried and looked at them to see if they understood.

Roberts turned to Fay, took her scabbed hand, and said very softly, "Me and Mai'll go and scout it out. You *rest*. This might be it."

18.

*T*hat same morning, with the early sun already fierce above the village, Lacey dangled his feet off the edge of a little deck built out from the porch as a drying rack for firewood, for the hundreds of tiny silver fish to be pounded with hot peppers into a paste, and for the strands of cotton to be dyed and woven into the colorful stovepipe leggings that Lawa women wore with their loose shifts. Still wearing his white shirt and white, canvas, rope-soled shoes from Spain, but having discarded his seersucker pants for dark, baggy, drawstring Lawa trousers, Lacey bent his neck to the hot sun and happily wrote in one of Johnson's old Cheyney notebooks. He was writing a poem, an event that in recent years had become rarer for him, and was usually filled with threat of failure, interruption, and corresponding irritability. As he sat here now on the deck near the ripe smells of dead fish and drying wood and penned livestock, assaulted at the ports of all of his senses, he was serenely composed, busy with the poem, alert to the village, and, to use a phrase of his philosophical friend, Vivian Bloodmark, "manifestly aware of his own manifest awareness." A rat rustled in the buffalo straw beneath his feet. Clucking bantams pecked the dirt road, still puddled here and there with yesterday's rain. And while most of the villagers were transplanting rice seedlings in the terraced, flooded fields above and below the village, a few others were still about. Across the way, a man was kneeling on his porch baiting a cone-shaped fish trap with crickets. Down from the mountain to Lacey's left, a kerchiefed woman was waddling home with large bamboo tubes filled with spring water, an awkward and heavy burden of about ten three-foot tubes lashed to a shoulder yoke. She sloshed past a ten-year-old girl flashing a long machete down upon a stob that she was cracking into kindling. Ahead of the water-carrier, a young man was leading a black-and-white, quasi-pinto pig off to the valley market; and near him, across the way and under some house pilings, a water buffalo rose up off its huge knees and tossed its horns when a boy with a switch came to lead it out to pasture. Next door, behind Lacey's house, a bare-chested man and his wife, both smoking pipes, were treadling a rice mill and tossing the chaff to a trio of pigs grunting around their feet and sliding their blubbery noses in the dirt of the threshing shed floor.

At the end of the village, just before the mountain's rounded, tree-shorn brow dropped off in steep ravines, a stream sparkled in the sunlight. Across the stream lay a bridge, and by the bridge a long pole had been planted, and from the pole—to mark a Haw trader's shop—fluttered a bright red banner. Lacey's senses took all this detail in, and let the abundance inform, breathe into, inspire his poem.

Although the village was new, it was firmly established. The land was bought, titled, and taxed; the fields were terraced in the wet-rice manner of the lowlands, which meant the mountaineer Lawa were going to stay, planting year after year in the same paddies, breaking their backs, moving each seedling by hand, working, with their Karen friends, as a community. Although some of the mountain fields nearby were slash-and-burn plantings, the village had a stable, single crop for self-sufficiency. The presence of the Haw trader indicated this. He wouldn't have trekked in his family, his mules—his store of plastic basins, tin pans, bags of teas, kerosene in bottles and tins, lengths of rope, pieces of wire, matches and tobacco, jags of rough iron, steel plow tips—to raise his flag for a village that might disappear in a few years. When only Karens had lived here, the BPP, the Border Patrol Police, had helicoptered in, looked about for opium fields, found none, shrugged, and promised to build a school. Since Chom kept his camp some miles away in the steeper mountains toward Burma, the village was not marked as dissident; and, since it grew no opium, the BPP, as the main representation of the Royal Thai Government, was prepared to ignore the village as altogether insignificant: just another mountain tribe—the Nae Amphur and his Kamnan, Snit Puaree, didn't even bother to distinguish between the Karens and the Lawa in the village—scratching out a primitive life in the red dirt of the mountains, backward people who couldn't even speak Thai. Indeed, few of the villagers could speak Thai. But one did, Myt, a young fellow whose ear had been shredded by an angry parrot when he was a child. At one point he had been sent to work as a guard at the Doi Sam Sao border post. Myt was now Chom's link to Roberts and Fay, and it was he who had given Roberts the message that tonight Khan Su and about a hundred of his Loi Maw mercenaries would be coming down the Keng Tung road, crossing the mountains to Mong Kwan and entering Thailand from the Wa Creek valley to make a deal with the BPP at Roberts's prison. There would be a big party, lots of drinking, and too many armed men and hobbled mules inside the prison for an orderly defense. "Much confusion," Chom had said. When they hit, the BPP would first think Khan Su had double-crossed them; Khan Su would think the same. Chom said they would find ways to add to the confusion. Lacey was frightened.

Lacey looked up from his page, shining in the brilliant sun, and rehearsed the coming events as Chom had laid them out. *(Maintain,* Lacey said to himself; *maintain.)* They would move out at noon, after lunch, pick up Chom's troops camped two hours north of the village and then file their way across the pitched, tiny valleys and ridges, keeping clear of settlements, heading north into the spit of land where the Jan River flowed out of the Burmese mountains into Thailand. By late afternoon, they would be in place to watch Khan Su go by with his troops; they outnumbered Chom's force by at least four to one. If it looked too risky—if Khan Su decided to bring more troops with him into Thailand—they'd call it off; if not, they'd hit at night—late at night, well after the drinking had started. Lacey and Carlos were to come along. Chom wanted American voices calling into the prison from the darkened jungle. Lacey looked back again at his poem. The words that held him so powerfully moments ago now wormed off the page. He was good on grouse; he had never shot at a man. And although men had shot at him in Can Tho in 1967, he hadn't taken it personally. Just an accident: wrong place, wrong time, wrong war. No one had fired at him—how did Prescott phrase it?—no one he knew had "fired at him in anger." If all went well, they would get Roberts and Fay and go north as quickly as they could through the jungle at night, northwest to Mong Yawng, twenty miles away in Burma, where the men from Chom's other camp in Mong Hsat would meet them as reinforcement. As they ran northwest across the border, Chom and Beta would leave units of two or three men behind to set up ambushes for slowing down whoever pursued. Khan Su certainly. He couldn't lose face. Maybe even the Thai BPP, although they could not cross legally into Burma. Chom said that if they could just reach his own reinforcements in the jungle hills near Mong Yawng they had "a home run, all base loaded." But whereas Khan Su couldn't afford to lose face, Chom couldn't afford to lose men. He had fewer troops than any other opium smuggler, and the men were his friends and lineage relations, not mercenaries. Though less experienced, they fought better and, Lacey hoped, took fewer chances. Whereas Chom wanted everyone home alive, Khan Su paid bonuses for lost limbs; he could always buy more soldiers.

"My men in Chiang Rai say your wife beautiful." Chom was on the porch loading shiny, stubby .45 slugs into the long clip for the greasegun slung over his shoulder. He had been watching Lacey from the kitchen and had only come out now that Lacey seemed distracted from his writing. "Don't you like your wife?"

"Sure I do. Why?"

Chom walked across the creaky boards of the drying-deck and sat down next to Lacey. He continued to talk as he slowly took more slugs from a canvas bag and shoved them into the clip, one of a dozen that he intended to load. Each clip held thirty rounds. Chom's fingers moved methodically, automatically, as they had moved the night before when he had played with the palmetto bug. Chom looked about as he fed the magazines. He might have been whittling. He had bathed. He was relaxed. His baseball cap was doffed for once, and his long black hair, still wet, was straight and sleek in the sunlight. "Well," he said, "why don't you stay home with her?"

Lacey put down the notebook, sticking his pen in the pages to mark his poem. "You should understand that. You went off after a friend," he said, nodding to the house where Pae was still sleeping, "and I went off to look for mine."

"Yes, but you came ten thousand mile. I only trave'd one hundred."

"Your one hundred were hard. Mine were fun."

"Fun to be so fa' from home?"

"Fun *because* so far from home."

Chom held a short, heavy slug up to the sunlight, turning it to study a bevel that his fingers had discovered on the lip of the casing. "I doan understan' that. I think of Baw Luang alla time. My house.

The stream that runs in valley. Our fields. Elepha's bringing rice in big baskets. Our lam talking to field spirit."

"My home is not so interesting."

"How so?" Chom laid the questionable bullet beside him.

"It's boring," Lacey said by way of explanation, but realized that he had only confused things more. He tried then to describe what life was like for him: his committee and office obligations, the entertainments in a college town—the three movie theaters, cable TV, the one disco where the kids lined up outside in designer clothes, football weekends, his inert colleagues, two-party politics, owning a mortgaged home, paying income taxes, the ordeal of keeping a car, the *distance* from nature, the distance from other people, from a community where you had real concerns—love, marriage, birth, death. How unreal those concerns had become for him. The endless talk in a world stripped of any real action. He tried to explain Western boredom. Chom was uncomprehending.

"Boring," Chom repeated and paused, as if to see if the word would take on meaning once it passed his lips. None of the English-speakers he had known had ever used the word, not James or Beta or even the Reverend Thompson. "In Lawa we have word for 'idle' which rea'y mean 'sleepy-sad.' Idle is nice, not boring. You are quiet. You think. You get sad maybe." Chom stopped loading for a moment and looked directly at Lacey as they both sat dangling their feet off the deck. "When I get ol' I want to be samang in Baw Luang or maybe even lam. I sit on my por' and decide the lan' for my people or maybe drink whiskey and listen to spirits. . . . What the opposite 'boring'?"

"Excitement."

"You want e'citemen'?"

"Not just excitement. In the West, there's an old saying, 'Judge a man by what he says and does,' and, of course, by the possible discrepancy between the two."

"Discrepa'cy?"

"Difference." Lacey took an extra clip and helped Chom load. "The idea is that you have to see *both* to judge a man's worth. In modern lives, real actions are absent. We just talk."

"Here we no much like action man. So'diers not respected. Poets, maybe. Wise man sees things or makes things happen aroun' him. It is e'citing to be quiet, to listen to spirit. Very e'citing for me, because when I listen to spirit again, they will be many blood spirit. Because I spill blood. Angry spirit."

Wheel and deal, Lacey thought. Get in there and kick ass. None of that "sleepy-sad" shit or letting things happen around you like the eye of a hurricane. Then, as Lacey reached into the bag of bullets, another snippet of Western belief floated up from his memory. "We have another saying: 'Virtuous knowledge results in human action.'" Lacey rememberd Sir Philip Sidney, knight, poet, and Christian humanist. "Maybe that is what I am looking for. And it applies to you, too, Chom; I mean, the way you act as opposed to the way Khan Su acts."

Chom took Lacey's finished clip, thumbed the top round, and then smacked the clip up into the submachine gun. He took a two-inch, funnel-shaped flash hider out of the canvas bag and screwed it onto the short muzzle of the greasegun. "Khan Su," he said, "very smart but, like you say, he have no power here. I can beat him." Chom put his hand to his heart, or really to his stomach, the Lawa seat of compassion and the forces of the soul.

Across the road the young girl was still whacking firewood with the machete. She wore baggy pants and a white blouse and smiled at them with very white teeth, her short black hair flying up with each swing. Her fat, naked little brother—his tiny pecker fluttering like a moth as he ran to pick up the pieces after each of his sister's swings.

"You have chi'r'en'?"

"No. We don't want any." Chom's question, his answer, and the gun clip in Lacey's hands made him think of a night and morning last fall.

It was midnight, or so. November. Louise was half asleep, her back and buttocks snuggled warm against his chest and lap, his knees curved forward behind her calves. Under the quilt, he had thrown one arm over her, and his hand cupped about a breast. His dick, as his mind drifted through sleep and touch and warmth and smell and wakeful worries, swelled and shrank between her thighs. She wriggled backward against him, his dick grew and nudged forward out of its foreskin as his hand softly squeezed her breast. It was a Friday night; the worries of the week were whispering in Lacey's ears. Louise was breathing deeply and slowly with sleep. He gave her a kiss on the shoulder and slid his hand softly down her side to hold her hip, rubbing his thumb on the rise of her backside. Outside their bedroom, the wind picked up and walked the brittle, dead November leaves across the roof into the rain gutters. A fat, wobbly moon rose above the hemlocks across the field. Sputters of snow flakes idled down and caught in the dead cups of Queen Anne's lace. Birds' nests, the locals called it. The untilled field was thick with them and with blackberry canes, with rye gone wild, with dry black-eyed Susans, with dead daisies and, down at ankle level, with clover, strayed rustly alfalfa, and wild strawberry nets—all dead, dry, and crackly underfoot. By the apple trees at the edge of the field, three deer— casting dim moonshadows—were reaching up their necks to crop the wizened crab apples. Not far below the house, beavers were paddling across the flooded creek to their dam. Their wakes rippled the water against two mallards, just passing through, who pulled their heads from under their wings, blinked terror, and then paddled off on scaly, webbed feet.

Up on the knoll near the rutted, dirt driveway, snug in the shed that Lacey had built for them, the two stinking goats lay against each other in loyal slumber on a bed of straw as, down from the woods, a fox passed by the shed, padding softly toward henhouse smells drifting up from the chicken farm below the church across the road. Mice were rustling throughout the field. One of Louise's cats—the nap of its fur picked up by gusts of wintery wind—lay in wait by the hedgerow, wary of owls. The other cat was curled like a ball of dark yarn in the chair by the foot of their bed. The dog was snoring on the rag rug.

Louise awoke and reached down between her legs for Lacey's dick, which swelled harder and curved up and slipped inside her when she rocked against it. Outside, the wind rippled the creek water and scattered yellowed elm leaves onto the rising pond as a beaver floated a birch branch into the spillway. On a far hill, the fox paused to lift a delicate paw and scratch at a red mite itching in its ear. And high above, a barn owl dropped in a noiseless swoop to ravage the field below.

The following morning was powdered white with the first snow. Lacey looked out the bedroom window with rapture: rabbits and grouse would leave their tracks in the snow. He crawled quietly out of bed and went downstairs, followed by his dog, to perk some coffee, find his boots, locate his shotgun in its leather case at the back of the closet, pull on his baggy, rubberized trousers, snap on his red suspenders, stuff his deep pockets with heavy twelve-gauge shells, shrug on his yellow, briar-tattered coat, pick off an itchy burdock cockle from the cuff, throw his netted game bag over his shoulder, stuff his wool-stockinged feet into his boots, and lace them. Gathering up his gun, flooding his coffee with milk to cool it for a big sip, he called his dog—already tap-dancing its loud nails on the linoleum floor. Pulling on his Day-Glo stocking cap, he stomped happily out the kitchen door.

A wet snow. The heavy, fat flakes clung to twigs and branches, composed lovely arcs on the blackberry canes, refurbished the crab apples in white blossom, and filled the the chest-high weeds as Lacey strode across the field, his boot laces snagging, knocking down showers of snowflakes. "Bobby. Bobby!" he called the Brittany spaniel off a cottontail that had sprung out of a bayberry bush and bounded across the field. Lacey drew up his shotgun and sighted, but did not shoot. He wanted to surprise the grouse that might be coveyed in the hemlocks at the edge of the field. But the dog—heart wild, legs pumping, nose all filled with Rabbit—chased the rabbit into the hedgerow, where it popped down into a hole among the line of limestone rocks picked out of the field and laid there by German farmers a century before.

As Lacey neared the hemlocks, the dog trotted back. Her little tail was up and wagging and she looked at Lacey to be forgiven. "Now, stay." The dog wagged her whole backside. No cuff, or snout slap, or boot in the ribs: what a generous master. Just as well, Lacey thought as he kneeled down to give the dog a pat. Better she run wild in the field than in the grouse woods. He wiped the snow from his gun butt and stood up.

Farther on, up in the hemlocks, but farther from the house than Lacey had guessed, Bobby pointed on a mess of fox-grape vines draping some young evergreens. Lacey looked for a clear shot. Said, "Get 'em." The dog shot forward into the clump and the grouse thundered out the other side. Three. One, Lacey never saw; another was just a drumming blur behind the pines; but a third rocketed out into the clearing and Lacey, leading it a foot, banged off a shot that kicked it over in the air and sent the bird plummeting down past the snowy branches onto a bed of needles.

"Bobby! Back!" The dog was already mouthing the bird. Lacey called her off, and this time Bobby minded before she tore the feathers and skin. When Lacey walked over, the spaniel was barking and dancing about the bird, whose red, dark, beady eyes fluttered with terror until Lacey picked it up and whacked the back of its head against a birch trunk. Its eyes shuttered and its neck dropped. It slumped in his open hand as Lacey held it out—beautiful, and brave, and wild, and dead—for the dog to sniff. "Good work, Bobby." The dog licked the trickle of blood that seeped from the bird's beak and snuffled the feathers, one of which stuck to the dog's muzzle until she pawed it off.

Lacey felt the gizzard sack to see if it was full. He rolled it between his thumb and finger like a bag of marbles and then he slit it with his pocket knife to see where the bird had been feeding. He saw purply, raisinlike grapes fall into his hand along with some bright, red bayberries. And, finally, checking again that the bird was dead, he dropped it into his game bag and cinched the drawstring. What was it like to kill a man?

Chom paused from loading clips to look at Lacey, unsure if Lacey weren't teasing him. "Doan want?"

Lacey shook his head no and tried to explain how he and Louise didn't think America in the seventies was much of a place to raise children.

"Lacey," Chom began, "I doan know America, but I think you talk crazy. When was there ri' worl' for chi'r'en'?" He gestured to the surrounding mountains. "You think *this* is ri' worl' for them? With TB, malaria, cho'ra, plague, worm, fevahs, lep'osy, bad food, no medicine? I afraid to bath in rivah now because of James. Lucky Lawa doan know disease—they think spirit kill James. May be if they know about disease, they think crazy like you. How can a man refuse to live his life? Should those chi'r'en' "—he pointed to the pair of little woodcutters—"not be born?"

Lacey sighed a large sigh of hopelessness.

"You know Nee Chee?"

Lacey shook his head.

"Yes. Yes. You know him. Famous German writer. Johnson give me his book."

Nietzsche! Lacey had thought he was hearing about some Chinese.

"He say, 'Whoever consent to his own return, participates in the divinity of this worl'."

Lacey was smiling.

"You like that?" Chom smiled too.

Lacey was smiling at Chom, not Nietzsche. He felt a little stupid. He would like to set Chom down on an American interstate at night, with a CB walkie-talkie in his hand, and let him listen to the insane, hopeless, disoriented chatter and the reports of random violence. He wanted to tell Chom about what it was like to grow up in the U.S.A. —the inanity of American schools, the drugs (!) and booze, the aimlessness, how everything seemed punctured by impending nuclear war. But all that seemed stupid to talk about. Here there were *no* schools, and children grew up educated in the complex modalities of their tribes. Here opium was always at hand, and everyone seemed to understand that it was dangerous, that only the weak and those desperate for defeat took it and, moreover, that they would take something else if opium weren't available. And here warfare was never far off, and yet for centuries the power of the mountain peoples to fill up the high valleys with peaceful communities seemed far stronger than the power of death and mayhem to sweep away their upland utopias—the terraced hills, the tiny spirit houses, the shared labors in the fields, the wrists tied in marriage strings. No TV, no "parenting" lectures. Here the kids were live on all channels, and the whole village loved them, taught them, chided them, plotted their marriages, reviewed their sorrows, and called them into the flooded fields, into the common scattering of splayed feet and bending backs, into the unchanging song of the harvest. Lacey felt a little stupid, and very remiss, spiritually remiss. He knew why Chom's beliefs were almost reflex, instinctual, unquestioned, and he envied Chom his instincts. What was Dowson's phrase? "Between the idea and the act, falls the shadow." Chom lived in the sunlight of enterprise informed by tradition—he had *fucking spirits* telling him what to do. Throughout Lacey's world fell the shadow. He wished he could translate Chom's world—perilous to the flesh; empowering to the spirit—into his own life. Instead, he was doing the reverse.

A good-sized lizard with a bright blue head scuttled across the deck, slipslapping its tail as it made a madcap escape from nothing in particular. Lacey jumped and Chom laughed at him, handing him the submachine gun. "Can you shoo' this?"

Lacey took the submachine gun in his hands. It was a heavy mother, weighing about ten pounds with the loaded clip, and it was very ugly. They called it a greasegun because the dull, gray, cheap, stamped parts assembled into something that looked more like a garage tool than a firearm. The U.S. had turned them out by the thousands at the end of the war. And the OSS, the CIA's forerunner, had ordered thousands more for Asia. Lacey's gun had been around a long time. It was slow-firing—about four hundred rounds per minute, comically primitive in comparison to modern light machine guns and assault rifles—and it wasn't very accurate at a distance; but it fired a big slug and was brutal at short ranges. Lacey had never fired one, but he knew all about them, had carried one, even slept with one, for days during the Tet offensive in 1968. For a whole day he had guarded an operating room in a province hospital while the war raged beyond the hospital fence and water splattered the sandy courtyard all about him when the hospital's water tower took a drilling in the cross fire. But he had never fired one. He was proud of that. He had sat there all day near the electrician's shack and the barking generator, looking at the *Playboy* pinups, looking nervously around the hospital grounds and one-story wards for the VC, who were supposed to be prowling for medicines and perhaps to kidnap a surgeon. To Lacey's immense gratitude none ever showed. How could he shoot someone whose cause he supported? Well, he could. He had agreed to. If he wouldn't have, the surgeons would have quit operating, and the hundreds of shredded and bleeding civilians who lay sprawled in the sun about the court would surely have died. Of course, he could. Shoot at me, I shoot at you. He wasn't a nitwit. But he never fired one. He sat there all day, looking at the girly photos, looking around the buildings. Later in the day a Vietnamese nun and nurse came and put a red-cross band, *hong thap tu*, on his left arm. Perhaps she thought he had earned it. He wore it like decoration, the greasegun still across his knees. Nee Chee! "Yes," he said, pressing the metal stock extended against his shoulder. "I know how." The reliable piece of shit in his hands had cost about $22 to make. How many people had it killed? "Will I have to shoot, too?" He tried not to sound afraid.

"May be three."

"No, I mean—"

"Yes, yes. If they chase us through mountain, you may have to shoo'. But I tell you when. Sometimes not shooting get better resul'. We'll see."

"Okay." Lacey sounded overly grave, even to himself.

"Lacey, want to hear a poem?" Chom said this with enthusiasm, as if to perk up their conversation.

"Sure."

Chom's poem was a folk song. He sang it. Each word a syllable so that the notes coincided with each word. Chom translated:

> *"Phoenixes compete; so do sparrows,*
> *They call before the shrine, behind the chedi.*
> *I can use men who are loyal, if not elegant."*

"Lacey," Chom's tone was serious, "you elegant. You must be loyal or you fuck up everything. You listen me, okay? Carlos, he listen Beta."

Lacey nodded. "Okay," he said.

"Now, tell me your poem." Chom's voice was enthusiastic again. "When I see you writing, you happy. He is writing to his wife, I think, or he is writing poem."

Lacey opened his notebook and read his poem; he did this without fanfare, the first sign of his loyalty.

> *"Under the tattered umbrellas, piles of live eels*
> *sliding in flat tin pans. Catfish flip for air.*
> *Sunfish, gutted and gilled, cheek plates snipped.*
> *Baskets of ginger roots, ginseng, and garlic cloves;*
> *pails of shallots, chives, green citrons. Rice grain*
> *in pyramids. Pig halves knotted in mushy fat.*
> *Beef haunches hung from fist-size hooks. Sorcerers,*
> *palmists, and, under a tarp, thick incense, candles.*
> *Why, a reporter, or a cook, could write this poem*
> *if he had learned dictation. But what if I said,*
> *simply suggested, that all this blood fleck,*
> *muscle rot, earth root and earth leaf, scraps*
> *of glittery scales, fine white grains, fast talk,*
> *gut grime, crab claws, bright light, sweetest smells*
> *—Said: a human self; a mirror held up before.*

That's called 'Chiang Rai River Market.' "

"Market like a mi'ah?" Chom said reflectively.

"Yes."

"I like it. But the English too hard to hear. You read it to me again tomorrow after we get your frien's. Ri' now, you come inside. Eat. Drink lots of water; take sal' pills; take quinine pills. James never listen to me 'bout that. He say if I doan take, he doan take. But James not a Lawa; he a white man—yes, rea'y he a white man—in a way. We leave after lunch. Lacey, sometime you wri' a poem about James, okay?"

19.

"*H*im, Khan Su." Mai had thrown her arm around Fay's waist and she whispered those words although the figure she pointed at, as the three of them stood and watched through the bars, was quite a way off and by no means awesome: Khan Su, alias Chin Shan-fu, was a tubby little man in green fatigues with a green peaked cap pulled down rakishly to his left ear, but much too far, so that the effect was silly. He rode a Yunnan pony, a sturdy little creature like the men of those mountains; but even on top of the dwarfish, well-behaved horse, Khan Su looked insignificant and small as he crossed the bridge over the scummy moat bordered by the flowering vines that had overgrown the coils of concertina barbed wire. Holding the reins too loosely and his elbows too far out at his sides, he looked a bit unsteady on his mount as he passed through the formation of his troops who lined either side of the path from the prison's orchards and gardens below the jute field—part of which had been cut by the valley people, who had laid the flower-tipped sheaves to soak in a makeshift retting pool—and all along the road, onto the bridge, and right up to the prison gate. Roberts and Fay and Mai watched as Khan Su grinned and offered his heavily armed troops goofy salutes as he passed through their ranks. Behind him, on the metal-mesh pad between the gardens and the jute field, the Nae Amphur's American-made Huey helicopter lurked importantly in the blue-green shadows spreading from the jungle at dusk. The opium warlord was making his entrance; the Nae Amphur had made his, leaving his wonderful machine sitting like a powerful totem on the landing pad—against police rules, to be sure, for the chopper was supposed to return to base each night in the province capital and not sit exposed at Border Patrol outposts. But the Nae Amphur, like the overly jaunty warlord, required some show of authority as each extended to the other the protocol that would establish their new agreement.

Neither was a fool, although Khan Su liked to play the slow-witted, good ol' boy from the China hills. Each had already made sure that no double cross would wipe him out. Behind new screens of bamboo thatch in the watchtower, the Nae Amphur had placed two men on the BAR so that it could cover the route from the jungle, the bridge, and the whole courtyard inside the prison, where a Loi Maw advance party had picketed their mules and ponies. Three more police were posted by a huge, rusting, yellow D-6 Caterpillar road plow, and, over by the chopper, Myt—the Lawa sharpshooter with the torn ear—had been placed along with another guy beside an M-79 grenade launcher. And so, with security matters settled, Khan Su made a relaxed entrance, exaggerating his ease with his new Thai friends as if he were embarrassed about all these silly precautions, but in reality confident, since now that his troops were inside the prison compound, they far outnumbered the Thai police and could easily turn any ambush into a massacre. He knew the Thais knew that, and the Thais knew that he understood how simply he could be picked off. They had reached the first stage of their friendship: détente.

At the prison gate, Khan Su, helped by a lieutenant, slid off his pony. He steadied his feet, joggling his paunch back under the belt of his baggy fatigues, and saluted the Nae Amphur and the Kamnan, who both stepped forward to shake hands. Behind them stood the Haw trader. In Thai, Khan Su shouted a greeting to the trader as if he were almost surprised to see him there. In Chinese, he asked about his health, and the trader replied by laughing and patting his belly. Snit Puaree stepped back and gave his prisoner a hearty slap on the back. When they all turned to go through the gate, Fay and Mai and Roberts had to leave their moatside window to watch through the curtained window facing the courtyard, since all the prisoners, except of course the trader, had been locked up. Some of the cells, like that of the two Shan opium addicts and the empty cell of the dead Karen, concealed BPP men, who were positioned to open fire on the courtyard at the first sign of trouble.

This *was not* what Roberts had anticipated. A fucking dink picnic. With roundeye entertainment, no doubt. He plunked down despondently on the edge of the bed as Mai and Fay hurried to peek out the other window. He coughed, which hurt his sides so much that he held them. And then he grimaced, blurted out an "aagh," and scrubbed and clawed his scalp for a moment. Through Mai they had learned who Khan Su was. As far as Roberts could see, the party held no interest for them. He took a swig from a bottle of Mekong whiskey. Several cases had been flown in by chopper. He was drunk. He had been nipping at the bottle by himself since late afternoon. Fucking Lacey, he thought. The guy was a nerd. How the fuck could *he* get them out of jail?

But from another perspective, farther out in the jungle, behind the lines of Khan Su's troops and the guards at the helicopter, things were looking just fine. Lacey and Chom and three of his men were hunkered down in a damp gully behind a wall of screw pines. From there they had watched Khan Su's troops file slowly past them, edging down along the creekbed from the jungle to the north and left of them and finally emerging onto the forest road where it skirted the pond and headed toward the prison. They had counted seventy-five soldiers, most of them Shan and Chinese, all properly outfitted in jungle boots and fatigues, some with matching caps, others with their long hair tied back under silk bandannas or cotton headbands. About half had ridden out of the forest, rocking on mules or ponies—the regulars sharing rides on the opium caravan mules; the officers riding the ponies. Many were still damp and muddy from the rivers they had forded after crossing into Thailand from the Wa Creek valley. In Burma, they had traveled openly along the Keng Tung road, obliged to look out only for ambushes from their Kuomintang rivals. But once in Thailand they had to travel the more difficult routes in order to keep clear of other Border Patrol posts, the Royal Thai Air Force and, most especially, American intelligence. The Americans were powerful enough to have the Nae Amphur removed and queer the whole deal.

Khan Su's men were well armed. Several had Soviet rocket-propelled grenade launchers, RPG-2s, slung crosswise on their saddles; others carried American mortar tubes and American M-79 grenade launchers, which looked like sawed-off shotguns. The rest were armed with an expensive array of semiautomatic weapons: Chinese AK-47s, American M-16s, carbines, greaseguns, a few M-1s. Along with their regular arms, they were weighed down with canteens, bayonet knives, and an assortment of clay amulets, gold Buddhas, and silver Asian swastikas pinned to their bandannas or dangling from their necks. Then there were various grenades—the Soviet kind with the throw handles or the grooved, fist-size American kind with a side pin—strung around their necks or fixed to their belt webbing.

Dusk was falling. Lacey wriggled a stiff leg on the bedding of upas bark that Chom's men had stripped from a tree earlier in the afternoon when they arrived for the long wait. The large rolls of upas bark not only kept them dry but also repelled ants and spiders, earwigs and beetles. Propped on an elbow, Lacey watched as some big red ants trooped up to the bark edge, reconnoitered, and turned away.

"Tree poison," Chom whispered, looking at Lacey. He had been watching the neatly rowed pepper field where the tail end of Khan Su's column was breaking ranks to follow their commander into the compound. "Some tribe," Chom said in a more normal voice, "like Lahu, still make poison for arra' from this tree. At ni' in forest', they sleep on tree bar' and bugs stay away."

Lacey nodded appreciatively, gazing at the bark on which he lay and the gray machine gun lying on the bark next to him. He darted a glance through the root stilts and across the pepper field to where the bamboo tree line was lifting and falling now with an evening breeze.

"No prob'em," Chom said, "we eat now." He spoke softly, as if he were still listening as he spoke.

Lacey let out a huge sigh. He felt as if he had been holding his breath all day. (PROFESSOR DISAPPEARS IN THAILAND. He could foresee the local headline and his colleagues' smug glee. Not that they wanted him dead necessarily: they just wanted anyone punished fatally who did out-of-the-way things.) For hours, it seemed, he had lain on his back and concentrated—even as Khan Su's troops began to appear—on the brilliant green-and-chartreuse bee eater that was working the yellow orchids clustered high up on a large fig tree near their gully. The bird appeared and reappeared through the fanlike canopy of screw pines about ten feet over their heads. Methodically, the bird's long, curved bill probed the whole cascade of flowers for ants and insects. When one blossom tumbled to the ground like a broken butterfly, it seemed to Lacey, as he was forced to bring his mind back to the soldiers filing by fifty yards away, that a great event had just ended. Now he took a really deep breath, filling his lungs with the sweet compost air of the forest, air thick with oxygen and the smell of breathing roots. Chom's men, as they pulled out their pouches and bamboo cylinders of food, were smiling at him. He guessed thcy could see how scared he was. He didn't care. He was, in fact, glad to see them smiling and he grinned back. Surely their smiles and their food canisters indicated that everything was okay, that danger was past, that he would not be told to jump up screaming and firing through the net of roots, that he would not have to flee and fire and hide with the family of rhesus monkeys inhabiting the stalactite grottoes of mammoth banyans, whose great, depending roots seemed to occupy a half acre of the surrounding forest. Had they been discovered in the afternoon light or now in the evening dusk, Khan Su's troops and the Border Police, who together outnumbered them three to one, would have chased them down and wiped them out as methodically as the bee eater had plucked insects from the sweet tongues of the orchids.

Over by the bamboo thicket, which nearly blocked their view of the pepper field and the road and the prison below, a bamboo rat —oblivious to them for hours as it worked at extending its tunnels —now popped up as Chom spoke and blinked at them with trembling whiskers and weak eyes before diving into a burrow. They laughed. All of them, including Lacey.

As dusk fell, the balance of terror shifted. Just as Khan Su's circumstance had changed once his troops were inside the police station, similarly Chom's advantage grew as dusk thickened in the lower reaches of the forest and night shadows spread around the prison where the enemy was gathered. Once it was dark, it would be extremely costly to launch an attack through the main gate toward a dark jungle scattered with Chom's platoons. Lacey was with Chom's artillery group: Two American M-19 mortars were already set up on their bipods and base plates and two RPG-2 launchers lay beside them along with finned grenades and bandoliers of mortar rounds.

They huddled together in the gully and opened their food. Chom offered Lacey a drink from a bamboo cylinder stoppered with a banana leaf and, from a similar canister, he indicated a helping of dried pork, boiled greens, and cold, sticky rice. Lacey was given a broad leaf for a plate and he opened the C-ration that Beta had given him earlier: a can of beenies and weenies whose little pop-top explosion stiffened the backs of his messmates for an instant. Like the others, Lacey ate with his hands, with trembling hands. They ate greedily. Chert, who had guided their boat upriver from Chiang Rai, found a rice bug in his food—pale green, stalk legs, red, protruding eyes. Rice bugs stank. You could smell one a foot away, and usually people threw away food stunk-up by rice bugs, but Chert merely plucked this one out and just as quickly shoveled his fingers into his sticky rice. Another fellow—a Karen, Lacey thought, from the man's smooth, flat headscarf—offered Lacey a little clay jar filled with a red paste and silvery specks. A flat stick, like those he used to get as a kid with Breyer's ice cream cups, stuck out of the jar and Lacey used it to scoop some of the paste onto his rice as he had seen the others do. It was salsa hot. And fishy. Carlos would like it. He wondered how Carlos was doing. He and Beta had moved through the forest like deer, whereas Lacey had stumbled on roots, clanking to the ground with his greasegun, once ripping his shirt on the jagged woody teeth of an otherwise delicate palm. But Uncle Sam could be proud of Beta and Carlos, now off somewhere closer to the road and the prison gate. In the early nightfall of the jungle's triple canopy, Lacey couldn't see any of the other men scattered in squads throughout the edge of the forest.

Night gathered under the ten-foot palms, in the banyans, and in the stilt-legged trees. Fireflies were beginning to blink in the blue-green shadows. The last daylight played high above in the seventy-five-foot figs and teaks and coffin trees where noisy flocks were quieting down. Lacey squatted beside the bandannaed men with whom he had trekked for miles that day. They had marched on sandals, some on bare feet. Lacey's Spanish tennis shoes were muddied and torn. His chin was smeared with pork and beans and smelly fish paste. He wiped his fingers on a rubbery leaf that had served as a food stopper. Far off, he heard a cuckoo calling through the foggy nightfall.

20.

*T*he moon edged out from behind the watchtower, full and hazed in a murky nimbus. Roberts, his head thrown back drunkenly in his chair at the banquet table, yelled "Go away!" and tried to shoo the moon off with his hand. "You don' wanna see 'is . . . this . . . DINK COOKOUT." He smirked to himself and turned to lean on the shoulder of the Nae Amphur's chopper pilot, a neat little man with a fastidious thin mustache and a shiny jumpsuit spattered with all sorts of bright patches. Roberts's mouth was close to the man's ear. "No moons allowed," Roberts said. The pilot grimaced from the stench of Roberts's breath and pushed him away. Not hard, but just the same he fell out of his chair to the ground and stayed there.

"His father knows the American president," the Nae Amphur said in Thai. Khan Su clapped his chubby hands and wheezed with laughter. The others, even those who didn't know Thai, laughed too.

Roberts lay there looking up. A haze of hot pork fat filled the compound, mixing with the stench from the overtaxed jakes and shit pond. Perhaps clouding the moon. The poor little fish. What was she saying? Fay leaned down from her chair, working her swollen lips, but the moon was now behind her head and her face was darkened. He couldn't understand her. She turned away. "Get up." Get up was what she had said. *Why?*

Roberts lay on his back and scanned the long row of stool legs, stools taken out of the prisoners' cells, along with their wooden beds, to provide seating for the Border Police and the "Shan United Army." Even so, only the more important police and Loi Maw had seats. The prisoners were left to sleep on their floors or look through the bars of their cells at the banquet, at the courtyard jammed with soldiers, and at the twenty or so mules and ponies that had been hobbled in the prison garden, now flattened by the churning of hooves and the foraging of the Loi Maw mounts. The soldiers were scattered in groups, chugging Singha beer and Mekong whiskey and tearing at chunks of pork from the old sow, now quartered and grilled on galvanized wire over an oil drum cut lengthwise and filled with charcoal. At the long banquet table made of rough planks set on oil drums and sandbags, Khan Su and the Nae Amphur were laughing at each other's jokes with booze-blotched faces and toasting to mutual good fortune. Across the court, the doors to the cells had been unlocked, and the women were being raped in the darkened rooms. Occasionally flashlights or kerosene lamps provided silhouettes of the soldiers standing at the cell doors. Some women were being pulled around the courtyard dust in approximate time to music from transistor radios or from a record player on which Snit Puaree was playing Chinese popular songs from Hong Kong. Seated with Fay and Mai were five of the younger women whose better looks got them to the table where the officers were pawing them. The women —a gold smuggler, a supposed tax cheat, a bar owner, the wife of a runaway subversive university student, and a woman who had murdered her husband by pouring molten lead into his open mouth as he slept—were, except for the student's wife, giggling and trying their damnedest to get their suitors too drunk to do them much harm. Fay was sitting next to the Kamnan, who was feeling her tits. She was nauseous and weak and muttering "bloody swine" and trying to get drunk; and Mai, who sat next to her, was pulling away Snit's hand and saying in English, "Hey, baby, forget 'bout her. She too ugly. You come here." And then Mai opened her blouse and shook her tits at Snit. The soldiers at the head of the table hooted and clapped, and Snit stumbled over to Mai and got both of his hands on her tits as she kissed him.

"Him number one soldier!" declared the Nae Amphur, pointing at Snit. "Kamnan big help me. Hey!" he shouted at Fay, "where you man?"

Once again they roared at Roberts, who lay in the dirt by the table. He would have lain there a long time if one of the drunken soldiers—who had been doing a hieratic monkey-dance to Cambodian radio music—hadn't decided to entertain his friends even more thoroughly by stopping to rouse the American. The banquet table howled when the soldier unzipped his fly, fumbled out his dick, and, rocking on unsteady legs, flooded Roberts's face and chest.

Fay was too exhausted, too burned out, to do more than watch as Roberts finally struggled up, sputtering and wiping his face and glasses with his bare arm. He leaned on his chair and vomited, splashing the chopper pilot, who this time jumped up and smacked Roberts hard behind his ear so that his glasses fell into the pool of vomit. This raised another roar of laughter from the crowd. Roberts swung a haymaker at the pilot's head that missed completely and only landed him on the ground again, where they left him, face down. The pilot then held up a quart bottle of beer as if toasting the table before turning the bottle over on the fouled chair seat to rinse off the vomit. He leaned over and with his right hand picked out the glasses with his thumb and index and laid them next to Fay's plate. He stood back and snapped her a salute. The table applauded.

Fay turned and looked at the pilot, wondering if she could get him to get her out of there, decided not, and with blistered lips she simply said, "Wog."

The pilot took this to mean "thank you" and sat down.

Over the laughter of the others, Fay heard Koi's high-pitched giggle. She looked at the guard as he fetched two beer bottles to their table; she looked closely at his eyes and at his mouth, missing teeth and wide open now in a hyena cackle. Really, was *he* the one? Was there anyone? Surely, she thought, the whole thing was a horrible joke cooked up by these monsters.

Then came the main course. From inside the district police office, two young guards carried out the *le plat*, or at least its head, as each held a rudderlike pectoral fin on either side of the huge, whitish, hacked-off head—perhaps three feet across—of a giant river catfish, a *pla buk*, that had been netted by villagers on the Kok River down where it flows into the Mekong.

Khan Su applauded slowly and deliberately, clearly impressed by this head brought for his inspection. He stuck his chubby arm deep into the toothless mouth. "O-oh," he said, approvingly.

The Nae Amphur beamed and struggled to his feet. Even in the whitish light thrown by the gas lamp hung from a porch beam and hissing near his head, his face was blotched with remarkable half-moons above and below his eyes. The lobes of his ears were flushed bright red. The *pla buk* was, he said, extremely rare. In the old days, they were caught all the way from Phnom Penh to China, where they spawned in Lake Tali, a source of the Mekong, many thousand of miles away. The Nae Amphur paused here to lean against a porch pillar as he hiccuped and burped simultaneously, then he went on to say how it was only the female *pla buk* that made the long migration each year from the tidewaters of the Mekong to the cold mountain lake in Yunnan province. The males, which had golden scales, waited for them there in Lake Tali. The male *pla buk* was the elephant of fish, powerful and noble—which is why the Cambodians called it *trey reach*, or "royal fish," and why the Thais and Laos called it *pla buk*, "huge fish"—and because these qualities reminded him of his friend Chin Shan-fu—here the Nae Amphur used Khan Su's Chinese name—he had decided to offer him a true mate for this evening: this female had been over six feet long.

The Loi Maw and the police all clapped and with boozed and slitted eyes nodded in approval to one another at the Nae Amphur's elegant speech.

And now, clapping his hands twice, the Nae Amphur called in Koi, who carried yet another delicacy, a platter heaped with the salted, two-and-a-half-foot-long ovaries of the *pla buk*. The dinner was a coup for the district chief. Among those privy to this meeting, it would be known as the *pla buk* feast. The platter was placed before Khan Su, who, using a knife and spoon, cut into his section of ovary, chewed it solemnly, and then waved both arms over his head in appreciation. At that, more guards emerged with tin basins of baked fish, baked in Chiang Rai and flown in with the booze.

When the fish head passed by Fay she glanced at its baleful, clouded eyes sagged at the corners of the great jaws, below the angle of the mouth. It looked like a cross between a whale and a shark. The vast, bald brow of the fish was knobbed and pocked; the under-jaw was flat; the fleshy lower lip looked like a car bumper, dented and banged. It was an old bottom feeder, scrubbing algae and scum off rocks throughout its long, innocent life.

"Him mouth look like woman!" shouted one of Khan Su's men, pointed at Fay's swollen lips, crusted in fever blisters. The guy was young; he had a belligerent, prognathous jaw and rather puffy fat lips himself. He had been silent that evening, but had now got up enough nerve to show his wits before Khan Su. But without luck.

"Hey, baby," Mai yelled across the table, "she too sick. Look like pig." She leaned across the table, her breasts wobbling out of her blouse, and said, as she offered him a slice of ovary, "Suck on this.

Make you a *man*. We talk 'bout it later." Mai was on top of the evening. The guy couldn't think of anything to say just then, and he shut up and swigged sullenly from a bottle of beer, wrapping his own ugly lips around the neck, while a Chinese friend who knew English poked his shoulder and laughed.

When Roberts woke up he found himself slumped forward in his chair, face down at the table, with his glasses again on his nose. Fay was screaming. He heard her screaming but she wasn't next to him. Instead, just beyond Fay's empty chair, he saw the student's wife lying on the ground, her face shimmering in tears and moonlight, as the young Loi Maw with monkey lips raped her while she rocked her head left and right. Her blouse front was ripped and her sarong pulled open and shoved up around her hips. Blood caked the inside of one thigh. A bruise swelled her cheek.

Roberts shook his head to clear his vision and looked about for Fay. It seemed that the screaming was everywhere. He coughed and grabbed his sides with pain. Scanning the yard to his right, he saw dozens of soldiers passed out on the ground, their weapons not stacked so much as heaped beside them. And although he had a slamming headache and buzz-on, Roberts considered the guns and figured he could grab an M-16 and make it out the open gate, even past the soldiers who were carousing there near the mules picketed by the road plow on the far side of the bridge. . . . But the screaming. He turned left and saw the pilot passed out next to him at the table and he heard clapping. Farther along the banquet table he saw that the party was still going on and not far away. Mai was on the opposite side of the table. She was stark naked and screaming Fay's name. From below Mai's almost hairless mons, nearly a whole pack of cigarettes stuck out of her vagina. Mai was screaming, "Baby! No!" Roberts followed her eyes to Fay, who was standing near the blaring record player and slapping Snit across the face and head and shoulders, trying to scratch his eyes as she gathered over him in rage and screamed, "You little pig! You bloody filthy wog!" She flailed at him as he tried to grab her arms and slap her back at the same time.

Roberts groaned, straightened himself, and started to come around the table. A few Loi Maw and the Nae Amphur were clapping. He couldn't tell whether it was for Fay or for Mai, who was now yelling, "Look! Look! I make smoke!" Bumping her pelvis furiously to the Stones' "Honky Tonk Woman," she was somehow making the cigarettes puff smoke from her cunt. It was her White Rose act.

But nothing was going to stop Fay. She was bigger than Snit. She was insane. Like the night, Roberts thought as he stumbled by the Nae Amphur, like the night she rode the Welshman's shoulders and clawed his eyes. And screaming hideously. "Oh, fuck," he groaned as he got closer, because now he saw, now he realized what had happened, because as he rounded the table he saw Khan Su leaning over a small table under which was strapped Nixon, the leaf monkey that Fay had sold for a day's outing. The monkey's arms and legs were tied down to cross struts. Even its head was fixed in place with leather straps nailed to the underside of the table top. Only its tail was free and thrashing. And it was screaming. Screaming furiously. Because the top of its head had been sawed off, trepanned, and through a hole in the table top the Chinese were eating its live brains.

Roberts put some speed in his shaky legs as Snit socked Fay straight on the jaw and she went down. Snit booted her in the belly just as Roberts got to him, spun him around, and hit the oily little fucker smash in the nose, crushing his septum and driving Snit down onto a turned-over stool, next to Fay, who, despite the pain in her stomach, rose up and drove her fingernails straight into Snit's eyes as Roberts aimed a kick of his sandaled foot into his ribs.

Now other guards jumped in. Koi was there first, bringing down a beer bottle on the nape of Roberts's neck. The bottle did not shatter, but the blood from the concussion at the back of his throat leaped out in a quick belch over Roberts's chin and throat and shirt front. The Nae Amphur was yelling. Mai and the monkey went on screaming insanely. With blood filling his mouth and dribbling from his chin, Roberts grabbed the old guard by his greasy ears and yanked his head into a cement porch piling. The Nae Amphur was yelling for guards but few were sober enough to respond, so Roberts kept slamming Koi's head into the rough concrete until Snit came behind him with his .45, and only the fact that Snit's eyes had been lacerated and his nose broken and his vision flooded with blood and tears saved Roberts from taking a bullet in the back of the head. That and Mai's naked flying dive across the table—cigarettes still fuming in her cunt—which knocked Snit over once again as he squeezed the trigger and sent the slug cracking into the ground. Roberts's punch, Fay's claws, Mai's leap—and the flare, whose parachute was heard to pop open above the prison in the momentary lull, broken only by the yowling monkey, that followed Snit's deafening report.

The flare hung high overhead beneath its little parasol, sputtered now and then in fierce white incandescence, and then settled into a smooth, hissing, reddish glare that drifted slowly across the compound, lighting the hellish scene in its glow and sending shadows walking about the yard as it began its languorous drift downward. Shadows traversed the guardhouse wall behind Fay and Mai, who clutched each other, sobbing. The smoke from Mai's cigarettes, which lay scattered at her feet, curled up around their knees in reddish wisps. Slowly, the shadows walked the length of the littered banquet table and crossed over the Loi Maw thug who was now trying to shove his stubby dick in the face of the student's young wife. The shadows stalked Khan Su and his officers, who had turned away from the silent, limp leaf monkey which had given one last scream as its motor reflexes died, scooped out with that part of its brain. Shadows moved over Roberts, and the red flare light gleamed on the dark blood on his chin. Shadows drifted across Koi, who was on his hands and knees at the foot of the pillar, trying to get up but helplessly dizzy with a badly gashed head. Shadows turned slowly, like the luminous hands on a watch, across Snit Puaree, who was lying on his back in a jasmine bush squinting uncomprehendingly into the bright light. In the eerie light that had commanded this odd silence, the Loi Maw began to rouse themselves from their drunken heaps about the courtyard, rubbing their eyes and staring at the light and groping for their weapons. By the shadow-stalking light from an infernal star, the prison women, including the student's wife and the gold-toothed murderess, gathered their clothes around their nakedness and crawled off like dogs.

"Who fired the flare?" demanded the Nae Amphur, but his tone already indicated that he knew it had come from the forest. None of his men would fire one, even as a drunken joke, because flares draw attention . . . from the Air Force, maybe even from the Americans. He turned to Khan Su and asked him if one of *his* men might have fired it, but before Khan Su could call out to his men, another flare popped overhead.

"Where's it from?" the Nae Amphur shouted to the watchtower.

"The jungle . . . to the west," said a small voice way up in the darkened tower.

"Shoot!"

Up in the watchtower, the gunner took aim at the spot in dark tree line where he had seen the flare swoop up and rocket into the sky. He chambered the first round and squeezed. The BAR fired, but just one round banged out as a small gas explosion sprayed from the front of the barrel and the big gun, an old American M-60, fell silent, its whole assembly jammed forward. The two men looked at each other and then examined the gas piston that powered the automatic action. In the flarelight they could see that the gas cylinder plug was missing and that its threads, judging from the shiny scratches all around the hole, had been reamed out.

"Fire!" the Nae Amphur yelled again. By now his guards were kicking the others up out of their stupors while the police and the Loi Maw gathered their guns. Khan Su was staring suspiciously at the Nae Amphur, who, in the hustle of the courtyard, could barely hear the sheepish explanation from the tower.

"C'mon," Roberts said. He pulled at Fay who was wide-eyed and still clutching Mai. The word was slurred in his mouth not because he was drunk, which he still was, but because several capillaries at the back of his throat were still firing spurts of salty blood onto his tongue. Fay and Mai pulled him close. Then, in a moment of friendship that he didn't think he had ever felt before—with Fay or with anyone for that matter, certainly not with Mai—the three of them embraced and Roberts could feel Mai shivering with fear and cold and Fay's back and shoulders shaking in sobs. Her mouth was swollen and split from the punches, and her clothes were torn. "C'mon," Roberts repeated. As they moved toward their cell, they looked down at Snit, who was drunk, beaten up, nearly blinded, and waving his hands slowly in front of his eyes as he squinted at the flare. He lay on his back like an upturned roach. Above them the flare floated serenely in magnesium dazzle. Roberts bent down slowly and picked up Snit's .45 from the dirt. No one noticed. "Le's 'o," he said, fighting his thickened tongue. He tucked the pistol in his jeans, and they moved quickly away along the line of empty chairs, stepping over drunks as other soldiers and police shuffled by them and Khan Su and the Nae Amphur shouted commands. Near the horses stamping in their hobbles, they noticed a woman lying in the dirt, on her back, naked. Her throat had been cut and the blood was now dried in hard, black bubbles along the slit. Her eyes were wide open and shining with flarelight. A Loi Maw soldier was curled next to her. He lay on his side and his hands were caked in blood. As they passed they couldn't tell whether he too was dead, or if he had only fallen into a whiskey dream after killing the woman.

In Fay's cell, as they gathered their clothes into two light suitcases, Mai sat on the floor and wailed. "What you do? What you do wi' zat? 'Ey kill us now. Now zey kill us all."

"Mai, darling, our friends have come for us. We're leaving." Fay pulled a blanket around her shivering friend and spoke softly.

"How you know?"

"We know," Roberts said. "Get dressed. Get packed."

Mai cried harder. "Zey kill me now. You go. Zey kill me."

"Get moving! You're coming with us. Move!"

"Rea'y?"

"Really," Fay said. She was jamming Prescott's notebook into her torn, silvery space-luggage.

Mai sat on the floor, thinking. She began to smile.

Roberts knocked the spiders and earwigs out of his shoes and shoved his bare feet into them.

"Baby, you let me wear you jean'? Jungle cut my legs."

Fay yanked the spare jeans out of her suitcase and threw them to Mai.

"Baby, you know I zink our fortune rea'y come true." Mai wiggled into Fay's jeans and began to consider what she wanted to take with her.

There were two explosions. One came from the courtyard and blew some debris against their wall; the other was a muffled blast from the jungle that sounded through their moatside window. They heard random small-arms firing from the prison walls. Silence. And then came a voice calling from the jungle.

21.

"*B*ro', I thought you quit the chiva?"

"Ah don't *shoot* it, you understand, but smokin' now and then won't hurcha."

Beta passed the red cigarette dot over to Carlos. His face flared as he took a drag, just a puff to ease the jitters. They sat at the crest of a plowed slope at the edge of the jungle, where a banana grove offered good cover. In the thick, misty dark, they squatted under the huge leaves. The full moon lit the slope falling away from them. Moonlight curled in the vapors rising off the pond above them and to their left, where Chom had set up the rockets and mortars. But no light played through the jungle canopy where Beta and Carlos and the main ambush unit crouched. Crickets shrilled about them, and then the two flares popped and floated above the prison triangle. The funnel of bright light spewed down upon the outpost. The whine of radios sang like mosquitoes.

Some flarelight seeped through the rubbery leaves and caught on Carlos's gold front teeth as he opened his mouth to exhale. The light caught on a grenade ring . . . on the dull glint of a carbine's wooden stock . . . on a trigger guard polished by nervous fingerings. The dark glow of Beta's hand pointed to Myt. Carlos handed on the joint, a tapped-out Marlboro refilled with No. 4 heroin. Myt took a drag and passed it on. About a dozen men were with them; some smoked and others didn't. This was Chom's main flank. The attack would move their way, for just above them was where the raw dirt road ran into the jungle, and just below, it curved past the Nae Amphur's helipad before jogging straight to the bridge where the mules were picketed and a few Loi Maw and Thai police huddled in the shadows of the big yellow plow.

The rest of Chom's force was scattered through the forest on the far side of the road. Anyone coming out the gate would be cut down in a cross fire. In the dark, before the flares went up, Beta and Carlos had already done a little road work, sapping the road just below them with Bouncing Betty mines. Now they squatted under the big leaves and waited.

Carlos was wearing James's fatigues, boiled clean and with about half a foot cut off each cuff. The shirt hung on him like a bag, and he had cut off the sleeves. His scraggly hair was tied back in the way the Lawas wore it, and his sharp cheekbones and the bridge of his nose were shadowed with charcoal. He had slung a bandolier of grenades over one shoulder, along with a canvas bag bulging with M-16 clips. A Spanish *madre* glittered in the hollow at the base of his throat; a coil of yellow, surgical tubing was tied to a front shirt pocket. He looked less like a human than a shadow, a shade, a mountain forest spirit.

Beta loomed next to him like a boulder rolled out of its streambed, a granite shape, a blue-black water buffalo settled on its knees. His big hands clasped the M-16 across his lap.

" 'Ey, bro', why don't we kill heem?" Carlos poked his gunsight into the neck of the Thai policeman who had been posted by the helicopter with Myt. "Cut his throat, you know?" Carlos's gold teeth shone in his smile.

The police guard lay hog-tied at their feet, trussed and gagged. His eyes stared wildly at the gun to his neck. Myt had brought him in, along with his grenade launcher and a flare gun and some charts from the chopper.

"No need."

Then one of the Lawa tapped Beta on the arm and pointed: Five or so torches were bobbing past the far side of the prison, beyond the moat. About a dozen valley people were headed toward the pond on an expedition to spear frogs. They were young people mostly, courting couples, both boys and girls in sarongs, the men bare-chested, ready to show off a little with their long spears tipped with jagged wires, jabbering in high-pitched voices as they moved up the creek to the pond, announcing themselves, curious about all the mules and the loud music from the prison. When the first flare went off overhead, the girls shrieked and then giggled at their fright. The Loi Maw stationed on the plow nearly gunned them down but were checked by the Thai guards, who knew the villagers and called out to ask where they were going. After all, nothing had happened. Just a ruckus of some kind inside the compound, two flares overhead, and now villagers out after frogs, stalking the banks and the sandbars, trying to catch the frogs with their lights and jabbing their spears.

Then came the single shot from the BAR in the tower. Then the whoosh of the rocket from the forest above the pond which blew out the prison tower in a ball of fire and a shower of timbers and thatch. The girls dropped their torches and screamed. Some ran, while others had the sense to drop down in the water as the troops at the prison walls opened up and the night air crackled with small arms and tracers sliced bright red zips into the dark jungle. A girl was shot near the retting dam and, moaning, she smacked into the sheaves of softening jute.

"*Sorry* mothers." Beta spoke to no one in particular, although he added "tha's a worl' fulla niggas." He turned to his men and told them to get down, flagging his hand just in case they didn't understand. He raised the grenade launcher taken from the police guard and, although this wasn't in the game plan, lobbed a grenade straight into the chopper, which blew apart in a double explosion that sent the rotor blades tumbling through the air. That diverted the fire from the prison to the area of the forest around Beta. The bullets ripped through the banana grove, shredding the leaves above their heads.

"Shit, bro,' why doncha wave a fucking flag," Carlos hissed.

But the firing stopped. None of Chom's men returned it. And now nobody in the prison could really be sure where to shoot. In the quiet, Beta's men heard a deer or something bark in the forest. A wounded villager thrashed in the waters of the pond. And, elsewhere, someone sobbed. But now even the crickets were hushed, and in the silence smoke drifted through the clearing from the smoldering tower and the crackling, collapsed chopper.

Now, across the pond, they heard Lacey calling.

22.

"*M*ajor Miang! MAJOR BUA MIANG!" With Chom crouched in the gully beside him, Lacey stood behind the upas tree and shouted the Nae Amphur's name across the pond where a torch was stuck in a sandbar and still guttered. Lacey shouted, then listened for a reply, but heard only the sawing pulses of the forest insects and the crackling of the burning chopper as the tubes and glassed dials of its control panel pinged and popped in the collapsed frame. He yelled again and raised his right arm to cup his hands to carry his voice. He winced—unwittingly he had stood too close when the RPG was fired, and his upper arm was burned and bruised where the back blast had roasted off his shirt sleeve.

A small voice floated up from the compound gate. "Who you are?" Lacey wondered if his own shout had transmitted that weakly across the clearing.

"I AM CAP-TAIN"—Lacey spoke each syllable slowly and loud —"JOHN LACEY, U-NI-TED STATES SPE-CIAL FOR-CES: GREEN BE-RETS." He waited for that to be considered, while the insects seethed around him and Chom leaned forward with his flare gun and fired another round over the prison. The first flare was now caught in the top of a tall fig and hissing bright magnesium sparks in the direction of their left flank, where Chom's other troops had so far remained undetected. The second flare on its tiny parachute was wobbling after the first.

"You say what?"

"U.S. SPECIAL FORCES."

"Why you shoot here?"

Lacey looked at Chom who was smiling and nodding for him to continue. "WE WANT YOUR TWO FOREIGN PRISONERS, PAUL ROBERTS AND FAY COCKBURN. REPEAT: WE WANT ROBERTS AND COCKBURN."

Once again the jungle gave long punctuation to his declaration: Grasshoppers, katydids, crickets and all the millions of stridulating bugs with leaf-crunching mandibles and rasping legs chorused with the frogs in the creekbed and the frogs in the trees and the legions of lizards stalking all the lacewings and flutterers of the night over boulders shagged with moss and branches smooth as wax where the long-tailed, long-tongued creepers paused to chatter and cackle as they flexed their leathery throats.

"They are crim'nal. Must stan' try."

"DON'T GIVE US NO JIVE SHIT," Beta bellowed from the forest to their right.

"MAJOR MIANG, YOU ARE SURROUNDED. YOU HAVE SEVENTY-FIVE LOI MAW BANDITS IN YOUR COMPOUND . . . AND THEIR HORSES." Lacey paused as he watched several of the villagers slip out of the water and scurry off. "YOU HAVE ONE BUNKER. WE HAVE ROCKETS AND ARTILLERY."

"You kill prisoners! U.S. ally Thailan'. What you do?"

"I HAVE MY ORDERS, MAJOR."

"YOU HEARD THE CAPTAIN," Beta roared from the banana grove. "GIT YO' ASS SHAKIN'."

"YEAH, BRO', YOU HEARD THE CAPTAIN."

With Carlos's shout, flares from the prison now whooshed up over the jungle where the men had been calling. Two flares popped and burned; a third hissed and hung dead on its chute. The tree line was illuminated, but the jungle still concealed them. Now, however, the prison troops had a clearer sense of how high to shoot, but without the BAR they would be randomly plunking at the forest wall. Still, there were a lot of them, and they were firing high-speed assault rifles, AK-47s and M-16s. They could rip up a lot of jungle, especially if they knew where to aim their grenades and mortars.

"MAJOR MIANG, I AM UNDER ORDERS TO LEVEL THE COMPOUND IF YOU DO NOT COMPLY. YOU HAVE TEN MINUTES TO SEND OUT THE PRISONERS."

"You say what?"

"I WILL DESTROY THE COMPOUND IN TEN MIN-UTES IF YOU DO NOT SEND OUT THE PRISONERS." Lacey turned around and leaned against the tree. He started to laugh, but gagged instead and threw up beside the tree. He wiped his mouth and raised his head and leaned against the tree again. His spine was shooting with chills. Maybe from the burn and the shock of the rocket blast; maybe from nerves. He started to laugh again, to laugh with immense relief, relief not that the thing was settled but that it was started right. He had done his number and they had bought it. He let his knees collapse and his back slide down the trunk. Chom and the others were sitting in the gully, watching him.

"You do well," Chom said. He took Lacey's arm and lifted the charred sleeve away from the wound and looked at it closely in the dim light trickling through the overhead canopies. "You good poet. No unnecessary words."

"Did you hear Beta and Carlos?" Lacey was laughing again.

"Yes, they make good speech."

"Captain 'Acey," called the Nae Amphur from the gate. "You wait one hour. I radio Chiang Mai for orders."

Lacey stood up once again beside the tree. "MAJOR, YOUR RADIO DOES NOT WORK. REPEAT: YOU HAVE NO RADIO. YOU HAVE TEN MINUTES TO RESPOND."

"Captain, come out, we talk like officers. Allies."

"YOU HAVE TEN MINUTES TO GIVE US THE PRISONERS."

What had saved Roberts from the Kamnan's bullet?

Roberts's punch that broke Snit's nose and blurred his vision, Fay's clawing that really spiked his eyes, Mai's bare-ass leap that knocked him down, and the first flare that paralyzed the troops in the compound like so many frogs in a pond. . . . But also the white ant . . . though no one of course recognized this as the true factor that had interceded in the equation of events and saved Roberts's life. Saved him from a bullet behind the ear. The white ant was a *phi zyaw*, a deadly forest spirit, and only Chom had seen it and recognized it as it crawled over the edge of his upas bark roll while he waited to start the operation. Another Lawa might have called things off on seeing the ant, but Chom was not another Lawa. One of his thirty-two *lambok* souls was a tiger's, which made him mortal but a little something more as well, something stronger, fiercer, wiser. This was common knowledge in his lineage, and this is why the Lawa and the Skaw Karen followed him into unknown jungles far from their homes and the protections of their local spirits. The white ant was the index finger on the trigger that fired the flare gun that the tiger spirit had raised at the walled fort washed in moonlight. Spirits had come to save Roberts's life. Only Chom really understood that.

The Nae Amphur stood in the radio room that was also his headquarters. A rusty file cabinet stood in the corner and, nearby, his canvas cot, and his little Sanyo refrigerator with a pile of girly magazines on top. On top of the broad table next to the refrigerator was the radio. In the glare of the gas lamp, his radio man was examining the torn-out wiring and the missing tubes. The Nae Amphur was drunk and hung over and rattled by the exchange with the American captain. He would have a lot to explain to the chief in Chiang Mai. His watchtower had been rocketed and its timbers collapsed on top of the sandbag bunker. Two men were dead in the tower and he supposed that the other two were dead by the chopper. The BAR was defunct; the radio had been wrecked. And the chopper. The memory of its explosion flooded him with pain. Furthermore he couldn't say a word about giving up the whites to the Green Berets, because no one in Chiang Mai knew about them. And all he had ever gotten from them was about five hundred U.S. dollars, a Japanese camera, and some clothing. He didn't mind letting them go. He had been planning to give the girl to Khan Su to take to Burma. Roberts was another matter; he was trouble. The Kamnan was right about him: shoot him and incinerate the body in a red barrel. No, he didn't care about losing them. He cared about losing them *by force* to Americans. That looked bad. No, he would say the Thahan Pa attacked from Laos, the Communists . . . and that he fought them off . . . losing the chopper in a crash landing. How he hated these big-mouthed, stinking Americans. Always pushing people around. They'd pay. This would cost them a new chopper, a BAR . . . what else? Well, surely he could argue for improving the outpost. A new tower. Extra bunkers, and cement ones, not sandbag and timbers, and he'd need a warehouse for Khan Su's opium. "Kamnan!" he called to Snit outside.

Puaree came in from the porch where he had been watching Khan

Su organize his troops. He entered the room squinting and blinking. His vision was blurred and his eyes were tearing.

"Tell Koi to get the Americans."

"We're giving them up?"

"Yes."

"Nae Amphur, Khan Su wants to chase the Americans in the jungle."

"Why?"

"He says there can't be many of them or his intelligence would have reported them. He says that probably there are only a few with some heavy arms. He wants those arms."

"It's night!"

"He says that's his advantage. He has more men."

"Time to earn your money, bodyguard." Beta reached into a rucksack and pulled out two green berets. He slapped one at Carlos's shoulder and, when Carlos took it, Beta slid the other over his own head where it perched like a beanie. In the drifting shadows and strokes of flarelight that momentarily broke through the forest canopy as the wind rustled the leaves, Carlos pulled his beret snugly over his headband and wiry hair. Then he gathered up his M-16, clip bag, and grenade bandolier and started to move out through the grove. He said nothing and did not wait for Beta to follow.

"Hey, man."

Carlos turned and crouched in the filtering light to look back at Beta through the banana leaves.

"Better tuck in that shirt. You're ah, what may I say, ah *representative* of the U.S.A."

"John Wayne, bro'. Dig." Carlos tucked in his shirt and turned to go.

"Hey, an' Carlos . . ." Beta paused while Carlos turned again. "Don't set yo' jaw so grim. Y'all git in trouble out there, don't play the fool, you know what ah'm sayin'? Just be cool, be quiet, and we'll git to you. Chom doan leave nobody behind. Huh?"

"Gotcha, bro'. I'm cool. I just get quiet sometimes."

"Tha's right. Ah think"—Beta reached down and threw one huge arm around the waist of the trussed-up Border Patrol guard, lifting him as he kneeled and rose up, throwing the little man over his left shoulder, Beta's right hand clasping his M-16 by its rear sight handle —"we goin' inta partnership, you understand." He joggled the guard's weight like a sack of feed and moved off behind Carlos. "Ah be right behind you," he said as they disappeared together in the grove.

"Not without her." Fay pointed to Mai, who carried cosmetics, toothbrush, and a pair of high heels that Fay had given her, all of it tied up in a big cotton scarf. The three of them stood on the porch before the Nae Amphur and the Kamnan, who blinked at them with runny eyes. Snit's .45 was hidden in the inside pocket of Prescott's flight bag.

The Nae Amphur looked at their suitcases and realized that they had been prepared to go. He made a mental note to search out the spy in his compound.

"Not without her," Fay repeated, taking Major Miang's silence for refusal.

The Nae Amphur snorted and made the same shooing motions at Mai he would with a fly. He couldn't care less about losing her, except for the possibilities of entertainment that she had shown that night. He motioned Koi over and nodded to the gate.

Koi glowered at them like a dog about to snap. The three of them had been his big chance at some side money and now they had ruined it. He remembered the prophecy book and was furious with himself for causing the whole thing by bringing them their fortunes.

The Nae Amphur walked off to confer with Khan Su, and the three released prisoners started off toward the gate behind Koi.

"See you around, Snit," Roberts said as the Kamnan squinted at them and hoped for a chance to kill them.

At the foot of the steps, near the end of the banquet table, the dead monkey hung limply in its straps. A spoon had been left in its head as in a cereal bowl.

23.

*L*ouise sat in the dark. From her chair on the clipped lawn of the Long Pine Inn, she listened to the waves washing up and rinsing the beach in a clatter of shells. The breeze off the Andaman Sea threshed the fans in the coconut trees by the beachfront. She heard a dull thunk as a coconut loosened and dropped to the ground. Offshore, boat lights bobbed on the moonwashed sea as local Malays set their nets off the head of the island. The hotel's bar had closed. Most of the guests had gone to bed.

She pulled her sweater down over her wrists and knuckles, a Norwegian sweater, a fisherman's sweater of heavy wool loaned to her by Madge, the English girl honeymooning with her chinless groom who worked for a pharmaceutical firm in Singapore. Louise was the only single person at the Lone Pine. After a week, she had become a topic of rumor and sympathy, for the other guests had heard that she was waiting for someone, something, a telegram. She never went into town to shop or play the casino, and if she walked the beach she was always within paging distance of the hotel. It was known that she had made several calls to New York from the desk phone. People did not know that she had given herself one more week to wait it out before declaring her husband lost.

Louise slouched in her chair and studied the sea: the white caps that tossed up in the moonlight before disappearing onto shore, the dark ripples that ran from right to left before the rolling lunge of a large wave, the boats rocking on their anchor lines, the moon over the sea. Only the moon could see she was crying.

24.

*T*hey stopped at the open iron gate crowned with coils of razory wire and crowded with Loi Maw weighed down with slings of rockets and shouldering long Soviet launchers. With the butt of his M-16, Koi punched Roberts in the kidneys and shoved him out the gate through the wedge of soldiers. He booted Fay in the ass as she and Mai followed. None of them looked back. Roberts coughed and caught his balance and stepped forward onto the road. The three of them stood clutching their luggage: Roberts's fake-leather flight bag, Fay's silver nylon space-luggage, Mai's bundled scarf. Under the drifting flares, under the full moon, they found themselves on the dirt road just before the moat. In the stagnant trench, spreads of duckweed shone in a pinkish glow. Roberts could hear his shithouse friends, the ducks, quacking nervously in the dark hollow under the timbers of the bridge where they had taken refuge in the earlier barrage.

"LACEY!" Roberts's yell stabbed the back of his throat with

pain, and he felt the blood trickle across the base of his tongue.
"WE'RE COMING OUT!"

"Come ahead," was the call that a breeze floated down the west-running road from across the pond. ". . . a man waiting for you. Across the bridge . . . at the edge of the gardens. WALK STRAIGHT to him. DO WHAT HE SAYS."

In the filtering red light and slow-moving shadows, Roberts's eyes traced the road across the bridge and past the luminous plow where soldiers, rifles at ready, were staring at them. His eyesight was shaky from the near concussion, the booze, and, of course, from the pumping fear, but he brought the gardens into his field of vision.

"There," Fay said, pointing to a lone figure standing in the seeping flarelight, below the smoking chopper. A small man was waving to them. He was standing off the berm of the dirt track near a cluster of shimmering papaya trees. He was out in the open. He wore a beret. His rifle was pointed to the sky, stuck against his hip, and with his other hand he waved them forward.

"Let's go, love." Fay touched Roberts's shoulder.

They started toward the man, crossing the bridge where their footsteps scuffed pebbles through the slats, spooking the ducks that thrashed and quacked below them. Across the bridge, beyond the rolls of barbed wire that trellised the mined banks of the moat, they spotted the Loi Maw mules and about a dozen soldiers huddled behind the road plow. The driver's cage was protected on both sides with bolted logs. The soldiers stared at them. Roberts fumbled his hand into the flight bag and clutched the .45. Someone called to them as they passed, "Hey, vuck. You vuck. Hey, you vuck."

When they got a few yards beyond the plow, they heard a commotion behind them as the gate swung out and Loi Maw troops rushed forward and split into two groups, some running up behind them and the others—including five or so on horseback—doglegging and charging north along the moat straight toward where the stream ran down from the pond. And straight—although they had no way of knowing—toward the other Lawa flank hidden in the forest north of the prison and the pond, cloaked in the tree line at the base of the Hmong foothills. Nobody fired a shot.

"Run! Run, goddamit!" they heard the Green Beret yelling. "Qué tienes? Run!"

They were running, running for their lives, Roberts yanking himself forward on spasmodic legs, on calf and shank muscles stripped of tone and power, and Fay and Mai running hand in hand, stumbling forward with their baggage, running on triphammer heartbeats and terribly shaky knees.

"HOLD FIRE. HOLD FIRE. Hold YO' FIRE!"

Beta yelled at his men but with their weak English (and in their panic as they crouched in the banana grove and saw the Loi Maw rushing out, breaking out of the fish barrel of the prison and getting away where they could close on them in the dark forest) Beta's men heard only "fire" and they opened up on the Loi Maw, who made it as far as the plow and dropped down to fire on the jungle as their comrades bolted north to the stream, on foot and on horseback, and got just that far as the other Lawa cut into them with automatic fire, dropping six or so men in the first fusillade and driving the rest into the cover of the bamboo along the stream as two horses went down screaming and kicking the air, and a third pony plunged riderless up the creek bed and into the forest.

"The DITCH! In the ditch!"

The three of them were running along the road just past the pepper field as bullets skittered the road behind them and cut slits in the long slender papaya leaves above their heads. Carlos was running toward them yelling "The ditch. In the ditch." And he dove, as if to demonstrate, into the irrigation ditch by the road as the troops on the plow tried to nail him.

But none of the Loi Maw were shooting at the runaway prisoners.

Khan Su needed them live and squirming, because dead they were useless in holding the American attackers in place while he got his troops clear and free of the prison, where a mortar barrage would destroy them utterly. It was Koi. It was Koi who, crazy with rage and whiskey and remorse, stood at the gate—as the Loi Maw surged out behind him—and blasted away at Fay and Roberts. Remorse for the new house that his extortions had almost bought him; remorse for the young wife he might have attracted if he could have gotten, say, one of their cameras. Whiskey ignited his remorse into rage. He stood there in the mayhem and popped off wild bursts at the three figures disappearing down the dark road, disappearing with his hopes into the western jungle. But, even sober, the old guard couldn't shoot.

Myt could, the Lawa with the torn ear who spoke Thai and had spent months inside the prison with Koi and his fellow guards. While his comrades fanned out through the tree line, Myt grabbed a carbine and dropped down on one knee beneath the man-size banana leaves that slapped and zippered with slugs as the Loi Maw peppered the forest. Taking aim, he squeezed off four single shots that splattered across Koi's chest and neck, shattering his sternum, his right clavicle and his voice box, spinning Koi around so that he dropped his rifle and spewed a swirl of blood. The old guard staggered into barbed wire, which tore his trousers and tripped him forward into the moat, where his extended hands detonated a claymore mine. The moat water rose in a furious jet and collapsed in a column of algae and slime, lilies and duckweed, fish and sundered flesh. Koi and several Loi Maw—some rushing out the gate and several near the plow—were blown away. A horse was splintered with shrapnel and the explosion had twisted off one of its front legs. It screamed and tried to lurch away, but fell over onto its side across the barbed wire and into the moat, tripping off another claymore. This explosion merged with a series of detonations as rockets roared in like trains rushing past a station. Chom's detachment had opened up and sealed Khan Su's flight to the jungle. The prison gate sagged, shorn off its heavy, welded hinges. The passageway was slippery with blood and foul water and pieces of dead men and horse. Khan Su, yelling orders from the center of the court where his men had set up six mortar pods, called his soldiers back. He was furious, but appeared calm. He hadn't calculated on Americans to the north as well. Why hadn't he heard of an American force in the Golden Triangle?

In what was left of the garden behind Khan Su, horses and mules were leaping and tripping on their hobbles as muleteers struggled to cut them free so they wouldn't snap their legs in panic. Khan Su was ready to go with his mortars. His men were pinned down behind the plow; the other group, badly dwindled, was creeping through the overgrown banks of the creekbed toward the pond and Chom. From the barred windows facing the jungle, the remnant of his troops still inside—their muzzle flashes stammering like a string of firecrackers —were withering the forest wall. His mortars, if on target, might get the Americans out of the creekbed and into the forest, but the Nae Amphur, the bungling fool, was yelling at him and waving his arms as he ran down the steps . . . and was nearly knocked down in the rush of horses stampeding back and forth across the courtyard.

"No mortars. No mortars!" Major Miang was screaming above the sound of the shooting. He started to shake Khan Su by the shoulders. "They kill us with mortars. Don't make them use theirs."

"Maybe they don't *have* mortars," Khan Su yelled back, pushing the Nae Amphur's hands away. "I must get my men out and into the jungle."

"You want to find out in here if they do have them? Did you know about their other troops? Yes? If they have rockets, they have mortars. And grenade launchers." The Nae Amphur remembered the distinctive slam that preceded the explosion of his beautiful chopper.

Khan Su sucked his teeth and reluctantly agreed. The Thai was right. One or two mortars fired in the tiny compound would cut them apart, and a good barrage through the flimsy roofs would wipe out the men crowded into the cells and police barracks. Khan Su called over the Haw trader and told him to stop the firing from windows.

"But," he said, shaking a finger at the Nae Amphur, "they will mortar to cover their escape once they get the three prisoners."

"Yes?"

"We have to be ready to get out of here. They'll leave a few men behind to stop us from chasing them."

Major Miang nodded agreement.

"My men will spread out and head them off. Which way will they go?" He fiddled with the peak of his cap.

"Burma. North; maybe west."

"You don't know of any Americans in Thailand?"

"No. None. I don't know who these people are. My chief would have told me." Miang wiped his face with his hand and thought of his chief and his blasted compound and the burned chopper.

"Good. We go north and west." Khan Su brushed the cloth epaulet on Miang's right shoulder. "Will you go with us?"

The Nae Amphur hesitated. The shooting had died along the moat wall. Khan Su's men were pulling down the iron gate, cutting through the snarl of barbed wire that had fallen with it and opening a clean passage into the night. Shots still popped off from the creek, from the plow, and from the jungle, but things were quieting down. A horse shrieked in the creekbed until a shot silenced it. Khan Su was brushing his shoulder the way spiders petted their prey.

"Yes," he said. "But only as far as Burma. I am in trouble enough."

This was probably the first honest sentiment to pass between them, and Khan Su recognized the fact. He paused from stroking the Nae Amphur's shoulder, barked a laugh, and slapped him on the back. They were in business again. "Good fish," he said. "Good monkey, too." He tugged the peak of his cap against his ear.

The Nae Amphur grinned and his gold teeth shone. They were in business again. It was good to have something to look forward to after all the mess.

The air over the irrigation ditch droned with mosquitoes while its warm water flowed with leeches, tadpoles, and little needle-shaped fish that batted against their arms and rippled off under the flare-lit surface. Fay was shivering. Roberts and Mai hugged her with their bodies, hoping that her fever was not running a cycle. " 'S okay, baby. 'S okay," Mai whispered. Roberts had flung his left arm over Fay's shoulders, and with his right he clutched Snit's .45 and rested it on the bank out of the water. Carlos was just above him, watching the soldiers at the plow. Carlos turned to look back into the ditch.

"Bro', you Roberts?"

"Yeah. Who are you?"

"I'm your fuckin' bodyguard that your mother or somebody hired."

"Mary?"

"I don't know *who*, bro'. I just come with Lacey." Carlos nodded toward the forest above them.

"Lacey up there?"

"You heard him. Say," he said, "who's the dink chick?"

"A friend. She saved my life." Roberts crawled farther out of the water onto the bank.

"Far out, bro'! Everybody tryin' to save your life. You must be a wonderful human being." Carlos turned and looked across the road. The plow was no more than twenty-five yards away. Everybody seemed to be staying put. He turned again to Roberts. "C'mon. We're movin' out. And, bro', you can put that thing away because you won't hit nothin' outside ten feet, you dig?" Carlos pointed to the .45. From the bandolier slung around his neck, he pulled off a fragmentation grenade and handed it to Roberts. "Cabrón, you know this shit?"

"Yeah."

"Throw it only if I tell you, dig? 'Nother thing—" He poked Fay's shoulder to make sure she was listening. Her hair was plastered to her neck and face, and her eyes lacked focus. "She listenin'?"

"Don't worry," Roberts replied.

"I am listening," Fay said, but her voice was weird and hollow.

"Okay, when we get out of the ditch, walk only where I walk. The road's been mined. You follow? You'll see a black dude by the chopper. He'll cover us if they start firing, so don't hit him with no grenade or nothin', okay?" Carlos's face was smeared with sweat.

"You're *not* Green Berets."

"No, bro'. If we was, you'd be dead by now. C'mon." Carlos dropped down into the ditch behind them. "Leave that shit here," he hissed.

Roberts turned and saw him pointing to the bags, so he deposited his own on the bank beneath the dirt berm, first taking out the .45 once again. The ditch ran along the field toward the jungle. If they stood up, the water was only thigh deep. Roberts now stood in the lead, holding the .45 and Carlos's grenade. Fay was behind him, clutching her bag against her chest. Carlos took Mai's bundle out of her hand and gave her a goose to get her going.

"Hey, beau," she said, "what you do?" She was already tuning in on Carlos. Pretty soon she'd have it right. Have him right.

They pushed forward slowly, trying to be quiet as their legs sloshed the waters and their feet were sucked down in the muck. Besides giving them away, their noise kept them from hearing any movement up on the road, so Carlos got out and crept along the bank beside them, keeping his eye on the troops by the plow and with his head moving along, just above the road, like a groundhog's.

Beta was waiting for them in a bamboo spray at the end of the ditch, where a culvert ran under the road to feed the field. The Thai guard lay beside him, still gagged, still trussed, still alive.

"Hand me that," he said to Roberts as they climbed out of the water. "Tha's right. The grenade." Beta took the grenade and told Carlos to take them down through the trees, skinny papayas with rotaries of long leaves over their heads.

They crouched for a minute in the shadow of the bamboo as the water trailed off their clothes onto the dirt. They looked at the guard who stared back at them listlessly, a bit like a mouse dragged around by a cat before the kill. Fay was trembling and staring widely at Beta. Roberts had lost one shoe in the ditch; he pulled off the other and threw it away.

"You lose any?" Carlos asked.

"Doan know yet. G'on ahead." Beta motioned to the orchard. "I'll folla." Then he noticed Fay staring at him. "Never seen a nigger before?" He sounded irritated, as men do when observed in a line of work that the world doesn't see as respectable. Beta was startled when Fay threw her head on his chest and her arms around his barreled midsection and began to heave with sobs.

"Thank you," she sobbed as she buried her face and her wet muddy hair into the curve of his chest just above his heart. "Thank you."

Beta was big. His large arms were warm and gentle as he held her and said, "Tha's alright now. Tha's alright," and then handed her off to Carlos, to whom she also sniffled a thank you as she touched his hard little face with her hand.

"C'mon, baby," Mai said. She reached for Fay's hand, and Carlos led the trio out through the orchard.

When they were gone, drawing no fire, Beta pulled the Thai up onto the edge of the road. Beta hunched below him by the berm, almost at eye level with the guard. He took Roberts's grenade and held it to the guard's face. Then he pulled the pin, activating the grenade, but keeping the tab depressed. He showed the guard this too. Then he pushed the man up, hooked the live grenade in the rope at his back, and eased the man down so that his body picked up the pressure on the tab. The man's eyes swam with fear. He whipped his head left and right and tried to talk through his gag.

"Now, I know you doan un'erstan' English. But I wan' you to know that the thing's settin' there, you see. You wiggle too much, Jack, and ka-boom. Now ah know you un'erstan' that."

Beta paused to look down the road. The night air seeped with the odor of exploded gasoline, burned plastic, burned rubber, burned flesh. They needed the rest of the night to make their getaway. He turned back to the guard.

"Now, like I say. Any numba things goin' happen. Yo' friens come up and right off they'll take the gag and you'll say 'look out, brothers, they's a live grenade un'er me' an' they fish aroun' an' fin' it. Or, what may I say, they come up and turn you over to untie you and kabloowie, y'all dead. Or you might see them comin' and try to roll off in the ditch as fas' as you can. Save yo' own ass, you un'erstan'. Or an angel might come down an' save you. Lots of things could happen. You figure out a lot more before the time come. My guess is you try the ditch."

Beta patted the man's shoulder and left him lying on the road.

Even in the dim light below the screw pines, Lacey was shocked by what he could see of his friends. He had last seen Fay in the London hotel the night before they flew off with Prescott, that drugged evening when Prescott lay like a corpse beside them, ghastly with cancerous bumps, nodded off on methadone. He remembered her nude pose in the bathroom doorway. He remembered her auburn hair, shiny and Sassooned, as Roberts combed it out while she sat naked on the carpet before his chair and Whiting filmed them. Her skin was so milky and soft. He remembered the first time he met her. She was naked and drugged, and she had dragged her ample fanny right under his nose and reached across his lap for the whiskey bottle on the floor. Now her hair hung matted, and sores blotched her scalp and seeped out through her hairline. Her eyes were puffy and shadowed; her lips, cracked with fever. The scabies had crusted her hands, the webs of her fingers, her elbows. And she was horribly thin. Roberts was not much better. He looked jaundiced. He jerked about like a puppet on tight strings. They would be a real pair of horrors in broad daylight. What was Roberts's boast in London? Reality is for people who can't stand drugs. Well, Roberts had apparently had enough reality to test the truth of that.

"Christ, man, what took you so long?" Roberts rasped.

"No one even knew for months. Hey, man, you're welcome."

They squatted in the gully behind the walls of roots. Just Lacey and Roberts and Fay; Mai was murmuring with Carlos in the deeper shadows; Beta was sitting on a piece of bark, studying the grenade launcher on his knees—the grenade launcher taken from the police guard he had left like a human trip flare on the road. Chom, the brim of his baseball cap pulled backward, crouched with his two rocket men and watched the prison. Everyone else was gone or ready to go. The men on the mortars had disappeared into the steeper reaches of the jungle where Chom had told them to listen for the rockets, give him time to get away, and then mortar not the compound but the edge of the jungle. There was a risk in this: If a breeze picked up, it could drift the mortars over the fleeing Lawa. They'd have to move fast.

His men north of the pond and those with Myt in the banana grove had orders to spread out in groups of two and three in a wide arc that would funnel together as they got to Burma, to the steep ravines near Loi Hia-Um, and to the footbridge over the Nam Yawng gorge. No one was to fire unless fired on and the target clearly spotted. And then they were to fire and dogleg off in false directions, gradually working toward Burma. They had to be at the Nam Yawng bridge by dawn. In the dark, the hunted had the advantage.

"We learned by an accident, a spook interrogated this Pathet Lao. The guy had Steve's driver's license with your name on the back."

"Christ," Roberts said, "I thought they were going to kill that guy."

"He escaped."

"And who's he?" Fay pointed to Chom. Her teeth were chattering, although one of the Lawa had given her his undershirt and another—now off in the jungle in his blue shorts—had given her his pants.

"Yeah, Hank Aaron over there."

"He moves opium and is a kind of revolutionary."

"Why . . ." Roberts checked the safety on the carbine Chom had handed him. "Why's he doing this?"

"Well, we paid him, but I don't think that's the reason."

"We?"

"Well, *you* did. Mary got the estate lawyers to break into your trust."

"Oh, fuck. How much will this cost me?"

"Probably fifteen or twenty thousand by the time we all get home."

Fay put her awful hand on Lacey's shoulder. She wasn't interested in hearing about the money. "What do you mean," she asked, "that 'it's not the whole reason'?"

Lacey looked at her. She looked like shit. He was grateful that Louise was safe on Penang. But, he thought, sometimes trauma turns out better people. Not Roberts, maybe. Pretty soon, if they made it o- t, he'd be griping about the money. But Fay, beyond the distress of her physical pain, was troubled by something larger. Steve had said something in his journal about living on the edge of the "two major categories," life and death. Sometimes it made you more human.

But Lacey didn't get the chance to answer Fay. Just then they heard the sputter, catch, and growl of the plow's engine as the police fired it up. While Chom waved his rocket men to get ready and they kneeled with the bazookalike launchers on their shoulders, Lacey pulled his friends out of the path of the backblast. His right arm was swollen and stiff and hurt like hell.

"Get ready," Chom whispered back to them.

Carlos, calling Mai "mama," pulled her up by the hand. She was wearing his beret. The others also stood up, gathering their gear or watching Chom as he peered through the veil of stilt roots. Behind Lacey and the rest, Beta checked his compass with a pencil flashlight that Myt had taken from the chopper. The flares were dead in the treetops; no new ones rekindled the sky. This was it.

Out on the moonlit road, the plow was now slowly clanking forward on its tracks while the police and their Loi Maw allies hugged behind it, using it like a tank or a personnel carrier. Farther behind them, across the moat, other troops were whisking out the gate.

As one of his rocketeers shuffled his weight on a knee, Chom raised his hand, paused, then dropped it. They felt two momentous whooshes with orangy backflashes and then heard the rockets slam home. One hit the corner of the prison wall, shattering cinder blocks and killing the men who ran by; the other exploded in an immense shower of sparks against the left track of the plow, throwing jags of linkage slashing through the air. Immediately, the prison troops opened up with rockets and automatic fire.

"Let's go!" Chom turned with his rocketmen and the race was on. Almost immediately they were all down on their bellies in the gully. A Loi Maw rocket blew apart in the banyan caverns to their right, billowing out in a big fireball and stabbing the air with shivers of wood. When they all got up to run again, they could hear the other Lawa opening up on the attacking troops. There was a grenade blast from the road, and screams momentarily pierced the din of the automatic fire. They were up on their feet. And running. Roberts stubbing his bare toes and stumbling across roots, Chom up ahead and Beta behind them. The two women and Lacey, linking hands as they ducked branches and the jagged teeth of palms, lunged forward after Chom in a *danse macabre*. They heard more explosions, and Beta yelled "tha's my Bouncin' Betty." And then Carlos heard something crashing through the trees over their heads. "Down!" he yelled and dove with Mai, pulling Lacey and Fay with them in a heap, and the thing came crashing clean through the canopy and slammed down in front of their faces: a boot with a leg in it broken off at the knee. Fay saw it and screamed, screamed and couldn't stop, couldn't stop until Beta scooped her up from behind with his huge black hands over her mouth and nose. He held her off the ground and hugged her close and whispered harshly in the back of her ear, "None of *that!* You scream all you want when we git home, but you shut yo' mouf on this run." Fay wiggled her head, and he set her down. She looked down at the boot standing upright with the remnant leg, and then Lacey grabbed her hand and pulled her forward and they were all running again through the night, climbing over, and under, large slippery roots, jogging around impenetrable thickets, sliding through big sucker branches rooted in the ferns, snagging their gear, their guns, extricating themselves to catch up with the others, fleeing after Chom—who glided like a tiger spirit through the forest. Twenty minutes later, as they groped along a creekbed's slippery ledges and lush ferns, they could still hear sporadic fire behind them and then the barrage of mortars.

The two Lawa, the Karen, and Chert had set up their weapons in a flat dish of stubby bamboo at the foot of a hillside poppy field two hundred yards above the prison. Reloading as fast as they could without burning up their mortar tubes, they caught the troops in the open. They could have wiped them out if they had had more units. But they had just two, and they fired these rapidly at high angles by simply dropping the mortars down the tubes onto the locked-out firing pins. They walked their sixty-millimeter rounds through the edge of the forest where the Loi Maw were now penetrating their abandoned hideouts. They worked their salvos across the pond, the gardens and orchards, the road, the moat— walking the bombs right up to the prison walls.

The police and the Loi Maw had nowhere to run. They dove like swamp rats into gullies and ditches and the sheltered banks of the stream. Their horses and mules either ran off or were blown apart on their tethers. Khan Su crouched in fury against the prison wall. The Nae Amphur, tagging after him miserably, was distraught; he saw his whole career atomized with each detonation and the cries of his men. But Khan Su, who had lost twenty or so men and his entire pack team, knew that he still outnumbered the Americans, that theirs was only a hit-and-run operation, that toe-to-toe he could wipe them out if only he could hunt them down. It was 3:15 A.M. Dawn was only two hours away.

He sent some of his men to capture the mortars on the hill. Like a gambler who has lost heavily, he would not quit, but instead upped the ante. He was in too deep now; he couldn't limp back to Burma on foot. His success as a warlord rested on a reputation that saved him from constant skirmishing. He depended on his dreadfulness: his eight hundred troops guarding his caravans, his ruthless execution of deserters, his intimidation of villagers. A more foolish man would have called it quits and exaggerated the American force, but Khan Su knew that word would get out—that he had been ripped apart without taking even one enemy soldier. And then he'd have to deal with the Kuomintang units or the rival Shan army that would come after him the way tigers run down a wounded stag.

When the barrage stopped and he could hear his own men firing at the hillside position, he sent up flares. In the infernal light he surveyed his losses—legless men, blasted horses, gaping torsos, gentle sleepers without a mark until you noticed the blood trickling from their ears. Dragging the Nae Amphur and his police with him, Khan Su ordered his fifty or so healthy men into the forest. He was going for broke.

25.

*A*s dawn rose and light seeped into the prison yard, the women moved to the doors of their cells and stood there, wordlessly, like wraiths, beside the broken walls and the burned tower. The awful night was over. The pale full moon floated above the coconut palms in a clear purple sky west of the prison; to the east, the jungle fowl were waking to fresh quarrels. In the gray light, the women looked out and saw the havoc: their friend lying dead near the trampled gardens, a guard draped dead across the sandbagged roof of the bunker, the prison gate lying off its hinges, and the dead men sprawled across the passageway near the gate. Some chickens pecked about the overturned banquet table. A rooster perched on one of their wooden beds and crowed. They saw the strapped-in monkey, stiff with rigor mortis and with the big aluminum spoon handle sticking out of the top of its head. A dog sniffed at the monkey's toes and then moved on to lift a hind leg against some turned-over cases of beer.

As they saw each other, they moved slowly together, still without speaking. Some of the men, however, called to them from their locked cells, called and told them that they were free, told them to search the headquarters for the keys.

The women moved uncertainly across the yard, crossing the devastated compound thick with the smell of urine and offal. They clasped their hands over mouths and noses as if to filter the stench. Some held each other by the arm. A few had been badly beaten. The student's wife's eye was swollen shut, and the side of her face was purplish. She walked timidly, like the others, looking about for guards. They found one: a young relative of the Nae Amphur, who was sleeping on the porch with his carbine cradled in one arm.

Somehow he woke to their slow shuffling steps. He shook himself up as if waking in a dream and stared at the silent women creeping slowly toward him. He bolted off the steps, slipped and dropped his gun, regained his balance and ran out the blasted gate. A shudder of energy entered the timid crowd of nine or so women, quickening their steps and urging a human murmur to start among them. The gambling lady said, "In the office," and she was the first to mount the steps. They stopped at the open door and peered in cautiously.

"Go in. Go in," the men called from their cells.

Inside they saw the radio pulled out from the wall and the wires tangled out from its back. They saw the Kamnan sleeping on the Nae Amphur's canvas cot. They entered. His face was gouged and his shut eyes swollen. They fell silent again. The young student's wife moved to the edge of his bed and the others shuffled behind her. They looked down on him—snoring with unwrinkled face, pudgy, his pompadour greasing the cotton bolster. They fell on him with a swoop and a screech.

The Kamnan screamed and opened his eyes. Through his blurred vision he saw who had grabbed him. He screamed again. Hands were on his throat, choking his yell to a gurgle. He kicked and there were hands holding down his legs and his arms and his head. The cot broke with the weight of the women. His face went red and then purple and finally he was no longer kicking to get free, but just kicking, spasmodically, as one knee jerked and twitched.

When he was still, they started jabbering excitedly, exultantly, refreshed and empowered. They broke apart and ransacked the office, pulling out files to find their IDs and looking for money, throwing papers about, knocking over the Japanese refrigerator. A barefoot woman in a tattered sarong and old cotton blouse found the heavy cell keys on a nail by the front door. She grabbed them and ran outside laughing triumphantly and jangling them before her as she padded across the yard. The men were cheering behind their bars. The other women ran out behind her.

In a few minutes the cells were opened. Even the two Shan opium addicts stumbled out like owls. Ten minutes later they were all out of the compound and on the road, hurrying past the dead horses and the blasted plow where a man hung backward out of the driver's cage. They saw the fat Haw trader lying face down in the dust surrounded by a dark birthmark of blood. Dead soldiers were dropped all along the road. One lay alive and moaning in the ditch water, his hands and feet still tied. Some of the escapees wanted to drown him, but others said not to bother.

Farther on they saw a village girl floating by the retting dam above a submerged pallet of jute sheaves. They wondered who she was. The retting pool was crimson. A horse had bled to death beside her.

They hurried past these horrors. Some of them knew the way to Chiang Saen and a village where they might beg for food.

26.

At dawn, Chom's troops were crisscrossing the steep ravines in Burma. Fay and Roberts had slowed them down, and although the higher terrain was easier to pass through—jungle foliage, roots and rubbery vines gave way to magnolias and squat oaks and tall silver figs and, higher up, to clusters of rhododendrons and pines—the hiking now was up and down ravines and across narrow canyons. Fay had given out altogether and was nearly delirious with fatigue. Beta was now carrying her over his shoulder, and although she weighed only about 105 pounds she was wearing him out as they hurried uphill to the crossing at the Nam Yawng gorge. Roberts had also given out; the opium and months of depletion told. With his arms thrown across Lacey's and Mai's shoulders, he worked his legs mechanically as they pulled him along. Khan Su was not far behind. They had traveled about fifteen miles in two hours.

Chom called a rest in a boulder field in an upland meadow about two miles from the gorge. The air was sweet and thin. Pine needles carpeted the clearing. In the spreading dawnlight they saw white trillium wavering among the shrill green tussocks fed by mountain springs. Rhododendrons with butter-yellow blossoms banked the cliffside behind them.

Shots rang out far below, and they could hear mortars thumping in the little valley they had just hiked out of. Myt and Chert and the others were still down there, holding off Khan Su and the Thai police until Chom and his group could make it to the footbridge over the gorge. At times, when the wind blew right, they could hear the distant rapids churning up from the bottom of the gorge. But time had run out. Khan Su had as good as caught up with them, having figured out their path, despite the ambushes and dogleg feints in the night jungle. They were north of Mong Yawng. There were only a few crossings of the gorge and, as they got closer to the river rift, only one was likely. There was time perhaps for Chom and his group to make it across, but only if the other Lawa dug in and held off Khan Su. All of them could not get across quickly enough, and Khan Su was going to wipe out those left already hemmed in—or soon to be —on the peninsular mesa on the wrong side of the river.

Chom conferred with Beta and Carlos, while Lacey and Mai and Fay and Roberts sprawled on the sweet pine needles. An early woodpecker throbbed at a dead tree nearby. Roberts drank from a bamboo canteen and promptly threw up. No one paid him any attention.

"They's 'bout two to one of us. We might be able to take 'em." Beta was leaning against a large boulder, his large chest heaved and clear streams of sweat dribbled from his cheeks.

A dove cooed in the tall pines. The sun was poking above the ridges they had crossed.

"Bro', what about some of us cross and the rest try to get out *behind* the fuckers. Everybody just stop shootin' and disappear."

"Forest too thin," Chom said. He wiped the sting of salt from one eye with the checkered scarf about his neck, then tilted forward with his hands on his knees and tried to catch his breath.

"Chom!"

One of his rocket men, posted on a boulder ledge, called urgently. Chom looked up where the Lawa was standing and pointing, pointing to a man walking down to them out of a cluster of scrubby pines that covered the hillside above their meadow. The man was in uniform, and his floppy hat was wreathed in sprigs of rhododendron. He was unarmed. He ambled toward them like an alpine hiker and smiled.

"He's North Vietnamese," Lacey called as he placed the uniform. Lacey scrambled to his feet and went over to Chom.

The soldier stopped about ten yards away and pointed behind them to the rhododendrons clouded with sand flies. They turned. There, about twenty yards distant, NVA soldiers began to rise up out of the shrubs. Then, all around, from behind boulders, from out of low-lying pines, from behind the trunks of the larger trees, North Vietnamese soldiers with camouflage greenery adorning their heads stood up, fully equipped and ready for battle. Perhaps a hundred soldiers appeared out of nowhere.

Chom told his men to drop their arms. Beta and Carlos merely lowered theirs.

The man now called to them in Lao and in Vietnamese.

"What he say?" Chom looked around for someone who understood.

"He wants to know who we are," Lacey replied.

"Tell him I progressive-minded revolutionary. They like that."

Lacey moved forward and translated into Vietnamese. Oddly enough, he wasn't frightened. He had had worse shakes walking into his office at the university. He just wasn't afraid of these men. In two years of work with war-injured children, moving them from province hospitals to Saigon and then onto hospital airplanes heading to the United States, he never once talked to a family or to a child who claimed to have been brutalized by the North Vietnamese. Well, once. He had evacuated a twelve-year-old boy, a trilateral amputee who had been on a public bus mined by the Viet Cong. But that was on a road that the VC had declared closed to travel. So he thought of them the way he thought of Chom: they would kill, but they were not killers. They did not wipe people out simply because they could or because they were crazy from battle fatigue. They killed with a purpose, and they could do that ruthlessly, even pedantically, as when they executed Saigon officials or mined a civilian bus. But their killings had a rationale. They never killed needlessly like Americans. He realized now, as he fumbled in his memory for words, that it was his sense of Vietnamese action that had made him chase after Chom—he had their style. *Nguoi khon ngam mieng; nguoi manh khoanh tay:* the wise man shuts his mouth; the strong man folds his arms. Lacey shoved his hands in his pockets and smiled back at the man who smiling at him, smiling at the European speaking passable Vietnamese.

"Cac ong la gi? Nguoi Tay lam gi o day? Tai sao linh My o day?" He pointed at Carlos and Beta and their uniforms.

"What he say?"

"He asked who we are, who the Americans are, and what American soldiers are doing here."

"Tell him the truth."

As Lacey spoke two other men came down. One wore civilian clothes, the other appeared to be the commanding officer. He had a Colt .45 belted to his hip and wore a light helmet with a chin strap. His uniform was neat, and he stood very straight on his car-tire sandals. He took over the questioning, asking Lacey about Chom's group and why they were there.

Lacey told them about Fay and Roberts, that Carlos and Beta were AWOL soldiers who belonged to oppressed minorities and who had refused to fight against the Vietnamese war of liberation.

"Yes, yes," the officer said in English. He said this with a polite but tired smile, looking over to see how his civilian colleague had responded to Lacey's description. Then he turned back and asked quite suddenly, "Khan Su o dau?"

"Do," Lacey said, pointing to the valley below where muffled shots could be heard from time to time along with the occasional slam of a grenade.

"Co bao nhieu linh?"

"What he say?"

"He wants to know how many troops Khan Su has."

"Tell him."

"Co the co nam chup nguoi Khan Su va ba chup nguoi Tai."

Lacey counted the way southern market women counted cigarettes or fish. The officer smiled at his colloquial *chup* and queried him about the Thais. "Ba muoi nguoi Tai? Tai sao?" When Lacey explained about the Nac Amphur, the officer smiled thoughtfully. "Tot," he said, "tot qua."

"What?"

"Good. He said 'Very good.'"

The interview seemed to be over. The officer told Lacey that he spoke good Vietnamese. Then he took notice of Lacey's arm, and of how sick Fay was, and of Roberts's stubbed and bloody feet.

"Tai vi bi thuong?"

Lacey explained about the rocket backblast. The civilian laughed. The officer called a medic down to have a look at them.

They all sat among the boulders while the medic cleaned Lacey's burn, applied a sterile compress—U.S. issue—and bandaged the arm. He looked at Fay and Roberts and found nothing terribly wrong with them. They were just exhausted, *met lam*, and weak. He gave them each some aspirin and a slug from a canteen full of some bitter concoction. For Roberts's feet he provided some gauze and antiseptic and, from his own pack, a pair of sandals, which, like the officer's, had been fashioned from an old Michelin tire.

Then the officer spoke again, nodding at Beta and Carlos but without expression.

"What he say?"

"He said that it would be more polite if Beta and Carlos put down their guns."

"Shit, bro', tell him we don't want to be fuckin' rude or nothing." Carlos laid his M-16 beside him; Beta, with a surly air, set his down next to him on a rock.

The officer thanked them and then told Chom to send a man down to the valley to bring his troops back up.

"And then?" Chom said. "What about us?" It would be a small matter to wipe them out after eliminating Khan Su and the Thais. Pathet Lao were sometimes to be found in the Golden Triangle but not Vietnamese—maybe they wouldn't want witnesses. Chom gazed intently at the officer, looking for something in his eyes as he replied; but those eyes were quiet and weary, weary perhaps out of mistrust and betrayal. No one spoke for a while.

The man looked, to Lacey, thirty-five or forty, but was probably forty-five. Vietnamese held their age until about fifty, and then suddenly their sleek black hair became a shock of white and large crow's feet streaked from their eyes. A plastic surgeon—Blake, to be precise—told Lacey it had to do with the particular texture of Vietnamese skin. So if the guy was forty, he had very likely spent half his life on battlefields. Maybe he had grown up on a small farm —now surely cratered by bombs or sown from the air with dragon's teeth mines—along the Red or Black rivers. He would have grown up during the Great Depression that brought mass starvation to Indochina as the French plundered their colonies to buffer their own failed economy. In 1944, at age ten, he might have seen the Viet Minh under Ho Chi Minh and his great tactician, Giap, driving out the Japanese troops with the help of American arms. Seven years later he would probably have married and started a family; at that point the countryside was peaceful as the Viet Minh in the North kept the French cordoned in the cities. Meanwhile Bao Dai had abdicated and ceded the royal mirror to Ho Chi Minh. The peace would last awhile. Farms were being collectivized in the North; maybe his family was poor. In that case it might have done them some good. But in 1954, he would have been called up in the general mobilization and sent south to fight the French—at age twenty. His wife and small children would have stayed on the farm with his parents. There was even a popular poem from that period, a folk lyric, that Lacey knew:

> Nen anh vac sung xong pha.
> Phan em la gai cua nha ruong nuong.

> So I shoulder a gun and head for the fighting.
> Your duty is a girl's: house, garden, and fields.

By 1960, when he was twenty-six, he might have headed home again during a lull. His oldest child, perhaps a boy, would have been nearly ten, old enough to tend the green rice paddy with his mother and father. But the elections agreed to in Geneva were overdue and so in 1964, at thirty, he would have been sent south again to fight Diem and the Americans, who, it was then clear, would honor no treaties and could be dealt with only by force. Our officer would be a Communist by now, commander of a company or, later, even a battalion in the highlands.

For some reason, now in 1974, with the war winding down, he had been diverted, with a third of his battalion, to set up an ambush for Khan Su. Why, was probably not entirely clear even to him. Somehow he had survived twenty years of war, including ten years of strafing by American jets, helicopter gunships and their rockets, B-52 carpet bombings, toxic defoliants, napalm, cluster bombs, land mines, heavy artillery, assault boats, riverine patrols, white phosphorus shells, Spooky Dragonships with their banks of .50-caliber machine guns, scorched-earth free-fire zones, and hundreds of thousands of healthy and brave but witlessly commanded American soldiers. Did he have a son? Had he survived the many battlefields only to have his family obliterated in their sleep? If he had a son, he would be twenty now and perhaps even fighting in his father's battalion. Perhaps he was one of those young soldiers with the garlands of flowered rhododendron sprigs, chatting and taking their ease while they waited to wipe out Khan Su. Was there a grandson? Would his generation ever walk the turned-up paddy behind a simple plow pulled by yoked oxen?

Lacey watched the officer, who now took off his pith helmet and brushed his hair with his hand. The man looked at Chom with sharp black eyes and said clearly, but in a gentle way, "You go your own way." He pointed to the gorge.

Then, with a glance to his civilian colleague, he added, "We support the liberation of oppressed minorities in Thailand and all over the world."

How awful! Lacey thought: to have gone through all that—and still be watched over by a political thought-policeman.

When Lacey was done with his translation, the officer continued. "And you," he said to Lacey, and Lacey translated for the others, "why don't you go home. The war is over. You Americans know that, don't you? Look at yourselves. See how much trouble you get yourself into here." He patted Lacey's good arm and chuckled.

Chom called over the Lawa rocket man who had been leaning against a boulder next to his launcher, smoking his little calabash pipe. Chom told him to call up the others and also to warn them about the Vietnamese.

But as the runner started to go, the officer raised his hand and said to Chom, "Make sure your men pass through this clearing. Let them drag their feet, leave a good path on the trail and in the pine needles. We don't want Khan Su to lose his way."

Chom picked at the letters on his baseball cap as Lacey translated.

Noting the hesitation, the officer added that Chom and his men would of course keep their arms. He called Chom *anh be*, "little brother," and added that when his men arrived, they were all to go to the gorge and cross. Khan Su would then be a Vietnamese problem.

Chom listened to this. He didn't have a lot of choices. While the Vietnamese wouldn't shoot them now because that would spring the trap before Khan Su was in it, they just might wait until his men arrived and then open up. But Khan Su might get away then, too, since he would be only a few steps behind the Lawa. So the order to pass directly through to the bridge would seem to be a sign of good faith. *But was there still a bridge?* Perhaps they had already dropped it down into the gorge. Practically, however, they could not disarm him without a shootout, so why not call his men up? Bridge or no bridge, their collective circumstances wouldn't be any worse. On the other hand, while he could think of no reason why the Vietnamese would want to wipe him out, he also couldn't think of any reason why they would want to wipe out Khan Su. Maybe the Vietnamese were moving into the opium trade—or ending the opium trade? No, they were too smart. Khan Su had somehow blundered with them. He had got in the way. With a ruined economy, Chom guessed they needed an exchange item for hard currencies. Johnson had said the Saigon generals dealt in opium, so why not the Hanoi generals too?

Chom gave his man the additional instructions and sent him off down the hillside, across patches of green tussocks marshy with alpine springs.

In the empty moment that opened up after the messenger's departure, Lacey repeated, out loud this time, the *tuc-ngu* proverb about the wise man shutting his mouth and the strong man folding his arms. The compliment was paid: true power has no need to display itself. Vietnamese were suckers for proverbs and poetical sayings. Even farmers composed them; everyone knew them, for despite the social disintegrations of the twenty-some years of continuous warfare, a lot more had held together in Vietnamese society than one might have guessed. Their Confucian order of respect went: king, scholar, worker, merchant, and, last, soldier. For centuries it had been this way; and now that they had no king, they chose their leaders—men like Giap, and Ho Chi Minh, and Pham Van Dong, and Xuan Thuy and Nguyen Khac Vien—from the traditional literati. They were generals who could write poetry, who could recite poetry in Vietnamese, Chinese, and perhaps even French. Marxist mandarins. Their sense of power lay in spirit and truthful appraisal, not in arms or blunt coercion: ". . . nguoi manh khoanh tay."

The Vietnamese were silent for a moment.

A yellow and black-spotted butterfly tumbled by their heads, over Fay and Roberts sprawled on the sweet brown carpet, over Beta slouched against a rock, over Mai sidling up to Carlos. It tumbled, for a bright moment while it got its bearings, about Chom and Lacey and the four Vietnamese, and pulsed off into the rhododendrons, passing as quickly as Lacey's two lines of verse.

The four Vietnamese—the soldier with the crown of greenery, the medic, the officer, and even the political cadre—were smiling broadly. "Tell our Lawa brother," the officer said, "that we would never harm you. After all, you are probably the only American ever to recite our poetry."

They laughed. Lacey beamed. And they laughed again when Chom grinned at the translation. Things were getting fairly light.

Then Lacey hit them with both barrels, a double whammy that he had memorized ten years before in Hue. It had been handed to him by a university student just before the kid was drafted into a disciplinary unit of dissidents whose work was to fetch munitions into battle and truck the corpses out. His truck had been blown up and Lacey memorized the poem in a kind of tribute. Ho Chi Minh had written it in prison. It was a rhymed quatrain, a *chueh-chu*, in the style made classical in the T'ang dynasty.

> *Tho xua canh thien nhien dep:*
> *May, gio, trang, hoa, tuyet, nui, song;*
> *Nay o trong tho nen co thep:*
> *Nha tho cung phai biet xung phong.*

The Vietnamese were positively troubled, and moved. The commander grabbed one of Lacey's hands with both of his and shook it. To hear their dead Chairman's words, in a poem that he had written in a Kuomintang prison, in China, in his youth, and to hear it on this lonely ridge, after many battles, and before a battle, hundreds of miles from their homes—and from an American—was an event that moved them and that they would talk about again and again, when all the tales of heroics and death had grown cold. It seemed providential, in much the same way that the first Puritans saw the workings of the divine hand in the surprising kindness of the Bermudas or in the coastal familiarities of the Massachusetts bays.

The commander called his men to attention in their deadly bowers and had Lacey step up on a rock and recite it again to as many as could hear the poem in that rock-ringed theater. It was called "On Reading the Anthology of the Ten Thousand Poets":

> *The ancients loved those poems with natural feel:*
> *Clouds, wind; moon, snow. Flowers, rivers, crags.*
> *Our poems today contain strong tempered steel;*
> *A poet, now, must learn to lead a charge.*

Lacey stepped down. The soldiers were applauding. As he paraphrased the poem to Chom and the others, the officers quieted down their troops and he could hear the political cadre saying something to them about "Khan Su . . . trying to kill our friends."

"Christ, man," Roberts called up, "keep it going. You're a hit. Better'n Bob Hope. Go for it!"

Chom was smiling broadly too. Yes, this poet knew how to lead a charge. After all that applause and camaraderie, there was no way the Vietnamese would harm them. The poem was a flak jacket.

Even Carlos was impressed, explaining to Mai, who was leaning her hip against him, that his boss really knew how to talk to these people.

"Uh-huh," said Beta. "Uh-*huh.*"

Then the political cadre turned to Lacey and said, "Tell the little brother that we have heard of his struggle to liberate his people . . ."

Lacey considered this extremely unlikely, but took it as a figure of speech with which such men began conversations.

"In Vietnam many mountain peoples live in peace and freedom under their own committees . . ."

Lacey imagined a horrible group of academics, living in the mountains, as the Department picnic stretched out into years. Lacey had to ask the cadre to slow down. His northern dialect was going by pretty fast, clipping through political jargon with utter familiarity— which was just where Lacey's ear was on uncertain timing.

The cadre paused to regard Lacey and then continued more slowly. "Ask the little brother if he would wish to join our revolutionary path. He could study with us at our institutes in Hanoi and, if he is capable, with our comrades in the Union of Soviet Socialist Republics."

Little brother had seen it coming. Chom replied that he valued their example on the revolutionary path and that their invitation was a great honor and opportunity. "But," he said, "I am leadah new village and cannot go. Lawa and Muong and Vietnamese come from same paren'. In two year, when my village is strong, I go Hanoi."

Then, as Lacey started to translate, Chom added in a quite normal tone, "Be careful how you say this, Lacey."

The Vietnamese, however, were pleased, and since it was now time to respring their trap, the commander and his colleague suddenly turned to shake hands all around. With Chom and Lacey. With Beta and Carlos, and with Mai, who the cadre said "looked as pretty as a Vietnamese." And with Fay, who they hoped would feel better soon and, lastly, with Roberts, who, before they could say anything Vietnamese and polite, told them to "whip Khan Su's ass." The two men looked back perplexed at Lacey and then laughed politely when he translated. Minutes later, Chom's group was seemingly alone on the sweet alpine terrace.

"No sense fightin' people like that. S'all cockelupwards, you see. They *got* somepn. You can see it."

"Shit, bro', we got something, too, man. We're *alive.*"

"Shit, yeah. We got *luck.*"

"And Lacey," Chom said, not so sure that things would be turning out so sweetly without Lacey's poems. "You do well."

"Loyal?" Lacey asked.

"Elegant."

"Bro', you really dig that monkey talk?"

Lacey grinned. He was feeling better all the time. He had won even Carlos.

"Zey kill us?" Mai asked. Along with the Lawa and the Karen, she had understood very little of what had just transpired.

"No way, mama. They said you was too pretty."

"I see some of them Lao, Pathet Lao."

"Mai, how do you know that?" Aside from his gratitude for her having helped him drag Roberts along, Lacey hadn't had time to consider Mai. It must have taken some courage to stand there quietly next to Carlos, wearing his beret, in deadly confusion while the North Vietnamese took over their lives.

She traced her memory reflectively and finally declared, "I sink I fuck one some day."

"Shit," Roberts said, as he tried on his new footwear over his torn, medicated feet, "she probably fucked the whole army."

The "bridge" was a long tunnel, a woven tube, of thick rattan ropes linked around a central alimentary tract about three to four feet in diameter. The ropes—some as thick as a human leg—ran the length of the bridge, were latticed concentrically by smaller weavings that circled and enclosed the walkway, giving it the effect of an elongated cocoon. The numerous strands radiating from the mouth were tied off on huge, gnarled, and wind-misshapen trees on the rocky ledges where the two cliffs yearned toward each other from either side of the gorge.

The gorge dropped six hundred feet below them to a thunder of spray and billowing mists that hovered above a stretch of Nam Yawng rapids. Down river, where the stream took a brief easterly jog toward Thailand, the gorge was cleared of churned-up clouds, and the river flattened out and calmed and winked back a bright ribbon as it caught the rising sun like molten mercury to disappear around the rocky bend. Standing on the ledge, they watched the bridge sway like a wind sock. Or perhaps like a spider's web because, from its mouth you looked into the circular center and, in peripheral vision, felt the ropes radiating out to their moorings like the weave of a spider's web. And then there was the sick helpless feeling—of a trapped fly perhaps—as you stooped and stepped into the bridge and the whole thing bobbed and swayed with the wind, drifting left then right at the cliffside and, farther out over the gorge, picking up lift and drop with each rip of the wind and shudder of heat rising from the steaming rift.

They went single file. Chom and Beta led, and the rest moved behind with antlike caution, while the bulk of the bandit troops grouped and chatted on the east ledge, chatted and made ready to cross. Some of Chom's troops—about a half dozen—had not come through. Myt said that he knew of none killed, but he couldn't be sure, since they had been cut off from each other in the dark jungle. Chert, whose stomach and groin were burned and abraded from hand-holding the mortars to trigger off individual rounds, said that he was pretty sure that some of the missing had ambushed Loi Maw and police and then had had to feint and dodge away and finally give up on joining the others at the Nam Yawng crossing. Instead, Chert thought, they had doubled back the way they had come. The final tally would be made at their base in Thailand.

But now the sure survivors were jubilant and the fright of the chasm dropping below them only spiked their joy. Fay, who had emerged weepy and shattered from her months of confinement and final devastating day, shrieked and whooped like a kid on a carnival ride. And Roberts, with his throat too sore to yell, shrilled hard whistles into the gorge, which echoed them back above the cataract thunder. They crept across, holding the cords that netted the sides and setting their feet cautiously on the thick bottom crossropes, while the wind surged between their feet and a white water bird sailed below on outstretched wings.

Burma, its mountains piling up quickly, lay before them across the gorge. On distant peaks, bald banks of scree topped the tree lines and, farther to the north they saw bright peaks shining with tips of snow. At the edge of the green bowl of Mong Hsat, Chom's Burma camp would be waiting with mules and horses.

Whooping now, they clambered through the long sock of ropes, feeling the cool air about them mingle with sudden blasts of jungle heat. Carlos, trying to scare Mai, halted and gripping the ropes— his M-16 slung around his neck with his grenades—whipped his ass from side to side. Mai shrieked appreciatively, but Beta bellowed back, real fear in his voice as he and Chom swayed in the middle of the chasm, "Stop that shit!" And Carlos was delighted at having his big friend in a tight moment and whip-sawed his ass some more and yelled up ahead, "Chíngate. Chíngate, maiate. Chin-GA-te."

The sun rose, and its light fell on wave upon wave of the forested ridges that lay ahead. As the gorge seethed and thundered and exploded below them, they turned their backs on the meadow they had just left, where they could still hear the machine guns rattling and the grenades whoomping as yellow rhododendron and sprinkles of white trillium were splashed crimson as eighty-some men struggled briefly and died.

27.

*L*acey, sitting on bags of fertilizer, stretched out on the sun-washed deck of the old freighter. Its anchor ports leaked tears of rust as the bow crashed into swells, booming splatters of bright spray on the patched and plated deck and rinsing wave suds over the coaming just before the first hatch. The ship, which Chom's Chaozhou associates had put Lacey aboard in Moulmein, was loaded with fertilizer and chemicals, including acetic anhydride for the heroin labs in Malaysia. Gulls were toiling overhead, keening and bobbing on the updrafts; others, plundering the ship's wake for churned-up fish, folded their wings and dropped into the white water and were left behind. The old tub shuddered and strained across the brilliant waves. It was bound for Singapore, stopping first at Penang.

They had traveled by horse to Mong Hsat, a dirt-rut town in the upland valley, where they ate and bathed and rested overnight before taking the dusty road to Mong Pan. Just before Mong Pan they stopped at the Salween ferry crossing to wait for the riverboat, a relic from the British Empire—its rails sharp with blebs of rust and lifting peels of paint, its decks crowded with livestock and kerchiefed men and women struggling with yokes and woven trays of produce. The old boat took a full day to bring them down the muddy river that wound slow and deep through Kayah and Kawthule states, in the shadow of the Dawna Range. Finally it docked that night at the municipal wharf in Martaban, where the river ran into the sea. There Fay and Roberts were taken to a wooden Chinese hotel, its old teak surrendering to termites that shimmered in a dense flickering cloud around a dingy streetlamp. Lacey had immediately boarded a fish-stinking launch and crossed the Martaban Strait to Moulmein. He left that night. It was that or wait several more days for another ship, and that was unwise since none of them had passports.

And now he dug his thumbnail into the flesh of a grapefruit the captain had given him. Lacey examined his arm, pulling up the bandage and then taping it over. The sun and the salt air would do it good. A nervy gull hovered over his head and side-spied the grapefruit.

The old Italian's skin was as rough and thick as his pungent gift. Sun-burned and leathery from years at an open bridge, the night before—as they waited to set out—he had served Lacey espresso and grappa in his cabin. His wife was Chinese. He hadn't been in Italy for over thirty years.

The plan was for Roberts and Fay to go on to Rangoon and for Lacey to head home to Louise, who he hoped had not jumped the gun and alerted American officials, who he hoped would still be there. Louise had his passport and their tickets. Carlos's tickets could now be cashed in.

From Moulmein they entered the Andaman Sea, leaking oil along the southbound shipping lane, nudging the coast, chugging past the Tenasserim reefs, passing the small junks in cabotage. The Singapore man-lion snapped in the breeze above the bridge, and Lacey thought of his tiger friend. At their good-bye at the Salween river, Chom had again urged him to stay. He said he'd think it over, seriously.

"Not as bandit, Lacey. You not skill at that."

"Yeah, how then?"

"Oh, I doan know. May be my Chinese frien's get you job university in Singapo'. May be Kuala Lumpur. You can do some quiet thing for us."

With Khan Su gone, the little brother, the little tiger, might be branching out, expanding his hunting grounds.

Moulmein. Then the Tenasserim coast, marked by a thick blue horizon line from the fogs of its rain forests. He had lunch with the captain, who sucked his noodles from a bowl like a Chinese. Dusk. Chugging into dusk as the twilight arc mounted across the clear sky. They ran all night, plowing the moonlit waters. Just off the Mergui Archipelago, where tiny lights trembled toward them from the distant island wharfs, the captain came down with a hurricane lamp to check his deck gun hidden under a large packing crate marked in Chinese characters. "Pirati," he said and showed Lacey, who was tipsy on Algerian wine, an old Japanese Nambu machine gun from 1939, an imitation French Hotchkiss mounted on a tripod and swivel. Pirati. Later that night when Lacey was rocked in his cot in the captain's cabin, he counted wave splashes instead of sheep and smelled the jungle air blowing through the porthole.

In Rangoon, he thought, as the morning sun warmed his belly and the gulls cried overhead, one of them actually swooping down to perch on the packing crate—in Rangoon, Paul and Fay would go to the British consulate, telegram Louise, and check into a hospital, while the embassies reported them to the xenophobic Burmese, who had admitted them legally six months before. There'd be some explaining. But they'd have a record of their entering the country. They could say they had been kidnapped near Keng Tung. Robbed. Passports taken. Lacey doubted the authorities would even investigate. Miss Fay Cockburn and Mr. Paul Roberts would be put in a hospital for foreign diplomats and get new passports within a week. Within two weeks, Roberts would be on a talk show.

Lacey tossed a peel at the gull on the crate, and his right arm ached with the sudden jerk. When Fay had said good-bye, she had given Lacey the rest of Prescott's journal, the part he had finished after London, in India. She said, "He was rather wonderful, you know—finally." She didn't seem so full of herself as she had in London last Christmas. Fay had lived for a while between those "two major categories," lived in that rare condition, on that bright edge, where inner clarity reigns. How would she adjust to London? It would be like walking on the moon. When their old river barge had sloshed off from the creaky dock at the Salween ferry crossing and Mai was crying—didn't Fay feel odd to see Mai throw her face on Carlos's shoulder and sob? Mai had made love to Fay; now Mai would make love to Carlos. It seemed to Lacey both chilling and odd. *Vaya con Dios*, bro'!

Yes, going back would be like coming down on the moon. Coming down again. "All my times been spent. Where are all my friends? Coming down again." Prescott's swansong vibrated up in Lacey's memory like a loose screw on a deck plate. He smiled and closed his eyes and felt the sun and the bounce of the waves against the bow.